D1350062

BRIEF ENCOUNTER, 1944

The chair next to him was still vacant when
the impromptu lights were dimmed and the
curtain went up. When someone came and sat
down alongside him he didn't even look round.
His attention was fixed on the stage where six
girls in skimpy costumes were dancing.

'Enjoying it?'

For a moment he froze, wondering if his
mind was playing tricks.

'It *is* me!' came the whisper as a hand slid
across his knee and took his.

Unable to believe his ears he glanced
sideways, and then doubted even his eyes. Kate
was sitting there, prim and efficient in her
khaki uniform, a clipboard on her knee.

Officers' Ladies

MARION HARRIS

This title first published in Great Britain 1987 by
SEVERN HOUSE PUBLISHERS LTD of
40–42 William IV Street, London WC2N 4DF
by arrangement with Sphere Books Limited

British Library Cataloguing in Publication Data
Harris, Marion
Officers' ladies.
I. Title
823'.914 [F]   PR6058.A68/
ISBN 0–7278–1473–7

Printed and bound in Great Britain

Chapter 1

Kate Russell found herself chattering nervously to her companion as they drove out of battle-scarred London towards
Somerset. Normally quiet and self-possessed there was an
unusual brilliance in her dark brown eyes and her mouth
was taut as she chewed uneasily on her lower lip. Ever
since she had so rashly invited Robert Campbell to come
home with her she had been trying to determine how she
was going to handle things once they arrived at Walford
Grange.

When she had found him waiting for her at the Barrack
gates, just as they had arranged, with the bright May sunshine turning his fiery curls into a banner of gold, her
apprehension had turned into excitement. With his strong
square face, and compelling green eyes under sandy brows,
he was handsome in a rugged rawbone sort of way. Kate tried
to imagine what he would look like out of uniform, dressed
in jodhpurs and hacking jacket, sitting astride a hunter as
powerfully built as he was himself.

It had all started a few weeks before. Halfway through
dinner, her father, General Sir Henry Russell, had needed to
return to the War Office for an emergency meeting.

'My driver will run you back after he has dropped me off,'
Sir Henry had told her as they finished their coffee.

'There's no need, it is not dark yet,' she protested.

'I would rather you used the car. It will worry me to think
of you wandering about London on your own.'

After depositing Sir Henry at Whitehall, Kate was startled
when the driver turned the Humber round and drove off
down the Mall towards Hyde Park.

'You are going the wrong way,' she said sharply, leaning
forward and tapping him on the shoulder.

'It is such a lovely evening, I thought you might like to come this way,' he answered without looking round.

She was so taken aback that she found herself at a loss for words and unsure of how to handle the situation.

A tall slim girl, self-possessed and confident, her aristocratic features were softened by enormous brown eyes and a wide generous mouth. She wore her dark brown hair in a smooth page-boy roll beneath her army cap and her creamy complexion bore only a light trace of make-up. Now, however, her cheeks were stained with an embarrassed flush, her poise shaken, as she tried to ignore the soldier's familiarity.

It had been a day of brilliant April sunshine and in Hyde Park, daffodils and crocuses pierced the grass and the pink and white blossom of the many flowering trees glowed luminously against the darkening sky.

She suddenly felt homesick. Her thoughts ricocheted back fifteen months to January 1942, when she had received her call-up papers. The memory was so vivid that she could almost hear her mother's voice ringing in her ears as she passed the letter across the breakfast table for her to read.

'This is utter nonsense! You must tell them you can't go,' Lady Dorothea had exclaimed in outraged tones.

'Mother, they're not asking, they're ordering me to report!'

'It must be a mistake! Let your father see it.'

Nudged into action, Sir Henry had put down *The Times*, and scanned her letter, then passed it back with an imperceptible shrug.

'York. In six days,' he commented as he shook out his paper and resumed reading.

'It's out of the question,' Lady Dorothea said imperiously. 'You must speak to someone at the War Office. The idea of Kate dressing up in that awful khaki uniform and pretending to be a soldier is preposterous.'

'Nonsense! It's high time the Russell family was represented on active service,' he announced decisively. 'If we'd had a son he would have been in the front line long before this.'

Interrupting her reverie, the driver commented: 'I used to live in the country once. I can still remember the day we moved there. I was only about five years old and as we

2

walked up the track to the farmhouse the grass on either side was chin high. I was scared stiff in case I got lost in it and no one could find me. Have you ever been to Cheshire?' he asked. 'On a fine day you can see the Welsh mountains, like enormous purple shadows away in the distance.'

'And will you go back there when the war ends?'

'No! My father died before I joined up and the farm was sold. My mother has married again so there's no future for me there.'

'What will you do then, stay on in the army?'

'I had thought about that.' His green eyes locked with hers. 'I wouldn't mind . . . if I could get a commission. Perhaps if you were to put my name forward . . .'

'Me! I couldn't do that. Your application would have to go through your CO.'

'I've tried that, he wants me to stay as a driver.'

Amused by his audacity she agreed to do as he asked . . .

It was two weeks before she dined with her father again and as they left the Savoy she noticed it was an ATS driver holding the car door for them.

After Sir Henry had barked instructions about where they wanted to go he leaned back in his seat with a snort of irritation.

'Don't know what's happened to my usual driver,' he grumbled. 'Probably on leave, I'll have to check it out. Hope I haven't lost him, one of the best I've ever had. It is always the same, if they're any good they seem to move on to something else,' he muttered as he settled himself more comfortably.

Kate was tempted to tell him that his usual driver was probably on an Officer's Training Course. Knowing that she would also have to explain how she knew, and the part she had played in his getting there, made her hold back and the moment passed.

As her father's car pulled away, Kate was startled when a tall, powerfully built man materialised out of the darkness and spoke to her. Then, as she recognised Robert Campbell, although her heart continued to beat wildly it was for a very different reason.

'What . . . what are you doing here dressed in civvies?' she exclaimed in bewilderment.

'Waiting to take you for a drink,' he grinned.

Before she could protest, he steered her briskly away from the Barrack gates and down the road towards a nearby pub.

She sat down at a corner table, trying to sort out the thoughts hammering inside her head. Instead, she found herself studying him as he towered over the other men standing at the bar. Without his forage cap, his hair seemed almost flame red. His army hair-cut left the back shaved close to the nape of his neck, but the rest curled crisply and thickly over the top of his well-shaped head. His lean tanned profile had an angular strength that gave him a bold, handsome look. Yet there was a ruthlessness about his mouth that she found disturbing.

With that colour hair he probably has a fiendish temper, she mused.

Their eyes met as he turned round and her heart raced as she met the challenge in their brilliant depths. As he sat down beside her, his muscular thigh brushed against her leg and she felt a tingle of excitement pulse through her.

'What are we drinking to?' she asked nervously as she picked up her glass of sherry.

'I just wanted to say "thank you" for putting my name down for an OTC,' he told her, raising his glass of beer in her direction.

'To your success on the Course.' She raised her own glass towards his before taking a sip. 'Do you know when it starts?'

'In ten days' time. After my leave.'

'I see.' She took another sip of her sherry. 'Where are you spending your leave . . . back home in Cheshire?'

'No, I'm staying in London. I was hoping that we could meet again. Go for a meal one night, maybe.'

'I am going on leave myself tomorrow.'

'To Walford Grange?' he asked, his eyes narrowing.

'Of course.'

'Stay in London. We could spend some time together . . . get to know each other.'

'That's impossible.' She stood up, checking her watch. 'I must get back.'

'I'll walk to the gates with you.'

'We had better say goodnight here,' she said, stopping a short distance from the pub. Although he was not in uniform, being with him was still breaching the rules.

'I understand.'

'Thank you for the drink,' she murmured and self-consciously held out her hand.

He held it firmly between his own. Then, without warning, he bent forward and before she was aware of his intention his mouth was on hers.

The sweetness of their kiss left her breathless. His mouth encompassed hers like a band of steel, enmeshing her in its warmth, melting all her resistance. She found herself swaying towards him so that when one of his hands encircled her waist, steadying her and at the same time holding her tightly pressed against his long lean body, she closed her eyes and gave herself up to the magic of the moment.

'I wish you were staying in London,' he breathed.

'It's out of the question,' she answered, quickly, her thoughts in turmoil, fighting back the tantalising prospects such a suggestion offered.

'When do you go?'

'Tomorrow, as soon as I come off duty.'

She found the naked longing in his green eyes so devastating that it made her feel guilty, as if she was deserting him. She fought against his magnetic hold on her then hated herself for being so weak.

'Look,' she said, struggling desperately to make amends, 'why don't you come with me? . . . if you have nothing better to do.'

'To Walford Grange!' His astonishment was as great as her own.

'Why not? You would probably quite enjoy it,' she said defensively.

'I'm sure I would, but what about the rest of your family?' he commented softly and his thin lips twisted in a sardonic smile.

'You already know my father.'

'Yes!' he gave a short harsh laugh. 'I do, but I don't suppose he knows me. To him I'm just a khaki-clad robot who drives him from point A to point B.'

'He speaks very highly of you,' she contended. 'He was quite annoyed to find you had been replaced by an ATS driver.'

'Yes, I can well see that wouldn't please him,' Robert Campbell agreed with a derisive laugh. 'Nor would it please General Sir Henry Russell to find me facing him across his breakfast table.'

'If, as you just said, he thinks of you only as some kind of khaki-clad automaton then he isn't likely to recognise you, is he,' Kate said mischievously.

'He just might.'

'If you're too scared to accept my invitation why don't you say so,' she taunted. Although she recognised the truth of Robert Campbell's remark she very much resented its implication.

'You really do mean it,' he said pulling her back into the circle of his arms. His green eyes shone like diamond chips as they searched her face before he accepted the challenge. 'Very well, I will come. Where shall we meet . . . Waterloo Station?'

'No, meet me here. I come off duty at twelve.'

'Looking for someone to carry your kitbag, are you?' he mocked, kissing the tip of her nose.

'No, it just seems pointless going all the way to Waterloo Station when I can drive you home from here,' she told him coolly.

Before he could reply she was walking towards the Barrack gates, her heart racing at the enormity of what she had just done.

Now, as the mellow outline of Walford Grange became visible through the long avenue of trees, she didn't dare think what her father's reaction would be. He could hardly order a guest out of their home, she thought defiantly. Yet, knowing her father's strict adherence to regimental protocol, she knew he might well be tempted to do so.

'We've arrived,' she informed her passenger briskly as they

turned into the wide gravel drive and stopped in front of the house. 'Come and meet my mother.'

'And the formidable nanny,' he grinned.

On the journey down she had explained about Mabel Sharp, her ex-nanny who was now more of a companion and housekeeper to Lady Dorothea. She also warned Robert not to mention to either of them that he was Sir Henry's driver. Time enough for that revelation when her father arrived home in two days' time. By then, with any luck, Robert would have charmed them both over to his side.

Nervously she pushed open the studded oaken door and led the way into the lofty panelled hall. She heard Robert whistle softly as he paused, feasting his eyes on the massive stone fireplace, flanked by antique guns and powder flasks.

'Quite some place,' he murmured as she hurried him past the wide sweeping staircase lined with gilt-framed family portraits. 'Elizabethan?'

'This part is. The rest is late Georgian.'

'It is certainly impressive.'

'Come on, you can look round later,' she said, leading the way through an arched doorway towards the back of the house.

She made straight for the morning room. Because it was a warm day the french doors, which looked onto a flower-filled walled garden, were opened back and the drone of insects, mingling with birdsong, drifted in.

Her mother, wearing a white cardigan over a royal blue cotton dress, was sitting out on the terrace reading, two black spaniels sprawled at her feet. Her smile when she saw Kate softened her rather severe features.

Heart in mouth, Kate introduced Robert Campbell. To her relief, Lady Dorothea accepted that he was an 'army colleague' and asked no awkward questions at all.

Mabel Sharp was not won over quite so easily. Her beady hazel eyes riveted themselves on Robert. Her quick fire questions left him speechless. It reminded Kate of the days when Mabel had been her nanny and she had brought a new friend home from school.

'That was worse than my OTC interview,' he breathed to Kate when Mabel Sharp eventually left them together.

'Never mind, I think you came through it OK,' she smiled. 'I did warn you she was quite a formidable character. I know I never got away with very much when she was in charge of me.'

'It's a wonder you have managed to grow up as normal as you have,' he told her with a wicked grin.

Although he had passed Nanny's initial interrogation, she continued to regard him with suspicion. She allocated him a bedroom as far away from Kate's as possible and seemed to go out of her way to see that they were never left alone for more than a few minutes.

'I don't think she trusts me,' Robert remarked rather irritably later that first evening when, for the third time in less than an hour, Mabel Sharp came into the sitting room where they were playing records. 'She's making me quite nervous.'

'Nanny's got a heart of gold, really,' Kate soothed.

'And a highly suspicious nature,' he remarked rather sourly.

Mabel Sharp's antagonism worried Kate. It meant she must contrive for her father to learn the identity of their guest without Nanny being present and the only sure way of doing that was for them to meet him off the train.

Lady Dorothea looked mildly surprised when Kate told her on Friday morning that they were going to spend the day in Taunton.

'I thought we could meet Father's train, afterwards,' Kate explained. 'Be a nice surprise for him.'

'More of a shock than a surprise, I would think,' Mabel Sharp sniffed, her sharp eyes fixed on Robert.

Chapter 2

General Sir Henry Russell was not just astonished, he was speechless when he realised that the man dressed in a tweed sports jacket and grey flannels, standing on the platform with Kate was none other than his army driver.

He alighted from the first-class carriage his florid face beaming with pleasure at the sight of Kate, slim and attractive in her belted white sweater over a knife-pleated red skirt, waiting to meet him. Only when his khaki valise was taken from his hand was he aware that she was not alone.

His perfunctory smile as he turned to greet her companion turned to an expression of incredulity the moment he realised who it was.

'Great heavens,' he boomed, tugging at the ends of his moustache. 'What on earth are you doing here, Campbell?'

'On leave . . . sir,' Robert volunteered.

'Robert is spending his leave with us,' Kate said quickly.

'Is he!' Sir Henry scowled. 'And how has that come about?'

'I invited him.'

Sir Henry stared from one to the other, his brown eyes hooded. Without further comment he headed for the Exit, leaving them to follow. When they reached the car, he settled himself in the passenger seat, leaving Robert to ride in the back. On the journey home he addressed himself exclusively to Kate, questioning her about the arrangements for the riding event he had asked her to organise.

By the time they reached Walford Grange he seemed to have recovered his equilibrium and even Mabel, watching with bird-like intensity, could glean nothing from his manner.

Robert and Kate, however, were both sensitive to the

atmosphere and aware that Sir Henry was anything but pleased at the turn of events.

'Keep cool,' Kate warned in a whisper as they went in to dinner. 'He will be fine once the riding gets underway tomorrow morning.'

Throughout the meal, Kate steered the conversation off any controversial topics. Sir Henry was curt and seemed immersed in his own brooding thoughts. She sensed Robert was feeling edgy so as soon as the meal ended she suggested they should take the dogs for a walk.

'Don't be late back,' her father warned. 'We have an early start in the morning.'

'I should not have come, I suppose,' Robert sighed ruefully, once they were clear of the house.

'It went off rather better than I thought it would,' Kate chuckled. 'I had visions of my father absolutely exploding.'

'I think I could have handled that,' Robert told her. 'It's Nanny's cold, suspicious manner that I resent.'

'She probably thinks you have some wicked designs on me,' Kate told him, her brown eyes dancing.

'And she would be perfectly right, of course,' he agreed, sliding his arm around her waist and drawing her close.

Gently but firmly Kate disengaged herself from his embrace.

'Don't tell me she has X-ray eyes and can see this far,' he scoffed.

'No, but we are walking past Home Farm so someone might see us and tittle-tattle to my father.'

'Can we stop for a drink, or would that be classed as incriminating evidence?' Robert mocked as they reached the village.

'I'm only being careful for your sake,' Kate flared. 'There is no point in antagonising my father is there!'

She led the way into the village pub. The bar was deserted and after one drink they left.

It was a clear night, but a chill breeze sent a shiver through Kate so she slipped her arm through Robert's, huddling close to him for warmth.

'That could be decidedly incriminating,' he said sharply as he disengaged himself. Taking her hand he broke into a jogging run. She allowed herself to be pulled for a few yards then broke free.

'What's up, no stamina?' he asked, looking down at her sardonically.

'Saving it for tomorrow,' she told him breathlessly.

'That will be another test for me, I suppose,' he snapped and his handsome face clouded.

'You ride, don't you?'

'Well enough.'

'Then what's the problem?'

'I've no riding gear.'

'I wish you'd mentioned it sooner. You could have borrowed something of Father's to wear.'

'I don't think it would help matters if he found me dressed up in his clothes,' Robert grinned. 'Anyway, I don't somehow think they would fit me.'

'You can hardly ride dressed as you are. Your jacket will do, but you need jodhpurs and boots.'

'I'm sure there are plenty of other things I can do to help,' he said drily.

The riding event passed smoothly enough. Robert made himself useful helping Nanny and Lady Dorothea with the refreshments. By the end of the day, the tension seemed to have gone out of the situation and everyone was much more relaxed.

Sir Henry, now recovered from the initial shock of finding his army driver was a house guest, tried to make up for his earlier boorishness. So much so, that after the two of them had spent all Sunday morning inspecting Home Farm, Kate felt rather neglected and was on the point of reminding her father that Robert was *her* guest, not his.

Over lunch, they discussed crops and cattle to the exclusion of everything else and after lunch, when the two men set off again, this time to inspect the piggeries, she felt it was time to protest.

'Leave them alone,' Lady Dorothea advised. 'It's not often there is anyone here for your father to talk to when he comes home at the weekends.'

The remainder of the week, after Sir Henry had returned to London to the War Office, was idyllic. Kate enjoyed showing

Robert around, exploring the picturesque villages, eager to share with him the surrounding countryside which she knew and loved so well. Because petrol was rationed they mostly either walked or bicycled. A couple of times they took the horses and cantered along the Polden Ridge from Marshall's Elm to Chilton Polden enjoying the fine panoramic view of Sedgemoor, the Brendon Hills and the Quantocks.

With each passing day, Kate became increasingly aware that what had started out as a casual friendship was developing into a much more serious relationship. She had fallen under the spell of Robert's charisma and she had never felt so happy. She found herself walking round in a blissful dream. Even the weather was kind to them. She wished the long idyllic May days, filled with warm sunshine, sweet fragrant air and joyous birdsong, could last forever.

But for both of them their leave was almost over. Although they had not spoken of what lay ahead, Kate guessed that when Robert had finished his OTC he would probably be sent to Italy which meant it would be many months before they saw each other again.

Alone in her room at night, remembering sweet moments of passion, and the strength of Robert's arms when he held her close, her mind was in turmoil. She had known plenty of young men at University, and since, but never anyone who had stirred her emotions so deeply. Until now her heart had been untouched. She rarely thought of marriage although from time to time her parents talked of one day having a grandchild so that the future of Walford Grange could be assured. And, she knew that they expected her to choose a husband from their own stratum. Someone who would combine his estates with hers to become even more powerful and wealthy.

It had always been understood that either Simon Nielson or Ralph Buscombe, sons of neighbouring landowners, were the obvious choice. And the one she didn't choose would marry her close friend Eleanor Anstruther.

They were both just a few years older than her. Simon had gone to Eton, Ralph to Marlborough and afterwards they had been together at Cambridge, both studying Law.

The future had always seemed so safe and settled that now she wasn't sure if she was really in love with Robert Campbell or merely trying to escape from a pattern that had been ordained for her since the day she was born. His mesmeric green eyes, deep northern voice and expressive mouth, stirred feelings in her that she had never even known existed. It took every ounce of her strength to restrain their love-making. Every fibre of her being cried out that she desired him every bit as fervently as he appeared to want her.

The feeling of euphoria that built up during the week, making the whole world seem bright and beautiful, was abruptly shattered when Sir Henry arrived home again on the Friday evening.

As they sat talking after dinner, Robert astounded the entire family by stating that he wanted to marry Kate. He hadn't even warned her of his intention to do this and she could only sit on the other side of the table and stare at him white-faced. Knowing her parents' attitude over such matters she was miserably aware that Robert had ruined everything by his impetuosity. If only he had told her what he intended to do then she could have warned him that he ought to discuss it with her father first in private and she would have arranged for them to be alone in the Library before dinner.

Covertly, from under lowered lashes, she watched the reactions of the others, her heart beating against her ribcage like a trapped bird.

Sir Henry's face was purple with rage, his dark brown eyes almost black with anger and a vein on his temple pulsed alarmingly. Watching him with growing concern, Kate thought he was about to have a heart attack. Lady Dorothea looked equally taken aback and sat tight-lipped and indignant, as if unable to believe her ears.

'Did I hear you correctly, Campbell?' Sir Henry barked.

A more prudent man might have pulled back, but Robert's shoulders squared, his cleft chin jutted and his eyes became emerald hard.

Kate ached to warn him to be careful what he said but her mouth was so dry she couldn't speak. When their eyes locked, he looked quickly away, his mouth a determined, grim line.

'Yes. I want to marry Kate.'

'Absolutely out of the question,' Sir Henry snarled, frowning darkly. 'Preposterous! You . . . you're not even an officer!'

'He will be, in a matter of a month or so,' Kate defended, hotly. 'Immediately after his leave, Robert is going on an Officer's Training Course, surely you have not forgotten.'

Sir Henry grunted disdainfully. 'Anyone can get on one of those damned courses. They're just looking for heads to make up the numbers. Officers are being killed like flies. They need some extra gun-fodder, nothing more. I'm talking about real Officers . . . gentlemen of breeding and quality.'

'That's unfair and snobbish,' Kate flared, her brown eyes blazing.

'It may be, but remember it is the aristocracy who are the backbone of our country,' her father reminded her sharply.

'Just a moment,' Lady Dorothea held up a hand. She looked disapprovingly at Robert and then turned to her husband. 'I seem to have been under a misapprehension,' she frowned. 'When he arrived with Kate, and she said he was an army colleague, I thought you knew this man, otherwise I would not have permitted him to stay.'

'I do know him,' Sir Henry told her drily. 'He was my army driver until he had the nerve to put his name forward for an Officer's Training Course. Damned impertinence! I would soon have put a stop to that had I known, I can tell you.'

'Robert didn't put his name forward, I did,' Kate said her face flaming with anger.

Sir Henry stared at her speechless for a few moments, then he pushed back his chair and stood up.

'Wait! Before you storm out and shut yourself up in your study, Father, I want you to know that if I can't marry Robert, then I will never marry anyone!'

Sir Henry paused, his hand resting on the door, his brown eyes boring into hers. She returned his stare without flinching and saw the fight go out of him. He seemed to age before her eyes. Her heart ached, knowing she was the cause of the disappointment that shadowed his face.

'You are making a grave mistake, Kate,' he said wearily.

'I think not. The war has been a great leveller, things will never be quite the same again. It is what a person is, not what his ancestors have been, that matters.'

Sir Henry smiled scornfully. 'Fine words, but with very little meaning. What you term "being in love" is merely animal magnetism. When that fades, as it always does, you'll find there's a great void unless you have married one of your own kind. Shared values mean a lot as you grow older. They are the only thing that lasts.'

'My mind is made up,' Kate said firmly, facing her father defiantly. Her heart was beating wildly and she refused to meet Robert's eyes although she could sense he was looking at her. She knew she was taking an irrevocable step and that she was doing it partly in defiance of her parents because she was so utterly ashamed of their bigotry. Until that moment she had not been sure about her feelings for Robert. The exhilarating emotions she had experienced during the past week had left her in a state of mental turmoil. Now she was convinced it was because she was in love and she couldn't bear the thought of Robert going out of her life.

'If you are old enough to serve your country then, I suppose, you are old enough to ruin your own life,' he told her harshly. 'There is nothing else I have to say.'

'But you can't let her marry this man,' Lady Dorothea protested. 'If he is not a gentleman, then he probably has no career prospects either.'

'Well, what have you to answer to that?' Sir Henry demanded, his eyes levelling with Robert's. 'How do you intend to support my daughter when the war is over?'

'I haven't thought that far ahead,' Robert admitted, 'but I am sure I shall manage quite well.'

'She has been brought up to expect the best, you'll find it quite a formidable task, I can tell you,' Sir Henry boomed sardonically. 'And I don't suppose you even have a job to go back to!'

'No, I don't,' Robert admitted quietly.

'Nor any worthwhile qualifications, I'll be bound,' Sir Henry added triumphantly.

'I come from a farming family so I have plenty of practical experience. I could come here and run Home Farm.'

'No you damn well could not! That most certainly is out of

the question,' Sir Henry exploded. Enraged, he flung back the door, his hackles rising. 'If that is what lies behind your idea of marrying my daughter you can forget it. When this damn war is over I will be running my own Estate! The best thing you can do is make a career for yourself in the Army . . . that is if you ever manage to get through the OTC!'

Chapter 3

Kate and Robert left for London immediately after breakfast next morning. Although she still had two days of her leave left there didn't seem to be much point in staying on at Walford Grange – the atmosphere was far too fraught. The weather, too, had changed; the morning was dull, misty and overcast.

Lady Dorothea came to see them off, trying desperately to bridge the gulf between them. Kate couldn't bring herself to meet her mother's reproachful blue eyes. The dark shadows beneath her own told their own story of a sleepless night spent going over the angry words exchanged between her father and Robert. Her heart ached to put things right. She didn't want to part like this but to stay any longer would impose an even greater strain on them all.

Sir Henry was nowhere to be seen when they left. Her mother had said he'd been up at dawn and gone off with the dogs, she was not sure where. As they pulled away Kate looked in her rear-mirror and saw him come around the side of the house and stand there in the drizzling rain, his shotgun over his arm, watching them drive off.

'Let's stop in Frome or Warminster,' Robert suggested.

'It is too early for coffee, I would much sooner push on,' Kate said, her mouth set in a grim line. She resolutely refused to meet Robert's eyes. She blamed him that things had gone so wrong. Although she resented her father's attitude, and his reasons for not wanting them to marry, she was equally annoyed that Robert had spoken out without asking her first. She resented being taken for granted. He had ruined everything by confronting her parents. If he had told her he intended speaking to her father then she could have asked her mother to prepare the ground with Sir Henry.

She was also incensed by their bigotry. It filled her with shame that they had displayed such open hostility towards Robert simply because he was from a different stratum of society. Until her father had denounced him as a mere driver, her mother had been ready to accept him as one of her army colleagues.

'I meant spend the day there. We could even stay overnight,' he added softly.

She shook her head, and accelerated faster. All she wanted to do was to get as far away from Walford Grange as possible. The thought of staying in Frome or Warminster and perhaps meeting someone she knew, was unthinkable.

'No!' Sensing that he was puzzled by her behaviour she kept her eyes fixed on the snaking grey road ahead, her hands tightly grasping the wheel as the speedometer moved upwards at an alarming rate.

'Well, slow down just a bit or we won't make London in one piece,' he told her grimly. 'Perhaps I should drive.'

'No! No one drives my car . . . ever,' she snapped, but she did ease off the speed.

She shot a quick sideways glance at Robert. He was staring stubbornly ahead, jaw set, his profile arrogant. She sighed. Robert's strength of character, the very thing she admired so much, might well prove to be an obstacle, she thought bitterly. The soft, subtle approach just wasn't his way. In that, he was as obstinate as her father.

As they caught up with a convoy of army lorries, Kate pressed her foot hard down on the accelerator again and swung out to pass. She was in no mood to dawdle. Speed provided exhilaration that helped to clear her mind and drive out the irritation and anger bubbling inside her.

She heard the bang seconds before she felt the impact. The wheel spun under her hands and suddenly she was being thrown forward, the breath knocked out of her, as her head collided with the windscreen. She was dimly aware that Robert had grabbed the wheel, steering the car so that it scraped along the side of the lorry while at the same time he wrenched on the handbrake. As they came to a juddering stop she found she was trembling uncontrollably.

'You all right, mate?'

18

The driver of the army lorry jumped from his cab and came running to the car.

'I think so,' Robert muttered. 'I'll just get out and have a look.'

'Smashed your wing in pretty badly,' the driver commiserated. 'Hang about and I'll get a couple of the lads to help, we might be able to straighten it out. We'll get a brew going. You look as though you need something,' he said nodding in Kate's direction.

Within minutes Kate's car had been pushed onto the grass verge and half a dozen khaki figures were at work on it under Robert's wary eye.

Kate sheltered from the drizzle inside the back of one of the trucks and sipped strong sweet tea from a tin mug someone had pushed into her trembling hands. By the time Robert returned to report that apart from a dented wing there was no real damage her nerves had steadied. Even so, she made no objection when he took over the wheel. She knew the mishap had been her fault and she was still feeling shaky.

'We'll be in London in less than an hour,' Robert announced. 'Shall we stop for a meal? You don't have to report back until tomorrow and I still have another two days' leave so neither of us is in any hurry.'

'What?' Kate looked at him blankly. Then, as Robert's words registered, she shook her head.

'Why not? Are you all that anxious to get rid of me! I can understand it in a way. I did rather put my foot in things with your father.'

'It wasn't really your fault, but if I had known what you intended to do I would have warned you it was not the right moment.'

'But it hasn't changed your feelings?' he asked cautiously.

'How could it!' She reached out and squeezed his arm reassuringly.

'Then let's stop off somewhere . . . just for a meal,' he added hastily, afraid she might feel he was pressurising her. 'It would give us a chance to plan what we are going to do.'

'Can't it wait until we get back to London?'

'No! If we do that we'll both end up back in Barracks

feeling we've spoiled each other's leave. Let's talk things over, and make some plans for the future.'

'Where do you want to stop?'

'I don't know. I'm sure we can find somewhere pleasant. The rain seems to be stopping. I'm not too sure where we are, mind you.'

'Just outside Reading. Perhaps we can find somewhere near the river,' Kate told him.

In the end, they lunched on Woolton pie and spotted dick smothered in a thin ersatz custard, in a small café in Marlow High Street. Afterwards, they walked along the towpath towards Medmenham. The wide smooth stretch of the Thames was so peaceful that it was hard to believe that bomb-shattered London was no more than an hour's drive away.

As they sauntered back, squinting against the brightness of the sun on the sparkling sheet of water, admiring the slim spire of the church and the graceful lines of the suspension bridge alongside it, they saw the hotel.

It sprawled on the far side of the bridge, its green lawns dipping right into the Thames. It was old and mellow and welcoming.

Relaxed, and once more in harmony after their quiet stroll, they looked at each other enquiringly, the same idea in both their minds.

'We could just *ask* if they had any rooms,' Robert murmured.

There was only one room available. A small double on the third floor, its tiny window tucked up into the eaves but with a wonderful view out over the river.

'It's fine,' Robert told the porter in a firm voice. He turned to Kate. 'Wait here and I'll bring up our things from the car.'

Left alone, she felt a surge of panic. What was she doing! She had only known Robert for a few weeks and here she was planning to spend the night with him. She had never even contemplated anything like this in her life before. Her parents would be outraged if they knew.

There was still time to change her mind. The thought of returning to Barracks two days early made her hesitate and then it was too late. Robert was back carrying both their kitbags.

'We won't need those,' she said in a tight voice. 'We don't need our uniforms!'

'I know,' he grinned, 'but I thought it would look better if we appeared to have some luggage. Not that I suppose anyone will give a damn as long as we pay for the room. It's only four o'clock. What do you want to do? I've booked an evening meal but that's not until seven.'

'We . . . we could go for another walk. I'll just freshen up first.'

When she came back from the bathroom she found Robert had taken off his shoes, jacket and tie and was lying on the bed with his eyes closed. He was breathing with a deep rhythm, almost as if he was asleep. As she moved closer he suddenly opened his eyes and reached out, grabbing her, and pulling her down onto the bed.

She started to struggle but he was so powerful that her muscles turned to rubber beneath his grasp. As he pinioned her to the bed, and rolled over so that he was lying partially on top of her, Kate's only struggle was for breath. As his mouth came down over hers, she felt a slow tingling of desire spread through her limbs and a small moan of surrender escaped her parted lips.

His green eyes gleaming, Robert slowly drew away and raised himself on one elbow so that he could look down at her. With a forefinger he gently outlined her brow, pushing the dark hair back behind her small, neat ears. Tenderly he kissed the tip of her straight nose, traced the curve of her cheekbones and chin, then ran his finger down the length of her throat until it met the neckline of her dress.

'Take this off!'

The whispered request startled her. A flicker of fear shadowed her dark eyes. Before she could voice her objection his mouth was covering hers, transporting her back into a sea of desire where pulsing waves of longing submerged her reticence.

His lips were gentle, tender and sensuous as they saluted every inch of her body, implanting light kisses spasmodically, wherever his eyes lingered.

Kate felt a mounting passion invading her entire being, rocking her senses. Her shyness forgotten her fingers began to undo the buttons of his shirt.

He released her just long enough to shed his clothes, dropping them into a heap on the floor. Without the warmth of his body against hers she felt a sudden chill and with it came sobering thoughts about what she was doing – a feeling of guilt.

The moment passed as Robert took her in his arms again, his long lean body a burning fire that re-kindled the erotic desire within her.

With quick-breathing eagerness his hands began exploring her body. As he felt the tips of her breasts hardening his own body responded.

His need built up into a crescendo. Strange heats burst inside him with every throb of his pulse and every breath he drew so that he found it hard to control his actions. With great tenderness he kissed her throat while his hands stroked and prepared her. His love for Kate was so great that he wanted to make this first occasion something she would remember with joy.

He sensed the passion building up in her, and that she was aroused and ready for him. The last delicious shuddering moments came on them simultaneously. It was a blending of minds and bodies, a unique joining of hearts, more permanent than any marriage ceremony. Vitality flowed from one to the other, like intermingling electric currents. And when it ended neither of them spoke, they simply clung to each other, overcome by the magic of the moment.

They made love again before they went down to dinner. Afterwards they strolled along the towpath, hands entwined, watching the silver crescent of the moon reflected on the shimmering River Thames.

They said very little. It was a moment for dreaming, for relishing what they had, not for planning the future. Time enough for that next day when they returned to London. This one night was for enjoying the wonder of being together.

Chapter 4

'Lieutenant Russell, there's a call for you on the outside line.'

'Can't you deal with it, Corporal?' Kate frowned, looking up from the mound of paperwork on the desk in front of her.

It was late afternoon but the July sun was still blazing down, turning the small office into an oven. Although she had rolled up the sleeves of her khaki blouse, Kate still felt hot and sticky. She longed for the day to end and to have the chance to get outside and breathe fresh air. At times like this, she hated London and being confined to an office where she was under pressure from the moment she sat down at her desk at nine each morning until she finished at six.

And even then she was not always free. Although the air-raids had ended, there were still doodle-bugs which meant that in addition to Barrack-room duties, regular drills had to be carried out or supervised. It was very time consuming, yet sometimes, she thought, this was all to the good. It meant she had less time to think and to brood on what might have been.

It was almost two months since she and Robert Campbell had last seen each other. After their memorable night in Marlow he had gone off on his OTC, promising to keep in touch, but she hadn't heard a word. She was not even sure where he had been sent for his training, only that it wasn't London or Sandhurst. So many additional courses had been instigated, in a frenzied endeavour to replace officers who had been killed in Italy and North Africa, that it could be anywhere.

Remembering her own training, she was not really surprised that she had not heard from him. She had found every minute of the day had been taken up by drills and lectures and at night she had been almost too weary to prepare for the next day. The army, she reflected, seemed to be divided between those who kicked their heels waiting for something to happen and those who were expected to cram at least twenty-five hours work into every twenty-four. And she came into the latter category, she thought grimly, as she reached for another folder from the pile in front of her.

'Lieutenant Russell, the caller won't leave a message. He says it's personal,' the corporal interrupted her apologetically.

'Do you know who it is?'

'No ma'am, he refuses to give a name.'

'Oh, very well, I'll take it.' Still talking she picked up the receiver.

'Kate? This is Second-Lieutenant Campbell speaking.'

'Robert! You've passed. Congratulations! Where are you? Can we meet somewhere . . . and celebrate!'

'I am afraid that is impossible. All leave has been cancelled. I'm on standby. The rumours say there's to be a European invasion. You probably know more about that than I do!'

'I don't know anything . . . I couldn't even find out where you were!' Her relief at hearing from him was marred by her disappointment they couldn't be together. 'If you can't get leave then shall I come and see you?' she suggested.

'If you can! I'll phone again as soon as I know where I'm being sent. Kate, I do love you.'

'And I you. I want to see you . . . soon!'

'Marlow was wonderful,' he said huskily. 'I can't wait for us to be together again. I've thought of nothing else! Has your father . . .'

The line went dead before he could finish. Kate jiggled the receiver impatiently but the only person she managed to make contact with was the switchboard operator who told her, 'There is no one on the line. Replace your receiver and I'll reconnect you when your caller comes through again.'

Although she waited hopefully all the afternoon, Robert didn't phone again. The frustration of not knowing where he had been phoning from, or where he was being posted, made her edgy. To make matters worse, it was her night for dining with her father.

The excellent food, the glass of white wine and the strong

black coffee at the end of the meal did much to restore Kate's spirits.

'You look better now than when you arrived,' Sir Henry said, leaning back in his chair and twirling the ends of his moustache. 'Had a hard day?'

Kate hesitated, wondering whether to take him into her confidence or not. Since the disastrous episode at Walford Grange, neither of them had mentioned Robert Campbell.

After she had returned to Barracks, Kate couldn't put the incident from her mind. She had desperately wanted to phone home and straighten things out. She wasn't used to quarrelling with her parents. She had even wondered if her father would even want to dine with her the following Tuesday.

When he didn't phone, or send a message either, she decided to just turn up at the Savoy as if nothing had happened. He had used the same tactics, waiting for her as usual in the foyer.

Now, when they were both relaxed after their meal, might be just the right time to talk, Kate decided.

'I had a phone call from Robert this afternoon. He has passed his OTC,' she said guardedly.

'Who?'

'Robert Campbell. You can't have forgotten him,' she added with irony. 'You said he was the best driver you had ever had.'

'Oh that fellow! Passed has he.' Sir Henry gave a dismissive shrug. 'Well, we've lost so many young officers they are giving commissions to the most unlikely chaps.'

'He'll make an excellent officer.'

'Maybe!' Sir Henry tugged at the ends of his moustache, a frown furrowing his brow. 'Not still seeing him, I hope.'

'I haven't seen him since he's been on his course but I shall as soon as he gets some leave, or when I find out where he has been posted. I don't suppose you'll have any objection if I bring him home now that he has a pip on his shoulder.'

Sir Henry signalled a waiter to bring him a cigar. Kate watched impatiently while he took a gold cutter from his pocket and meticulously removed the end. When it was going well, he gave a satisfied sigh, then said in a heavy voice:

'Damned impertinence, asking me if he could marry you!'

'We are in love with each other,' Kate defended.

'I've already given you my opinion on that,' Sir Henry said sharply. 'I was hoping you would let the subject drop.'

'I won't talk about it if you don't want me to,' Kate said quietly, 'but I will be seeing Robert again and nothing you say will stop me. We are going to be married, just as soon as we can both get leave.'

Sir Henry had only to look at the serious set of her face to know that Kate's mind was made up. He was an expert at planning battles and saw this as a small-scale skirmish, one he could easily win if he planned aright.

'Fine, just as long as you are sure you know what you are doing.'

Her father's agreement completely stunned Kate. She had been all keyed up for a fight, expecting every possible obstacle to be put in her way. His cool acceptance left her indefensible. It was as if the enemy had capitulated without firing a single shot.

'You don't mind?'

'If it's what you really want . . .' he left the sentence unfinished, putting the onus squarely on her shoulders.

'And I can bring Robert down to Walford Grange?'

'It *is* your home. When is he next on leave?'

'That's what I don't know . . . do you think you could find out for me?' she pleaded, her brown eyes desperate. 'Please! It is very important. I don't even know where he's being sent.'

'You'd better give me the relevant details.'

'That is the problem, all I have is his name and service number. I don't even know which regiment he's with now,' she said dejectedly.

'I'll see what I can do.' Sir Henry looked at his watch. 'Time we were moving,' he said abruptly. 'I told my driver to be back at nine o'clock and it is almost half-past.'

She phoned her father three times the following week but he had not managed to unearth any news for her, nor had she heard from Robert again. With her next leave barely a fortnight away, Kate felt a sense of panic. She had made enquiries from all of her own contacts but no one seemed to have any news of a newly commissioned officer called

Campbell. Troop movements were both chaotic and erratic. Units, platoons and even divisions were being moved from one field of operations to the next. The posting of newly commissioned officers to make up depleted strength was going on all the time, he explained, and records were not always up to date.

When she met her father the following week, he was negative about Robert's whereabouts. 'He may have already been sent to North Africa or Italy,' he told her.

Kate still had no news by the time her leave was due and felt torn between staying at her desk, so that she would be on hand if Robert phoned, or going home for the break she so desperately needed. In the end, she took her leave but left instructions with the Duty Corporal that if Lieutenant Robert Campbell should phone to be sure and contact her with details of where she could get in touch with him.

Walford Grange seemed like another world. Apart from rationing, which was amply supplemented by local supplies of eggs, chickens, rabbits and freshly grown vegetables, the war seemed to have passed them by. There had been no air-raids, or any major upheavals. None of the heavily laden bombers that set out each night for Europe ever passed overhead.

Kate found the slow pace of life consolatory and spent the first few days relaxing, contentedly soaking up the August sunshine, dozing, dreaming and half listening to her mother as she gossiped about local happenings.

It seemed that although most of the evacuees had gone home, now that the air-raids on London and other big cities had abated, the village was still over-run by 'strangers'. Land Army girls and Italian prisoners of war were working on the farms, replacing local men who had been called up. But, the really big news was that the entire area had been flooded with GI's from the 8th US Army Air Force. Girls were eager to befriend them because they handed out silk stockings, and their generosity with gum and chocolate bars had won over most of the sweet-starved villagers.

In their smooth, well-tailored khaki uniform even the ordinary soldiers were as well dressed as a British officer. American officers went one stage better and looked incredibly suave in their well-cut olive jackets and beige trousers.

'You'll be able to meet some of them at the weekend,' her mother told her. 'Your father has invited several of them over for drinks.'

The news surprised Kate. Her father was not gregarious and generally resented any kind of intrusion into his home. She even felt suspicious about his motives when on the Friday evening two Majors and a very young Captain arrived. After introductions had been made and drinks served, Sir Henry cornered the two majors and settled down to discuss the different strategies employed by Eisenhower, Marshall and Montgomery and the effect the exchanges between Churchill and Roosevelt would have on the outcome of the war, leaving Kate to entertain the Captain.

Marvin Greenberg had a round baby face and a soft southern drawl. He told Kate he had been a musician before he'd joined up. His supple hands, with their long slender fingers, looked as though they had never known hard physical work. There was a dreamy look about his pale blue eyes and his soft brown hair was a shade longer than even the American Army permitted. When she took him through to the drawing room and suggested he might like to play the baby grand he was as delighted as a child receiving an unexpected treat. He played beautifully and she listened entranced even though she didn't recognise any of the tunes. When she mentioned this afterwards he smiled shyly as he told her he had composed them himself.

'I had just begun to have my work published when the Japs attacked Pearl Harbour.'

'And publishing stopped?'

'Life stopped, or at any rate, changed completely.'

'You abandoned your career to fight for your country!'

'I had no real choice. My mother claims to be a distant cousin of Lieutenant-General Joseph Stilwell, so there is family honour at stake.'

'And when the war ends you'll go back to composing music?'

'Who knows,' he shrugged expressively. 'I might even stay on here in England.' He closed the lid down on the piano. 'For the moment,' he said gravely, 'all that matters is winning the war.'

The next evening, four different officers came to the house. One of them, Major Potac, a thick-set man with compelling dark eyes and jet black hair professed an interest in horticulture and asked Kate to show him the garden. Once they were away from the house he grabbed her by the shoulders, spinning her round and crushing her to him in a bear hug. Although she was taken completely by surprise, Kate had no intention of giving in without a fight. As his mouth came down over hers, his breath so redolent with tobacco that it almost made her gag, Kate found her army training stood her in good stead.

She might look feminine and slim in her light pink silk dress and high-heeled shoes but her leg muscles were like steel. Months of 'square-bashing' gave power to the heel she brought cracking down on his instep. The moment his grip slackened, she sped light-footed, leaving him to find his own way back to the house.

After that, she regarded American visitors with suspicion. Her father recognised the signs and tactfully conceded defeat.

When they next met in London for dinner, he told her that he had located Robert Campbell.

'For security reasons I am unable to say where he is,' he told her, watching her reaction from under hooded lids.

'Does that mean he will be sent to North Africa?'

General Sir Henry Russell looked round anxiously, then leaned closer, lowering his voice to barely a whisper. 'I don't think so. A new offensive is being planned, he will probably go on that.'

'You mean he's still in this country?' she breathed excitedly.

'Somewhere in the South,' he said in clipped tones. 'I have no idea where. This is highly confidential . . .'

'I understand. Don't worry.'

Her heart was dancing at the news. For the rest of the evening she hardly heard what her father was saying. She was far too busy trying to work out how she could find Robert. She felt wonderfully optimistic. As long as he was still in England nothing else mattered.

Chapter 5

August became September, the leaves turned yellow then golden or red and finally, before they fluttered to the ground, became a crisp crunchy brown. Hidden away in the densely wooded countryside, somewhere in the south of England, Lieutenant Robert Campbell of the Guards Armoured Division fretted and fumed, irked by the seeming futility of the endless drills and field exercises. They went on relentlessly, often under cover of darkness, until men and officers finally achieved the superb precision and efficiency demanded of the Guards.

To ensure complete dedication, leave had been cancelled and all letters were censored. It was the nearest to being in limbo that Robert could imagine. There were times when he longed for the comfortable niche of his old job, driving General Sir Henry Russell to and from the War Office.

Remembering the imposing figure, with his receding grey hair and aristocratic features, only served to remind him why he was having to put up with mud and discomfort rather than the cocooned luxury of a staff car. Proving to Sir Henry that he would make a suitable son-in-law was a daunting task. Wearing the right uniform and sporting a pip on his shoulder, was only the framework.

It had not taken him long to realise that the other Guards officers were well aware that he was a fake. His accent, his behaviour pattern, and everything else about him was a giveaway. He lacked their aplomb and their specific brand of bantering humour. His voice was not authoritative when he issued orders and he found it difficult to accept services rendered in a nonchalant manner. He was too ready to do things himself instead of ordering someone of lower rank to do it; and automatically he treated the men under him as equals. As a result, the men, NCO's and fellow officers all regarded him with varying degrees of contempt.

He constantly reminded himself of Kate's spirited confrontation with her father, when she had said that war was a great leveller. It made him determined to master the nuances and prove himself to the General and everyone else.

Spit and polish became almost a fetish with him. No one could fault him on that score. His argument was that it kept the men alert and in a constant state of readiness. For what purpose he didn't really know. The most popular rumour was that they were destined for Operation Overlord, the cross-channel invasion that would seal Hitler's fate and bring an end to the war. He wished fervently that they would get on with it.

Even Kate's letters often disturbed him. When she had mentioned that some American officers had visited her home while she had been on leave he had seethed with jealousy. Why should they be enjoying her company when he could not! His reply had been so recriminatory that she had stopped mentioning such incidents, which only made him worry more.

If only they could meet once in a while and spend an hour or so in each other's arms. He wanted to hear from her own lips, not just from words on paper, that she still cared as much about him as he did about her.

Christmas 1943 came and went and he was still in England. The huts they were living in were heated by coal stoves which smoked erratically and emitted choking gaseous fumes. Even the officers' quarters were primitive and colds and bronchitis were rampant.

In late January, Robert went down with a dose of flu. He was so ill that he was moved into the sick bay. As soon as he was feeling a little better he began scheming how he might find out precisely where he was. The night nurse was young, not very pretty but amiable and approachable.

'We're not allowed to say,' she murmured uneasily.

'I'm not asking you to tell me, just to let a friend of mine know,' he pleaded.

'No! I can't even do that,' she told him shaking her head. 'I'm being moved from here tomorrow,' she explained.

'All the better! If I give you her name and telephone number you could get in touch with her. Please! It means so much to both of us. I'll pay for the call.'

He reached for his wallet and drew out five £1 notes and pushed them into her hand.

'I don't need that much!' she gasped, colouring.

'Now you know how much it matters to me,' he grinned.

When he returned to his unit at the end of the week he lived in a state of suspense. He didn't know just how Kate could contact him but he was confident that she would.

The news that an ENSA concert party was to visit their camp revived everyone's spirits. Some jokingly said that it was only a propaganda stunt to make up for the fact that their mail had been held up for the past month. As junior officer it fell to Robert to be responsible for organising the seating.

There was no lack of volunteers to help and the men were all in their places almost an hour before the curtain was due to go up. The first two rows were reserved for officers but even these filled up early and Robert had difficulty in keeping an end seat reserved for the concert party organiser who, he'd been told, wished to sit out front.

The chair next to him was still vacant when the impromptu lights were dimmed and the curtain went up. When someone came and sat down alongside him he didn't even look round. His attention was fixed on the stage where six girls in skimpy costumes were dancing.

'Enjoying it?'

For a moment he froze, wondering if his mind was playing tricks.

'It *is* me!' came the whisper as a hand slid across his knee and took his.

Unable to believe his ears he glanced sideways, and then doubted even his eyes. Kate *was* sitting there, prim and efficient in her khaki uniform, a clipboard on her knee.

They had an hour together before the ENSA concert party was ready for the road again. Afterwards, he wondered if it had all been a figment of his imagination.

Knowing everyone was at the concert he took her back to the Mess. Even when she was in his arms, her love-filled dark brown eyes gazing into his, her slightly parted lips waiting invitingly for his kiss, he still couldn't believe that she was actually there.

They made love, urgently, primitively, unaware of the cold hardness of the bare wooden floor their need for each other was so great.

Afterwards, breathlessly, Kate explained how she had influenced the ENSA concert party to arrange a show and then had persuaded them to let her come along as well.

'Can't you stay . . . just for a few days. I'm sure I could manage to get out of camp,' he begged, his green eyes pleading.

'It's not possible, darling.' Her fingers tenderly traced the firm outline of his face. 'The security checks are too stringent. As it was they didn't want me along because it meant getting special clearance.'

'When am I going to see you again then?'

'Soon. Now that I know where you are, I'll come back. On my own, though, without involving anyone else,' she assured him, her brown eyes dark with love.

He accepted her promise, confident that what she had achieved once she would manage again.

Only it was not to be. Two days later his division was suddenly ordered to move out. Hours of tedious convoy driving, and just where their final destination was, Robert had no idea, except that it must be near the coast because he could smell salt in the air.

Again came the interminable wait, with only drills and exercise to relieve the monotony. Spring turned to early summer and although he continued to hope, Kate didn't manage another visit and once again he found himself engulfed by loneliness. Apart from Kate, no one else wrote to him. And, although he was surrounded, day and night, by other men, there were none of them that he regarded as a close friend, no one he confided in.

When he was not on duty, Robert spent hours lying on his bed reading, thinking or scheming. He brooded about the past . . . his past and how everything had changed so abruptly when he was fourteen and his father had died.

They had been so close. His father had always treated him as an equal, talking to him about everything he planned to do on the farm, even asking his opinion. When they had ridden side by side on the horse-drawn wagon his father would hand over the reins to him, showing him the right way to control the great animals. On his fourteenth birthday, his father had even let him drive the tractor! Within a few weeks, Robert's whole world had crumbled. A shotgun accident and his father was dead.

Without even telling him what she intended to do his mother had sold the farm and moved back to Liverpool where she had grown up. Within a few months she had re-married and they moved to New Brighton, on the other side of the Mersey, to a big Victorian house near the promenade where they took in summer visitors.

From then on, he had felt an outsider. He hated the broad-vowelled boisterous Lancashire mill-workers who came there on holiday and escaped whenever he could, spending hours messing about on the shore alone. He didn't particularly like the sea and longed to be back farming.

When he left school, he managed to get a job delivering milk. The horse that pulled the float was old and weary but he groomed it and cared for it as his father had taught him. When it died between the shafts, he wept. A week later he left the dairy. He was nineteen. There was talk of war so he joined the army.

'You must be mad, Robert, to go before you are drafted,' his mother snapped when he told her what he had done.

'Good riddance to bad rubbish, I'd say,' his step-father grunted. 'He never does a hand's turn around here so we won't miss him.'

'It means we'll have another room to let,' his mother agreed thoughtfully, her face suddenly brightening.

He cleared out his room, burning all his childhood books and games. The only thing he kept was a photograph of him and his dad, sitting on top of a haystack, the Welsh mountains a dark smudge in the background.

As he caught the train from Liverpool's Lime Street, he vowed to himself he would never return to New Brighton. It was going to be a new life as far as he was concerned. Someday, he vowed, he'd even have his own farm.

He never had much time for girls. The bright-eyed young

women with their made-up faces, who hung round the camp, reminded him too much of his mother, shallow and out for all they could get, he thought cynically.

Kate had been different. Right from the very first time he had seen her he had been impressed by her calm quiet manner. He was curious as to why she was dating someone as old and pompous as General Sir Henry Russell. He was puzzled by her manner. She was so very much at ease as she sat chatting with the General in the back of the Staff Humber. And their outings always followed the same pattern. Dinner at the Savoy then straight back to her Barracks with just a brief kiss on the cheek as they parted.

He made discreet enquiries, and was startled to learn that she was the General's daughter. After that he took an even greater interest in her, daydreaming of what it would be like to know her, to date her, to take her out, even. Not that there was the remotest chance of that ever happening, or of even speaking to her. As far as she and the General were concerned he was just an extension of the Humber, a robot who took instructions and carried them out without question.

The night General Russell had been recalled to the War Office and left him to drive Kate back to her Barracks, had been like the hand of Fate intervening. Afterwards, whenever he thought about it, Robert wondered what would have happened if she had reported him for insubordination . . . or worse. But she hadn't. She had reacted just as he had always dreamed she would.

Things had gone so well for him from then on, that he was confident all his other dreams would also be fulfilled. He accepted that Sir Henry didn't intend letting him run Home Farm at Walford Grange but he still hoped he might find him another farm close by.

Kate was his trump card. From conversations he had overheard when he had been driving them both he knew how fond the General was of his daughter. Everything would eventually work in his favour, of that Robert was quite sure. Meanwhile, he watched and waited, learning all he could from his fellow officers, so that when the day finally arrived he could take his place alongside Kate with confidence and aplomb.

When he learned that along with the rest of the Guards 8th Armoured Brigade they were to join up with the 43rd Wessex and several other Divisions, to become XXX Corps in readiness for 'D-Day', Robert felt fresh hope. They would be under the command of Lieutenant-General Horrocks and he was sure that General Sir Henry Russell would know about this through his job at the War Office and must surely mention it to Kate.

Despite their exhaustive training, the crossing to France for the invasion proved to be something of a fiasco, it was so disorganised. Once they landed on the Normandy beaches, however, the months of drilling and survival exercises began to pay dividends.

In their first major battle, Robert's unit faced fierce machine-gun fire and short range mortar attack. German tanks milled around on all sides and casualties were heavy. They moved on through extensive minefields to Mont Pincon, the 'Little Switzerland' of Normandy; his sense of achievement when they finally gained the crest of the hill was intense.

With Caen in ruins, they pushed deeper into France, and Robert found that his energies were so taken up in fighting and surviving that he no longer noticed the passage of days. When he did sleep, it was from sheer exhaustion; dreamless hours from which he wakened still unrefreshed.

By late August, XXX Corps, now the spearhead of the British Second Army, was crossing the Seine. They established a bridgehead on the east brink, jubilant in the knowledge that their disruption of the German armies was a tremendous success.

They moved on through Belgium, heading an army that stretched back over 250 miles to the Normandy beaches, where men and supplies were still being landed. The fighting was spasmodic. It was like 'Indian Country', Robert thought grimly, it contained more German than Allied troops. Then came the bold drive north into Holland, dividing the country in two and taking possession of the Northern gateway into Germany.

As they drove through Eindhoven and reached the bridge at Nijmegen they became involved in difficult fighting over open boggy country. The situation seemed to deteriorate, pockets of Germans seemed to be everywhere and the entire enterprise seemed to be fraught with difficulties. There were problems with supply trucks and Robert found his work cut out trying to bolster the spirits of his men. It left him no time for his own worries, not even after they'd won Operation 'Market Garden' at Nijmegen by mid-September.

After Arnhem there were intermittent fighting and stiff counter attacks throughout October. Christmas came and went without any real celebration. The weather was bitterly cold. During January and February, the Rhine rose and flooded the 'island' between Nijmegen and Arnhem, floods made worse by the Germans deliberately breaching the dykes so that in places the land was up to six feet under water. When this froze over, and snow added to their hazards, movements became treacherous. Spirits eventually lifted when the thaw came in February, followed by crisp clear March weather that dried out the flooded land in no time at all.

There were fresh problems and tough resistance when they attempted to cross the Rhine in late March. Their job as an Armoured Division was to advance and support the 43rd Wessex Infantry Division, even though the Germans still held most of Holland. Several assault crossings were attempted, both in daylight and during the night.

Robert, because he was used to working out of doors all year round, found he could stand the hardships of winter better than most of the other officers. It was the continual noise he found unbearable, the thunder of gunfire that extended for almost fifty miles from Nijmegen to the Ruhr. And, added to the sound of gunfire, was the noise of bombers and of German reconnaissance aircraft dropping flares over Nijmegen, and of tank convoys roaring along the roads to the Rhineland.

Eighteen days and 150 miles later, they took Kloppenburg. The Germans reacted strongly but with superhuman effort, Robert and his fellow officers rallied their men on to meet this fresh attack. Liberating villages was phrenetic stuff, he thought grimly. After fierce fighting the Germans either pulled back or waved a white flag of surrender, leaving many dead and countless prisoners in their wake.

The fighting was still not over. Bremen was finally captured, the first big German port on the North Sea to fall into Allied hands. As the Guards took over the peninsula between the Elbe and Weser, Robert found they had to deal with over 6,000 prisoners.

Rumours that Hitler and Eva Braun, whom Hitler had married only a few days previously, had taken refuge in their special Bunker in the Chancellery, brought fresh hope that the war would soon be over. Civil order was collapsing. German civilians had started looting abandoned trains, shops and stores, shouting 'Germany kaput!' as they did so.

The first few days of May were edgy ones. Everyone was waiting for the rumours that the Germans had surrendered to Field-Marshal Montgomery to be confirmed. When the announcement 'all hostilities will cease at 0800 hours tomorrow morning, 5th May', eventually came they celebrated with a firing of flares. Victory was assured. As Corps Commander Sir Brian Horrocks took the salute at a parade of gleaming tanks, guns and vehicles, Robert found it hard to believe that only a week before men and machines alike had been covered with the grime of battle.

Exultantly, Robert wrote to Kate. The long wait was over, she could begin making arrangements for their wedding.

Chapter 6

London was a scene of wild rejoicing. The Germans had finally capitulated, after almost six years of fighting, and victory in Europe had now been declared. 8th May was designated VE Day. And, ever since they had heard the news, people seemed to have gone crazy even though the announcement had been expected for almost a week. The previous Wednesday, newspapers had carried the headline '*Hitler is Dead*' and, on the following day, '*Army of 10,000 surrendered*'. On Saturday, placards everywhere declared '*Germans surrender inside Monty's tent*'.

From her office, Kate Russell could see the crowds gathering in the streets below, streaming towards Whitehall, like an army of ants, and she felt an overpowering urge to join them.

Concentrating on the masses of paperwork piled up on her desk was almost impossible. A handsome, square-jawed face with burnished red hair and tantalising green eyes blurred her vision. If the war in Europe was over then Robert could be home any day. In between signing letters and forms she day-dreamed about the future.

Just before lunchtime, her father phoned to ask if she could join him for a celebratory drink and from then on her day became a shambles.

Sir Henry was in a jubilant mood. He had been under pressure ever since the invasion had begun and it showed in his greying hair and bowed shoulders. With a pang, Kate realised that he was growing old and ready for retirement.

She stayed with him at the War Office to listen to Churchill's speech from Downing Street at three o'clock. After that, returning to work was out of the question. The sun was shining and it was as if everyone had suddenly gone crazy. Parliament Square was jammed with people, laughing and cheering, kissing and hugging.

It was early evening when she finally got away from her father and his friends. She had declined his offer of a car to take her back to Barracks. She wanted to be mingling with the ecstatic throng, enter into the spirit of freedom. On impulse she made her way towards Buckingham Palace, the point where the crowds were at their most congested. Groups were singing and dancing, everyone was rejoicing and happy. Complete strangers wanted to shake her hand simply because she was in uniform.

Suddenly there was a movement and Kate found herself being swept forward as the crowd gazed expectantly towards the front of the palace. Earlier in the day, the King and Queen, and the two Princesses – Princess Elizabeth wearing her ATS uniform – had appeared on the balcony and stood there on either side of Winston Churchill, the Prime Minister, waving to the crowd.

Now, as Kate stood there, hemmed in on every side by the milling crowd, she felt a thrill of excitement as a deafening cheer went up to greet the King and Queen as they again emerged. It was followed seconds later by a full-bodied cry for the two Princesses. When this went unanswered it brought murmurs of disappointment followed by a roaring chant of 'we want the Princesses'.

'I wonder what they would say if they knew we were down here with them,' a voice whispered just behind Kate only to be quickly hushed into silence.

Startled, Kate looked round, then caught her breath in astonishment. There, standing shoulder to shoulder with the crowd, were both the princesses! Concerned for their safety, she wondered whether she ought to report the matter so that they could be given professional protection.

A feeling of panic swept through her as she realised that, like her, they were jammed in so tightly by people that it would be impossible for the police, who stood at the outside edge of the crowd, to reach them.

Then, as she heard Princess Margaret giggling happily, she reasoned that since those around them were in such a joyous, happy mood there was unlikely to be any trouble. Anyway, she reminded herself, Princess Elizabeth had trained as an ATS officer and should be well able to take care of both herself and her sister.

The celebrations went on for days. London seemed to be one massive street party. Kate wished Robert could be there to share the incredible atmosphere with her.

No one seemed to know when the troops would be coming back from Germany. She asked her father for news but he was evasive, merely reminding her that though hostilities had ended in Europe, there was still fighting in the Far East.

'Don't forget there will be an army of occupation in Germany and it is quite likely that the Guards will form part of that,' he warned.

The war in Malaya and Korea entered a new traumatic phase a couple of months later, when atomic bombs were dropped on Hiroshima and Nagasaki, so it was almost with relief Kate heard from Robert that he was to stay on in Germany.

After VJ Day, when her own demob date was announced, Kate was afraid to sound too jubilant when she wrote to Robert knowing how frustrated he must be feeling. She wondered if there was any possibility of getting a job in Europe. When she mentioned this to her father he thought it a ridiculous idea.

'Be patient. He'll be back in next to no time and then you'll have a lifetime of each other's company ahead of you. Make the most of your freedom while you can – he probably is,' he added cynically.

She had four days' leave owing so she spent them at home, trying to visualise what life would be like when she was back there for good. Everything seemed so tame and drab. Her mother and Mabel grumbled constantly about food shortages, saying that things were far worse now than they had been when the war was at its height, now even bread was to be rationed. They also constantly bemoaned the fact that they both needed new clothes but lacked coupons to get them.

To escape from them both, Kate went to see Eleanor Anstruther, who had already been demobbed from the

WRNS. They had always been very close friends although they were exact opposites.

Eleanor was shorter than Kate with fair curly hair and deep violet eyes set in a heart-shaped face. At school, she had been decidedly plump but three years in the WRNS had slimmed her down and the light blue cotton dress she was wearing showed off her shapely figure to advantage.

Her effusive greeting confirmed she had lost none of her bubbly good humour. Kate felt her spirits lifting as she followed Eleanor upstairs to where they could talk without being overheard. As she entered Eleanor's bright airy room, with its chintzy armchair and matching curtains, it took her right back to the old days when they had confided in each other over just about everything under the sun, from boys and homework to parent problems.

'Are you going on a holiday or just coming back from one?' Kate asked as Eleanor lifted a half packed suitcase from the bed and dumped it on the floor.

'I'm off, but not on a holiday,' Eleanor said smiling mysteriously.

'Oh! What then? You're not getting married!'

'No!' A shadow clouded Eleanor's eyes and for a brief moment her smile vanished and her lower lip trembled. 'You probably haven't heard that Simon Nielsen has been killed.'

Kate shook her head, her brown eyes widening with shock.

'It happened on VE Day. So bloody stupid!' Eleanor exclaimed angrily. 'He went right through the war, took part in horrendous naval skirmishes in Italy and North Africa, and then, after peace has been declared, gets himself killed while out celebrating!'

'Whatever happened?'

'Someone dared him to walk along a parapet at the side of a bridge and he lost his balance and fell into the river and was drowned.'

'But he was a first class swimmer! Don't you remember how he used to win medals at the School Sports,' Kate declared.

'He drowned just the same. He was drunk, of course!' Eleanor sighed, her violet eyes misting with tears.

'Didn't any of the others try to save him?'

'They were as pissed out of their tiny minds as he was,' Eleanor said angrily.

'It's really upset you, hasn't it,' Kate remarked, gently touching her friend's arm. 'Is Ralph Buscombe all right?' she asked anxiously.

'As far as I know. He's an RAF Squadron Leader these days. What do we do . . . fight over him or toss a coin?'

'He's yours if you want him,' Kate said drily, 'I've found someone else.'

The two girls looked at each other dejectedly for a few seconds then suddenly they were in each other's arms, hugging, kissing, laughing, and crying until they both collapsed helplessly on the bed in a fit of hysteria.

Simon's death saddened them both. Not only had they all grown up together but it had been taken for granted in their tight knit social circle that someday Kate would marry either Simon or Ralph and Eleanor would marry the other one. They were both such suitable matches. All four families were local landowners, had the same standards and lifestyle. If the war had not intervened, the marriages would probably have already taken place, which was a sobering thought for both girls.

'So who have you found?' Eleanor asked when they had regained their breath.

Kate told her about Robert, sparing none of the details of how they had met and her parents' reaction.

'I'm amazed Sir Henry didn't kick him straight out of the house!' Eleanor exclaimed. 'Are you sure they'll let you marry him? Be awful if you'd stayed faithful all this time for nothing!' Her violet eyes quizzed Kate laughingly. 'That is, if you have. It *has* been ages and it *is* war time.'

'I have.'

'How noble!' Eleanor teased, pulling a face. 'And what a terrible waste,' she added cynically.

'I take it you *haven't* been wasting *your* time,' Kate commented.

'No, I've lived every moment of it,' Eleanor replied with a satisfied smirk.

'And what are your plans now?' Kate asked curiously.

'Aah. This is the *big* adventure!' She grinned. 'You

43

probably won't approve. Have you heard about the "Groundnut scheme"?'

'The what?'

'Groundnuts . . . monkey nuts? Britain is desperately short of cooking fat so the government is starting a scheme out in Africa, to grow groundnuts to provide oil.'

'But surely that's where they grow anyway,' Kate said in bewilderment.

'Yes, but they are going to send men and machines out to clear acres and acres of the land and then use modern methods and cheap African labour to grow vast crops and produce a bumper harvest. This will then be processed efficiently and provide an abundance of oil for Britain and anyone else who needs it.'

'And where do you fit in?'

'It's a government project so they offered jobs to Naval officers due for demob. A rather special friend of mine has taken up the challenge and is going out as a Field Officer. He needs a secretary so I said I would go along as well. I may as well be pounding a typewriter out there as somewhere in England.'

'You, pound a typewriter . . . I don't believe it. I thought you planned to get married as soon as the war ended!'

'We both did, remember? Simon or Ralph! Now all that has changed.'

'You mean it was Simon you wanted?' Kate asked softly.

'Not particularly. It was what our parents expected of us, wasn't it?'

'True! It was almost like these arranged marriages you read about,' Kate grimaced.

'I wonder what Simon and Ralph thought about it?' Eleanor mused. 'Was Simon really coming back to marry one of us? And is Ralph desperately trying to decide which of us he will choose now that he's the only survivor?'

'As I said earlier, he's yours if you want him,' Kate told her. 'I certainly don't.'

'Well, don't tell him yet. Keep him guessing. If my trip to Africa doesn't work out then I may come back and marry him.'

'Or you may stay out there with lover-boy,' Kate teased.

'Mm. If his wife will agree to it,' Eleanor said flippantly but Kate saw her face cloud as she turned away.

'You mean he's married already!'

'All the best ones are, or hadn't you noticed.'

'But Eleanor . . .'

'Look, don't start preaching,' Eleanor snapped. 'It's my life. He and his wife haven't seen each other for three years. She cleared off to Southern Ireland the moment war broke out and took their kids with her. Apart from letters, and the occasional snapshot of the children, they may as well all be dead as far as he's concerned.'

'What do your parents think about it?' Kate asked.

'Are you mad!' Eleanor mocked. 'They are the last people I want to find out.'

'But they do know you are going to Africa.'

'Yes, I had to tell them that!' The sparkle was back in her eyes and laughter bubbled as she added, 'They were full of dire warning about all the dangers, everything from lions roaming around at night to the fact that the ground is alive with snakes.'

'And is it?'

'Probably, but who cares. That's all part of the excitement.' She stretched her arms wide. 'Anything is better than returning here . . . yet.'

'But perhaps someday,' Kate murmured softly.

'I don't know!' Eleanor slid off the bed and walked over to the window and stood looking out at the garden beyond. 'I'm not placid and tractable like you are, Kate. I want a challenge out of life. I want to go places and see things not become enmeshed in parochial affairs like my parents. Honestly,' she spun round to face Kate, 'they really do believe that this is the centre of the universe. They don't know, nor care, what is happening in the rest of the world. As long as the hunting is good and the port properly decanted, the old man is perfectly happy. And when he is content, Mother can arrange flowers and have afternoon tea parties and together they live in perfect harmony. Ugh! That's not living!'

'But dodging snakes, fighting off scorpions and never knowing when you might be eaten by a lion, is?' Kate parried.

'When you are sharing the experience with the right

person, then yes, it is. Look, why don't you come along as well?' she challenged.

'Now I know you're mad!'

'Just for a few months,' Eleanor persisted, 'until this Robert chap gets his ticket. Come on, you'd enjoy it, it would be great fun.'

'Not for me. I like my creature comforts too much and living under canvas, in primitive conditions, just isn't my idea of a good time.'

'What *will* you do then? Can you stay on in the ATS? I know they asked us if we wanted to defer our demob date . . .'

'Eleanor, you really are wizard!' Kate exclaimed, her brown eyes widening with delight. 'That's the perfect answer. Why didn't I think of that?'

For the rest of her short leave, Kate could think of nothing else. Continuing in her present job would be the ideal way of filling in her time while she waited for Robert to be demobbed. She was perfectly happy working with Captain Graham Parkes. Although he demanded a high standard of efficiency, his manner was courteous and he had a whimsical sense of humour that she enjoyed.

She could hardly wait to get back to the office to find out if it was possible.

'If I do defer my demob date then I would want to be sure I could go on working for you,' she told him.

Graham Parkes looked positively startled. A warm friendship had grown up between them during the time they'd shared an office. He found Kate extremely efficient, and always cheerful no matter how much pressure they were under. He admired her greatly. He liked the way she wore her dark hair, her well groomed appearance, and her quiet competence.

Knowing that he was to be put in charge of a new department and that his work load would be greatly increased, he had been dreading the thought of her leaving. Now, the chance of her continuing to work alongside him was a bonus indeed.

'There shouldn't be any problem,' he said cautiously. 'What sort of period did you have in mind?'

'I hadn't really decided. Could we say three months to start with. It depends on how things work out . . .' she hesitated, colouring.

A feeling of unease went through him, as he saw the anxiety in her dark brown eyes, in case she was doing this because of her feelings for him. 'Look,' he blurted out, 'I don't want you to do this because of me . . .'

He stopped quickly as he saw her bewilderment and realised with a mixture of shock and dismay that he had judged the situation wrongly.

'I . . . I thought you'd heard that I was being given a new department and that perhaps you thought I couldn't cope,' he added lamely.

'No, I hadn't heard,' she said quietly. 'My reason for staying, as well as for being so indecisive about how long it should be, is that my fiancé is still out in Germany and I have no idea when he will be coming home.'

'That's fine. Couldn't be better.' His relief made him overly delighted. 'I'm sure we can arrange for you to leave whenever you want to,' he added quickly.

'Thank you.'

'Funny, we've worked together all these years and I never knew you had a fiancé.'

'No? Well, I suppose I'm rather like you, I don't talk about my private life very much.'

Her brown eyes were so candid as they met his that his heart thudded. For a moment he wondered if she knew his secret, then dismissed it as nonsense. A girl like Kate Russell wouldn't be so openly friendly with him if she knew the darker side of his nature, he thought ruefully. For one bitter sweet moment he felt cheated. Although he was almost twenty years older than Kate he knew that if he had been the marrying kind then she was the one woman he would have chosen.

Chapter 7

Robert Campbell groaned audibly as the curtains were whisked back and brilliant sunshine flooded the bedroom. It was almost as though someone had beamed a searchlight directly into his eyes. He struggled to sit up, but it felt as if a steel band gripped his head and he lowered it carefully back onto the pillow, dragging the covers up over his face to shut out the glare of the new day. Muzzily, he tried to remember where he was.

'Good morning, Lieutenant. Your morning tea.'

Tentatively he lowered the sheet as he heard the sound of china rattling. His mouth was parched and his lips felt cracked and dry. Propping himself up on one elbow he reached for the cup. The liquid was hot and sweet and as he gulped it down everything began to come back into focus.

'Thanks! I needed that,' he grinned at the plump German woman who was now picking up his uniform from the floor where he had dropped it the night before. 'Sorry about the mess . . . I had one too many last night.'

She nodded, her round face inscrutable as she walked towards the door, his uniform draped over her arm.

'Hold on, where are you taking my clothes?'

'To have it pressed. I will bring it back when you have had your bath, in time for you to take breakfast.'

As the door closed behind her dumpy figure he stacked the pillows behind his head, and lay back, eyes half closed, enjoying the comfort of his surroundings. It was a large airy room, tastefully furnished. The walls were papered in a delicate peach shade, that contrasted so well with the dark woodwork and pale green deep-pile carpet. The figured walnut bedroom suite was handsomely carved and the bed he was lying in was massive. He stretched luxuriously as it all came back to him where he was and why he had a hangover. Last night he had been drinking until almost midnight with a crowd of other officers from XXX Corps who were also staying at Bad Harzburg. He'd been there for almost a week and this would be his last full day, he thought with regret.

In pre-war days it had been the most fashionable resort in the Harz Mountains. Now, since they were not allowed home to England, it had been taken over by the British Army as a Leave Centre and was intended to provide a complete break from military atmosphere.

After almost two years spent either under canvas, in makeshift barracks, or requisitioned SS quarters, Robert was enjoying every moment. There were splendidly comfortable lounges, a dining room with panoramic views and several attractive bars, as well as excellent leisure facilities.

He took a deep breath of the scented air that wafted into the room through the french windows that opened onto a balcony. From where he was lying he was able to look down on the bright red roofs of the town below. Beyond them he could see the chequered fields, dappled by the bright early morning sunshine, rising towards the Bad Harzburg hills which were closely thatched with pine and fir. He could even see the cable carway which carried people to the top of Burgberg, outlined invitingly against the cloudless blue sky. 1,600 feet above sea-level, in less than ten minutes! All the benefits of mountaineering without any of the toil, he thought with a smile remembering his visit.

There was so much to do at Bad Harzburg that it was impossible to cram everything into just one week. The swimming pool, with its modern springboards, was one of the largest he'd ever used. There were also lawn tennis courts, a clay pigeon shoot and it had even been possible to go on a fishing trip with all the tackle supplied. He had thoroughly enjoyed that, especially since arrangements had been made afterwards to cook his catch.

As soon as the chambermaid returned with his uniform, he dressed and breakfasted, eager to be out of doors and making the most of his last day. After wandering around the town he ordered a coffee at one of the open-air cafés.

'And some cakes? They are filled with real cream, quite delicious.'

Although he knew it was really much too early in the morning for such delicacies, the pretty black-haired girl, in her tight-fitting red dress, was so persuasive, and her smile so winning, that he agreed to try one.

There was only one thing his holiday lacked to make it perfect, he thought as he settled back, and that was Kate.

He suspected she was as unsettled as he was. He had been very surprised when she had written to say she was staying on in the ATS and he still couldn't fathom her reason for doing so. Whenever he thought about it, his imagination worked overtime and he wondered what this chap Captain Parkes was like. He visualised a darkly handsome, polished type with a clipped military manner. The sort of officer who would fit in with General Sir Henry Russell's idea of what a future son-in-law should be like, he thought censoriously.

The memory of his last meeting with Sir Henry still rankled. Yet, in some ways he was almost grateful to him. His disapproval had acted like a challenge. He'd already been made up to full Lieutenant since he'd been in Germany. If he played his cards right, he might even manage to get to the rank of Captain before he was demobbed. That would impress the old buffer, he thought cynically. He wondered if Sir Henry had mellowed in any way now that he had retired from the War Office or whether he was still as aristocratic and arrogant as ever.

If only he knew when he was likely to be sent home, Robert thought as he drank his coffee. After VE Day there had been talk that they would be going back to England in just a matter of days.

He'd known that was expecting too much since there was still fighting out in the Far East. Now weeks later though, the Guards Armoured Division, like the rest of XXX Corps, still seemed to be no nearer to getting back to England and still had no idea when they were likely to be demobbed.

Patience had never been one of his virtues and he felt fed up and frustrated. Although the suspicion and resentment with which he had been regarded by fellow Guards officers when he had first been given his commission had long since vanished, he was still very much a loner. In battle he had proved himself to be a born leader. His men not only trusted his judgement but they liked him as a man and had given him their fullest support when under fire.

Robert spent a lot of time thinking about these things and wondering what the future held for him. The war had completely changed his life and it was pointless trying to pick up discarded pieces now. He still felt that his future lay with Kate and he hoped that Sir Henry would eventually relent and let him run Home Farm. The ambition to become a 'country gentleman' was still his main motivation.

When the waitress came to clear his table she was eager to tell him about the local amenities and he encouraged her to chat. She was in her twenties, black-haired and blue-eyed with a pale olive complexion and a ready smile.

Her English was hesitant but easy enough to follow since her voice had none of the usual harsh guttural intonations of the Germans. As she told him of the valet service where he could have his uniformed pressed, of the hairdressers who excelled in everything from a trim to a singe, he tried to work out whether she was Austrian or even Italian. Picking up one of his hands she ran her fingers lightly over the back of it, then studied his nails telling him there was a first class friseur should he decide to have a manicure.

'And what is there to do in the evening?' Robert asked.

Her sea-blue eyes widened expressively. 'There are many things. You can dine, attend a symphony concert, go to the cinema or even go dancing at the Kurhaus. The ballroom there is most romantic,' she added sighing prettily.

'And where is the Kurhaus?'

'It stands in lovely gardens on the banks of the River Radau . . .' she paused, frowning, a look of dismay on her face. 'But you could not go there!'

'Oh, why is that?'

'It is not for officers. Officers must dance at the Harzburger Hof Hotel, or at the Thirty Club here in town. That is used exclusively by officers, so of course I have never been there,' she said wistfully.

'Would you like to go to the Thirty Club?' Robert asked.

'Oh!' her eyes glistened. 'It is one of my dreams.'

'Then will you come with me, this evening?'

'Do you really mean it?' she breathed, excitedly.

'Where shall we meet. Here?'

'No, no. I will be finished work in time to go home and put on my prettiest dress.' She frowned. 'My home it is not easy to find so why do we not meet at the Club.'

'Just as you like. At seven o'clock?'

'That would be most wonderful!' She clasped her hands together delightedly, like a child promised a treat.

'Right. See you there. I must be on my way now.'

'You do mean it, you really will come?' she asked anxiously, placing her hand on his arm as he stood up.

'Of course, I will! By the way, what is your name? Mine is Campbell, Robert Campbell.'

'And I am Maria,' she breathed softly, lowering her eyes shyly.

As he walked back up the hill to his hotel, Robert wondered what on earth he could have been thinking about to invite the girl out like that. He didn't have to turn up, of course, but since he had been rash enough to tell her his name she could easily come to the hotel looking for him. Runnels of cold sweat snaked down under his shirt at the thought that Kate might get to hear of this escapade.

What if she does, he argued with himself. He only wanted some company for the last evening of his leave.

Later, as he got ready to go to meet Maria, the guilt came back. Surely Kate would understand how desolate he felt with her being hundreds of miles away, he thought gloomily. Anyway, she had her Captain Parkes to help her overcome feelings of isolation and loneliness.

The Thirty Club in Harzburg had been planned to provide the same sort of glamour and escapism as could be found in any first class London night club. Maria was ecstatic about the plush interior, the elaborate décor, the soft lights and the general opulence and feeling of luxury.

As they circled the highly polished dance-floor between courses, Maria smiled up into Robert's eyes, giving a little sigh of contentment. She had changed into a dress in a silky material that was the same blue as her eyes. The bodice was close-fitting with a heart-shaped neckline and the full skirt flared from the nipped-in waistline.

'This is just heaven,' she breathed, her face wreathed in smiles.

His arm tightened, pressing her shapely body closer to his. He was enjoying it too. As he looked down at her radiant face, framed by her glossy black hair, he felt a surge of longing. For a brief second he closed his eyes, shutting out Maria's Latin looks and imagining instead that it was Kate he was holding in his arms and her smooth brown head nestling beneath his chin. The wine and the music helped the illusion so much that he let his lips rest on her brow.

Maria's reaction was dynamic. Before he knew what was happening her mouth was pressed hungrily against his and her body moved sensuously in his arms as she responded fervently to his brief caress.

For a harrowing moment he fought the temptation rising within him. Then his own blood was afire and he made no resistance when she took his hand and led him off the dance floor.

They found a small annexe used as a cloakroom. Their lovemaking was swift yet satisfying. As he climaxed, her face was just a blur, he only knew it wasn't Kate.

Afterwards he felt an overwhelming self-hatred and knew he had behaved despicably. He refused to go back to their table. He knew she was hurt by his attitude but there was nothing he could do about it. All he wanted now was to be alone. There was no way he could possibly make her understand, so he didn't even try to explain his inner turmoil.

'We have not yet even finished our meal,' she exclaimed angrily when he said they were leaving.

'I'm sorry but the evening is over for me,' he said quietly.

'But not for me! I wear my prettiest dress for you, I wish to stay.'

Her warm smile had vanished, her eyes were glacially cold with angry sparks in their depths, as she squared up to him. At that moment he wondered how he could ever have likened her to Kate.

Their eyes met, held and clashed. There was such venom

in hers that he drew back, no longer sorry at having taken advantage of her, only despising himself for his weakness.

'You can stay on if you wish or I will take you home, now,' he told her.

Her answer was to pivot away from him on her spiky heels, tossing her jet black head defiantly as she minced her way back to their table, her body swaying in time to the beat of the music.

He remained where he was until she sat down, then thrusting his hands deep in his pockets, turned and left the Club.

When he returned to duty, Robert found that the break at the Harzburger Hof had unsettled him and that it was increasingly difficult to get back into routine. Part of the trouble was that there was not a great deal to do and what duties there were seemed pointless. His restlessness increased to such a point that he even asked the MO whether he could have some home leave on medical grounds.

'Not a ruddy chance, old boy. We're all in the same boat. It looks as though it's going to be at least another six months before any of our demob numbers come up,' he added gloomily as they stood chatting in the Mess.

Six months seemed to be a lifetime away and Robert was sure he couldn't stick it out that long. He was so engrossed in his own feeling of despair that he almost missed the Major's next words.

'. . . only fellows who are being allowed back to Blighty are those signing on for the regular army . . .'

Next day Robert checked to make sure he had heard correctly and then made an appointment to see his Commanding Officer.

'Didn't realise you liked it out here that much,' Colonel West grunted.

'I'm not exactly enamoured by the place, sir, but if I was in the regular army I don't suppose I'd spend the rest of my service life in Germany.'

'You might have a point there,' the Colonel agreed. 'Well, if you are quite sure I'll send in my report and we'll see what happens. You'll probably have to pop back to England to sign the necessary documents and they may decide to keep you there for some update training, I shouldn't wonder.'

Robert hid his feeling of elation. Stony faced he saluted and withdrew but inwardly he was gloating. As long as he got back to England and could see Kate everything would change. He had no intention of signing on for the regular army! He couldn't wait to get out!

Once he and Kate were married he was sure her family would see things in an altogether different light. Sir Henry was, after all, exceptionally fond of Kate so he should be overjoyed at the thought of them living at Home Farm and within a stone's throw of Walford Grange.

His optimism made the waiting bearable. When Colonel West confirmed that his application had met with approval, and he was to report to Wellington Barracks in London for an interview, Robert felt that once again Fate was on his side.

Chapter 8

The sky was overcast and oppressive and there was an ominous rumble of thunder as the plane landed at Brize Norton around mid-morning. Robert Campbell made a quick dash for the office buildings as a mid-summer downpour slashed across the airfield.

'If you want a train for London, there will be a truck going to the station in about twenty minutes, sir,' the Duty Sergeant told him after he had checked his papers.

'I am not going to London . . . not today. Is there any transport going Bridgwater way?'

'I can check, sir. If not, then you will probably have to go into London and travel back out again.'

Robert waited impatiently while the Sergeant made enquiries. He had managed to get a seat in the Transporter from Germany so the journey had only taken a fraction of the time allowed for overland travel. It meant a weekend at home and his plan now was to go straight to Walford Grange and surprise Kate.

'There is a truck going to Warminster, sir,' the Sergeant told him a few minutes later. 'They will be happy to make a slight detour,' he added with a grin.

As they drove through towns and villages, everything looked totally different to what he had expected. Most people seemed to have a shabby, despondent air about them as they queued outside the food shops. But the thing he noticed most of all were the giant hoardings, all trying to influence the voting in the forthcoming elections. It seemed almost as if there was another war going on, a fight for the right to rule Britain.

Although the main contenders were the Labour Party and the Conservatives, he noticed that in some towns there were strident red and black posters belonging to the Communists pointing out how prices of everything from food to homes would rise if either of the other parties managed to gain control.

By the time the truck dropped him at Walford Grange the sun was once more burning down. As he crunched his way up the gravel drive his spirits lifted at the sight of the well tended fields on either side of the neatly trimmed hedges and the herd of black and white cows grazing in a distant field. At least things here looked the same, if not better, than when he had last seen them.

Having pulled the iron handle set in the stonework along-side the carved oak door, and heard the bell clanging deep inside the house, he straightened his uniform.

The astonishment on Mabel Sharp's face when she answered the door should have warned Robert that his madcap scheme of arriving unannounced would go wrong.

'Hello, Nanny! Surprised to see me?' Without waiting for her reply he made to step inside.

'Miss Kate's not here,' Mabel Sharp said frostily and there was open hostility in her sharp hazel eyes as she barred his way.

'Is Lady Dorothea at home?'

'No!'

'Sir Henry then . . . someone must be here!'

'Sir Henry and Lady Dorothea are out campaigning. One of their friends, Sir John Buscombe, is putting up for Parliament. Miss Kate is with her ATS unit . . . in London.'

Robert's green eyes darkened with bewilderment as he stared at Mabel Sharp. For a moment he wondered if she was lying deliberately. He knew Kate had decided to stay on in the ATS but he assumed that now the war had ended she would work a five-day week, the same as her father had done when he had been at the War Office.

'Are you quite sure she isn't coming home for the weekend, Nanny?' Keeping his temper in check he smiled coaxingly. 'I have come all the way from Germany and I am only in England a few days . . .'

'I am quite sure!' Mabel Sharp's chin jutted aggressively. 'I have just said so!'

'Yes, I know . . . I was not doubting your word.' Robert removed his cap and passed a hand through his hair, so that it stood on end, glowing like a cock's comb. His thin lips twisted into a grimace. 'I don't appear to have planned this manoeuvre very well.'

'Well, I suppose you could phone Miss Kate . . . from here,' she relented, sensing the sharp disappointment in his voice.

'Right!' His mood lifted. The solution seemed suddenly simple. He would phone Kate, and see if she could come home for the weekend. If not, then he would arrange to meet her in London.

'You may use the phone in the morning room,' Mabel Sharp told him as she stood aside to let him enter the house. 'Do you know her number?'

His hand went to his breast pocket. Then he remembered he'd changed his tunic before leaving Hanover and he shook his head, feeling foolish and inadequate.

'I'll get it for you,' Mabel Sharp sniffed.

When he finally got through the connection was appalling and he couldn't believe it was Kate speaking. She seemed to be having similar difficulties at her end and it took him some time to convince her that he was in England and speaking from Walford Grange.

'I can't get home, I haven't any leave due,' she wailed.

'The war is over, you don't have to stay in the ATS,' he bellowed back irritably.

'I'm sure Captain Parkes will let me have some time off when I tell him you are home but I shall have to wait until tomorrow to check it out with him.'

'So what do you want me to do. Stay here at Walford Grange and kick my heels on the off-chance you'll be able to get home?'

'What does my father suggest?'

'He's not here. He and your mother are out canvassing. Nanny let me in . . . just to use the phone.'

The silence that followed was so long that Robert thought they must have been disconnected. When she finally spoke, her voice was full of doubt and he could tell she felt uneasy about the situation. He wanted to ask why but he didn't dare because Mabel Sharp was hovering within earshot, and would doubtless report everything that was said to Lady Dorothea.

'Look,' he said, suddenly decisive, 'I will come to London. Meet me at Waterloo Station when you finish work.'

He replaced the receiver. 'I want a taxi to take me to the station,' Robert said to Mabel Sharp as she entered the room.

'There is no local taxi service,' she told him. 'No petrol to spare. All right for you army fellows dashing around all over the country in your jeeps and wagons. The rest of us are rationed.' She sniffed. 'We have to rely on the local bus.'

'And when is the next bus to Taunton or Bridgwater?'

'Tomorrow!' she answered, a look of triumph in her beady eyes.

'I see.' Refusing to let her see how dismayed he felt, Robert replaced his cap and made for the door.

'What are you planning on doing then?' she asked. 'I only want to know so that I can tell Lady Dorothea and Sir Henry when they get back.'

'Don't bother. I hardly think either of them would be interested,' he replied cuttingly.

'How will you get to the station then? If you waited a while, Sir Henry will be back from his canvassing and he might take you . . .'

Robert gave a thin smile as he touched his cap in a salute before turning away and walking briskly down the drive, revelling in the crisp scrunch of the gravel, knowing that Mabel Sharp was still standing in the doorway, bemused by his action.

He had walked about a quarter of a mile when a car drew up alongside him.

'Want a lift? Where are you going?'

'Bridgwater.'

'Hop in. I am not going quite that far but I can drop you off where you can get a bus.'

At Bridgwater he just had time to buy a ticket and find the right platform before his train pulled out. When he arrived at Waterloo, his eyes raked the crowded platform looking for Kate, afraid they might miss each other. Then he spotted her, trim and attractive in her khaki uniform, her brown hair in a shiny pageboy roll under her officer's hat. Suddenly she was in his arms, hugging him and returning his kisses, oblivious of people pushing and jostling them as they hurried on their way.

For them both, time was unravelled as they remembered the hours spent together in Marlow when nothing else mattered except the love they felt for each other.

For Robert, all the hardships and frustrations he had experienced since D-Day were obliterated. All that counted was that he and Kate were together again. He was aware of the fragrance of her hair, the softness of her skin, and the pressure of her body against his, stirring up emotions that had lain dormant for so long.

Sensing the turmoil within him, Kate raised her face once again, her brown eyes searching his for confirmation of the love she felt brimming over inside her. The mundane routine she had become so involved in since she had agreed to stay on in the ATS suddenly seemed so futile. She wanted only one thing from life, the chance to be with this magnificent man who filled her thoughts, every moment of the day and night, and who was even more devastatingly handsome than she had remembered. Sometimes, when she was feeling particularly depressed, she had even wondered if he existed at all or whether he was just a figment of her imagination.

Now, it all seemed worthwhile. Robert was here, holding her in his arms and the future stretched ahead of them like an unrolled carpet.

'If only you had written and let me know you were coming!' she murmured between kisses, looking up into his vivid green eyes that were blazing with desire.

'There was no time. It all happened so suddenly.'

'When are you actually being demobbed?'

'Well, that is what I want to talk to you about,' he told her cautiously. 'Shall we go somewhere and have a meal. I have not had anything to eat since I left Germany this morning and I am absolutely starving.'

'This morning?'

'That's right. I managed to get a flight over on a transporter plane but I don't have to report in until Monday. That's why I had time to spare . . . and why I decided to surprise you. Let's go somewhere and eat . . . and talk.'

60

They chose a restaurant in a side street off Leicester Square and settled into a quiet corner. The fish pie was surprisingly good and Robert ate ravenously. Kate was far too excited to eat very much of the omelette she had ordered so, when he had finished, she swopped her plate with his empty one and smilingly watched as he cleared that as well.

As they drank their coffee, Robert began to expound on how he came to be in London. He had given it considerable thought since he had spoken to his CO and what had started out as a mere ruse to get back to England to see Kate had gradually taken on a whole new career possibility. Since he had no job to go to and not enough money to provide a home for Kate, joining the regular army had suddenly seemed one way of attaining both of these.

'Are you sure that army life is what you really want?' she asked apprehensively when he had finished explaining everything to her.

'Of course it is, why else would I be doing it?' he answered sharply.

'To please my father,' she said shrewdly as her brown eyes locked with his.

'Well, that may have had *some* bearing on my decision,' he conceded.

'Robert,' she leaned across the table, taking his hand between her own, 'please be sure you are doing this for the right reasons. I know something of army life. It puts a tremendous strain on a marriage.'

'We'll be together and that is all that matters,' he told her confidently.

'It is not that easy,' she protested. 'The long separations . . .'

'You will be with me,' he assured her. 'No matter what part of the world I am sent to you will come along as well. Look on it as an adventure, something we can enjoy together.'

She smiled wistfully, thinking of Eleanor. Remembering the joyously defiant way Eleanor had announced she was going to Africa just to be with the man she loved, she wished she could be more like her. And Eleanor was not even married to him so there was always the possibility that his wife would claim him back, or that he would be overcome with remorse and go running home to his family.

'When will you know if you have been accepted?' she asked, studying Robert's face anxiously.

'Possibly after this interview on Monday. I shall, of course, insist on staying in a Guards Regiment,' he added.

'You will. Why?' A frown knotted her brow.

'Surely, that's the whole point if I am to please your father!'

'So you *are* doing it to impress him!'

'Influence him, perhaps,' he agreed grudgingly.

'But you don't have to commit yourself to the army!'

'It is the only career for which I have any training.'

'Nonsense. You could always take up farming.' Her hand squeezed his understandingly.

'No.' He shook his head. 'That needs capital, something I lack. Remember what your father said when I suggested running Home Farm for him?'

'He hardly knew you then,' she demurred.

'The situation has not changed at all,' he said grimly.

'He has not had much of a chance!' she argued.

'No, Kate, I've given this a lot of thought and I know I'm taking the right decision. If I make a success of soldiering then perhaps your father will give me a chance to show my capabilities at Home Farm. I'll transfer to the regular army, as long as I can stay in the Guards, and just hope they will let me keep my present rank. As soon as I know will you name the day?'

'Is this a proposal?' her eyes twinkled. 'If it is, then it's rather matter of fact. I had hoped for something much more romantic.'

'You mean you would like me to go down on one knee?'

'Something like that!'

'Right!'

Before she knew what was happening, Robert had pushed back his chair and was kneeling in front of her, one of her hands clasped between his. 'Kate, my darling Kate, will you marry me?'

As she leaned forward and pressed her lips on his there was an outburst of clapping. Cheeks flaming, Kate looked round the restaurant. Most of the tables had been empty when they had come in but now they were packed with people and everyone, waitresses included, was looking over at them and applauding.

'I have far too many witnesses for you to back out now,' Robert laughed as he stood up and took his seat again. He was so overjoyed that he didn't even feel embarrassed.

Chapter 9

'It is utter nonsense to say that I shall be leaving you on your own, Mother,' Kate exclaimed in vexed tones. 'I haven't been living at home for years! And as for asking permission to be married that is absurd as well. I'm twenty-three! You were not only married but you had a baby before you were my age.'

'Things were quite different in those days and anyway my parents thought I was making an excellent match.'

'Are you trying to say that Robert does not meet with your approval?'

'Your father already had a career in the army and his future was secure,' Lady Dorothea said firmly.

'So what is different?' Kate asked quietly. 'Robert has a career in the army. Not only is he an officer in the Guards but he even holds the same rank as father had when you were first married.'

'It's quite a different set of circumstances,' Lady Dorothea insisted petulantly. 'And we really must stop discussing it,' she exclaimed faintly, dabbing at her brow with a lace-edged handkerchief.

'But, Mother . . .'

'You've brought on one of my sick headaches again. Draw the curtains, dear, I'll have to lie down for a while.'

Kate sighed as she walked across to the window. It was always the same. Each time she tried to explain to her mother that she and Robert intended getting married as soon as he completed his re-training her mother either dissolved into tears or feigned a headache.

Her father was not being very helpful either, she thought irritably. He either refused to discuss the matter or raised as many objections as he could.

She wished Robert would agree to her suggestion that they should slip away quietly to a registry office. Once they were actually married her family would have to accept the situation. But Robert insisted that they owed it to her parents to be married from Walford Grange.

She knew he was probably right. She didn't really want to do things in an underhand way. She had always dreamed of a white wedding in the village church, surrounded by family and friends. As children, she and Eleanor had enacted it all over and over again, using old net curtains for veils and collecting wild flowers to make bouquets.

Kate sighed. She wanted her own marriage to work right from the start. She loved Robert so intensely that it hurt. Eleanor had broken with tradition and it was proving disastrous. The African venture was turning sour and the threatened divorce, and problems over his children, made it seem probable that there would be a rather sordid ending to the affair.

Robert was quite the most handsome man she had ever known. Whether he was wearing his immaculate, well-tailored uniform, or in casual dress, with his broad shoulders, slim waist and long muscular legs he made heads turn and she felt inordinately proud of him. His swinging stride, his deep voice, that could also be so thrillingly soft and passionate, his lean tanned face, keen green eyes and burnished shock of hair made him seem like the reincarnation of a mythical Greek god.

Just to see him striding towards her, head and shoulders above the crowd, made her heart pound and her legs turn to water.

All this, combined with his impeccable manners and natural charm, should have made him the perfect choice and yet her parents' opposition to her marrying him never wavered.

'They don't want to lose you, darling,' Robert consoled her. 'I can understand their reluctance even though I can't accept it.'

Once his transfer to the regular army was confirmed, he became increasingly anxious to set the day for their wedding.

'Two months should give you enough time to arrange your demob and get everything organised for the wedding,' he told her.

'Absolutely impossible . . . if you still want a white wedding,' her father said emphatically. 'Far too great a strain for your mother to be rushed like that. Much better to leave it until next spring.'

'We want to be married before Robert is posted . . .' Kate began but her father ignored her interruption.

'Robert might have managed some promotion by then,' Sir Henry went on. 'At twenty-six he should hold a higher rank than Lieutenant if he's planning a career in the army.'

Kate bit back the angry reply that rose to her lips. There was no point in antagonising him now. Two months was perhaps rather optimistic but next spring did seem a lifetime away.

'What about Christmas . . . ?' she suggested tentatively.

'Absolutely impossible!' Sir Henry barked. 'We are involved with far too many local activities in December. Apart from that, who wants to be standing around outside the church ankle-deep in snow!'

Dispiritedly, she wrote and explained the situation to Robert. As the days passed and no reply came back she began to worry. Then, after three weeks' silence, by which time she was unutterably tense, she received a brief note telling her that their wedding would have to be postponed until after Easter as he was on a four-month tour in Italy.

Expediently, she turned this to her own advantage and told her father that she would take his advice and postpone their wedding until April or May.

Secretly, she was dismayed at the thought of a six-month delay and wished she hadn't already applied for her demob from the ATS. Then, early in December, Eleanor came home from Africa, alone.

Eleanor was so depressed and heartbroken that Kate spent as much time as she could trying to cheer her up. Wedding plans were pushed to one side, and barely mentioned for fear of distressing Eleanor even more.

At Christmas, Ralph Buscombe, who was now demobbed and working at his father's bank, came back into their lives and he and Eleanor slipped back into their old relationship almost as if there had never been a break.

Watching them together, Kate felt lonely and left-out and

threw herself wholeheartedly into perfecting the plans for her own wedding. The date was fixed for the first Saturday in May and afterwards they would drive to Cornwall for their honeymoon.

To ensure Lady Dorothea would not be overtaxed, Kate made all the bookings for the church, choir, organist and reception herself. She blamed her mother's poor health on the fact that her opposition to the forthcoming wedding amounted almost to paranoia. Mabel Sharp was also violently opposed but Kate was convinced that this was because she had been turned against Robert by Lady Dorothea.

With each new embroilment, Kate wished herself out of Walford Grange. Robert was now a Captain and expected to be sent back to Germany immediately his tour in Italy ended. He wrote such glowing accounts about what their home and social life in Hamburg and Hanover would be like that she couldn't wait to join him. Just to escape from her mother's plaintive voice, constantly complaining about the difficulties the wedding was presenting, would be a relief. They were fast becoming a daily trauma that she found hard to endure.

Now that Robert held the rank of Captain, her father had no further criticism to make on that score, only about what his prospects were after he left the army and, like Lady Dorothea, bemoaned the fact that he lacked breeding.

'He's a man, not a stallion,' Kate snapped angrily.

'Pedigree counts in both instances,' Sir Henry told her. 'Blood, background, breeding and wealth are the criteria by which you should judge a man.'

'How about looks, personality, and moral fibre?' she asked sarcastically.

'The first doesn't matter a damn and the other two will follow automatically if the breeding and background are right!'

Since it was pointless to argue, Kate usually changed the subject or found an excuse to take refuge in her own room.

She wrote to Robert most days, giving him a running record of the wedding plans, without mentioning any of the controversy.

April heralded in sunshine and showers. The bright green

of the lawn was a perfect foil for the masses of daffodils, jonquils, polyanthus and grape hyacinths, that overflowed from the borders. The hedgerows wore white mantles of sweet-smelling May and in the orchard the grass was showered with pink and white apple blossom that drifted on the light breeze like confetti.

Just before Easter, Eleanor said she was going away for a few days but promised to be back in good time for the wedding. When Kate learned that Ralph was also on holiday she suspected they were together. When they reappeared, glowing with happiness, Kate learned her friend had stolen a march on her and got married first.

'I'll have to be matron-of-honour instead of chief bridesmaid,' Eleanor laughed as she displayed the slim gold band on her left hand.

Looking at Eleanor's radiant face, Kate felt envious and even more conscious of the tremendous hassle that still lay ahead of her. If only Robert were near at hand to give her moral support, she thought wistfully.

As April drew to a close and the wedding was imminent Mabel Sharp seemed to have a last-minute change of heart and threw herself into organising everything with immense gusto. She persuaded Lady Dorothea to let her take on two women from the village to help with the extra cleaning and cooking and personally supervised everything.

Kate felt overwhelmed by everyone's generosity. There was a constant stream of callers bringing gifts. The stack of precious rations grew daily as people delved into their store cupboards, bringing out carefully hoarded sugar, tinned or dried fruit, home-made preserves and other luxuries.

Some of the villagers even brought along clothing coupons. And there were gifts of silk lingerie, hand-made from old parachutes and trimmed with exquisite hand-made lace.

When news leaked out that Kate and Robert would be motoring to Cornwall for their honeymoon, donations of petrol began to appear and Kate stored it up in black jerry cans ready for the journey.

One last minute hitch set her nerves on edge. Robert and a fellow officer, who was to be his best man, were due to arrive in England the day before the wedding and it had been arranged that they would stay overnight at Ralph and Eleanor's flat.

'It will be awfully cramped,' Kate protested.

'Never mind,' Eleanor laughed. 'It is the only way of making sure the two of you do not meet before you get to the church!'

On her wedding eve, Kate waited with unbearable excitement, longing to hear Robert's voice saying he had arrived.

A few minutes before midnight when the phone rang, she was disappointed when it was only Eleanor.

'Thought you would want to know that Ralph has just gone to Taunton to collect Robert,' she told Kate.

'And his friend.'

'No . . . just Robert. That is why I am phoning you. It seems the other chap was unable to come . . .'

'But what will we do!' Kate wailed.

'Don't worry, we've thought it through. Ralph will be best man. Now get some sleep or you will be arriving at the church with black shadows under your eyes. See you in the morning, Kate. I'll be over early to help you dress.'

Kate couldn't sleep. Her mind was in a turmoil, wondering what had gone wrong with Robert's arrangements and wishing he had phoned her himself with the news. She heard the hall clock chime midnight. Her wedding day had already dawned and it was too late to change anything now.

Kate's wedding was a scene of fairytale splendour. After the drabness of the war years, the sight of a bride in white, and a handsome Guards Officer waiting for her arrival, brought tears to the eyes of the many well-wishers who clustered outside the granite-grey Norman church.

The spring day was filled with sunshine and flowers. Kate and her father arrived in a horse-drawn landau. Sir Henry was resplendent in a grey morning coat and grey topper. Erect, and bristling with pride, he gave his arm to Kate as she descended from the carriage. She looked a vision of loveliness in her white lace dress, the heavy pearl-encrusted veil covering her dark hair. Tall and slim, her hand rested lightly on her father's arm as he proudly escorted her down the aisle.

The strains of the organ died away as she reached Robert's

side, and a hallowed silence filled the ancient church. Sunlight streamed in through the rose-window, bathing her in a kaleidoscope of colour. As Robert turned towards her, and she saw the love in the depths of his green eyes, she knew an exquisite peace. The moment she had dreamed about for so long had finally arrived.

The service, exchange of vows, signing of the Register, posing outside the church for photographs and the reception back at Walford Grange all merged into an incredible extravaganza, in which she did all the things required of her as if in a trance.

It wasn't until Eleanor had helped her to change out of her wedding dress into her blue woollen suit that she really believed it had all happened and she was married at last.

Once clear of the well-wishers who lined the drive, waving them on their way, Robert pulled over to the side of the road and cut the engine. Turning, he took Kate into his arms. They sat holding each other, not daring to speak for fear of destroying the enchantment of the moment. Then masterfully his mouth covered hers in a deep tender kiss.

With a light sigh she responded, relaxing in the warm reassurance of his arms. The long months of separation were erased by those sweet magical moments and when Robert restarted the car, and they headed west for Cornwall, Kate settled back in her seat filled with an overwhelming contentment and pleasurable anticipation.

The sun was dipping by the time they arrived at St Ives. Suspended like a glowing red ball it floated above the shimmering surface of the sea, until it finally sank from view.

Their room looked out over the sea and when they at last went up to bed, Kate went out onto the balcony. The air was fragrant with lilac and she stood there, momentarily mesmerised by the full moon, a golden shield, suspended high above the white choppy waves against a backcloth of dazzling stars.

Then Robert was at her side, his lips nuzzling her hair, his hand on her arm, drawing her towards him, back into the room and their long awaited night of love.

Chapter 10

Kate stirred to sharp sunlight, a crisp salt-laden breeze and the unfamiliar sensation that there was someone in the bed alongside her. For a moment she lay perfectly still, trying to collect her thoughts and convince herself that it was not just a dream and that yesterday *had* been her wedding day. As she turned her head, the shock of reddish-gold hair on the pillow beside her confirmed the reality of it all.

She had imagined this moment so many times yet it still had an air of unreality and even now she was afraid she might suddenly find it just a mirage. As she lay there, conscious of the heat of Robert's body where it touched her own, she became aware of a gradual sense of contentment. The early morning sounds outside, the unfamiliar lapping of the waves as the tide crept up the beach, and the scream of the gulls as they dived for food, all helped to crystallise the moment.

She raised herself on one elbow and looked down on the face that had haunted her thoughts for so long. Lightly, she traced the strong outline, running her fingers up into the fiery tousle of Robert's hair, staring down at him in silent joy.

With a blissful sigh she lowered her head to kiss Robert. As their lips met he grabbed her. Startled, she offered no resistance as he rolled her over pinioning her beneath him.

'Good morning, Mrs Campbell,' he breathed, his green eyes glinting with desire. He pulled away so that he could look down at her, feasting his eyes on her creamy skin and the soft curves of her body, tantalisingly hidden by the filmy nightdress. Then he began to gently caress her throat with his lips and to move in a slow trail down over one breast.

'I thought you were still asleep,' she murmured, wriggling one arm free so that she could stroke his face and bury her fingers in his hair.

'I know you did,' he smiled. 'I've been awake for quite some time. I enjoyed watching you sleep.'

'That's unfair!'

'Why is it? You were watching me!'

As she made to pull away he held her more tightly. The playful glint had gone from his eyes, replaced by purposeful ardour. His hands slid beneath the sheer nightie, stroking her body, sending delicious waves of pleasure rippling through her entire being. Intoxicated, she pressed closer, and the burning heat of his skin against the coolness of her own increased her excitement.

Time, place, the past and the future melded into one sensation as she felt his hardness touch her. With a tiny rapturous moan she responded. For them both, each moment became another step of discovery in the joy of loving.

Kate gave gasps of pleasure and surprise as his lips continued to explore her body, his teeth gently grazing in a manner so sensuous that he aroused her need of him until it was as great as his for her.

Kate's face was damp with tears – her body now so relaxed that when he finally entered her the completeness of their union filled her with joy. As the pulsating rhythm united them, she responded to every vibration and to every breath he drew, feeling his tremendous vitality seep through her entire being.

The sudden release of their passion was cataclysmic. An overpowering heat flooded over her, a great wave of happiness welled up, leaving her gasping as the last delicious shuddering moments came on them simultaneously.

Her cheeks flushed with emotion she lay quiescent, listening to the rasp of his breath, feeling its warmth in the nape of her neck, conscious of his weight as he lay there exhausted. When he attempted to move away she clung on to him, wanting to retain the feeling of completeness for ever. Tenderly he kissed her eyes, her brow, her mouth, then, still cradling her, rolled onto his side.

They lay there in each other's arms, her head resting on his muscular chest, for a long time, content to dream, to bask in their love for each other as they watched the sun shimmering on the blue sea beyond the open window. The light morning

72

breeze stirred the curtains and wafted over them, promising all the glory of an early summer day.

'What a pity it is too cold to swim before breakfast,' Robert murmured as he stroked Kate's pink tipped breast.

'Perhaps it will be warm enough after lunch,' she said hopefully.

'You mean after our afternoon siesta,' he teased, his green eyes challenging.

'We're not going to waste our entire honeymoon in bed!' she admonished. 'This has to be the holiday of a lifetime, we have both waited long enough for it.'

'Not a single moment will be wasted,' he assured her as his hands began once again to move caressingly over her body.

'Stop!' She captured his straying hand and held it tightly. 'If we don't get dressed and go down to breakfast we will probably find we have left it too late and I am ravenous.'

'So am I,' Robert agreed, 'but not for food!' He nuzzled her ear, pushing her dark hair to one side, and then his lips began a trail down her neck until his mouth closed over her hardening nipple.

The shrilling of the phone broke the spell. Frowning, Robert reached out and picked up the receiver from the bedside table. A look of anger crossed his face as he passed it over to Kate.

'For me!' she exclaimed in astonishment. 'Who knows we're here?'

'Mabel Sharp!'

'Nanny?' She looked bewildered as she spoke the word into the receiver. Then it changed to dismay. She reached out for Robert's hand and held on to it while the colour drained from her face as she listened without speaking.

'Very well. I'll come right away,' she promised in a small tight voice.

Tears streaming down her cheeks she handed the receiver back to Robert to replace in its cradle.

'What was all that about?' he asked as he tried to pull her back into his arms.

'We have to go home. We must leave right away,' she said, resisting his embrace and throwing back the bedcovers.

'Why, what has happened? We have only just got here!'

'Mother has had a heart attack. She collapsed last night. They have taken her to hospital, it sounds rather serious. My father is with her and he asked Nanny to phone and tell me. It seems . . . Nanny thinks . . .' the words choked her and she was unable to go on. The colour had drained from her face leaving it strained and white, her dark eyes confused.

Robert gathered her into his arms, rocking her tenderly in an attempt to comfort her.

'Come on, it can't be all that bad!'

'But it is,' she wailed. 'They don't think she will live. That is why we must be there. Nanny said they wouldn't have contacted me otherwise but the doctor thought I should be there . . . that is how critical they think it is.'

Placing the flat of both hands against Robert's chest Kate pushed herself free from his embrace and went into the bathroom. He heard the splashing of water as she bathed and within seconds she was back in the bedroom, wrapped in a towel, scrabbling through her unpacked suitcase searching for clothes.

His face set like granite, Robert shaved and dressed, anger bubbling inside him that this had happened. He tried to think of some way to persuade Kate to delay leaving.

If Lady Dorothea was already in hospital there was not much that Kate could do so it did seem senseless to make such a long journey without being quite sure that they were needed. If she phoned home again, later in the day, she could check whether it was absolutely necessary for them to cut short their honeymoon. By then the worst might be over and her mother off the danger list.

Kate didn't attempt to eat any breakfast. She drank some coffee and tapped her foot impatiently, waiting for Robert to finish his bacon, egg and toast.

'Why don't you try to eat something, it will save us having to stop on the journey,' he suggested.

'You won't need to stop on my account,' she said, getting up from the table. 'I'll go and stow the cases in the car while you finish.'

'Hold on. I shall only be a couple of minutes!'

'It is over half an hour since the phone call came through,' she said, looking at her watch impatiently.

'We will make that up when we get on the road,' he promised.

'I am going to drive,' she told him firmly. 'I will feel better doing something than just sitting there.'

'We'll take turns. You can drive first,' he said stubbornly.

'I will go and bring the car round while you pay for our room.'

Robert was still trying to explain to the manager why they were leaving after just one night, when Kate came back and snatched up the case resting on the floor by his feet. With an apologetic smile at the manager, Robert followed her out to the car.

Her speed along the narrow twisting Cornish roads frightened him but he thought it wiser to say nothing. He hoped that once they were actually on their way she would relax a little and slow up.

Once they were into Devon, and joined the main road heading towards Bridgwater, Kate increased her speed until the car vibrated under the strain. Her hands gripped the wheel so tightly that her knuckles shone white.

'Would you like me to drive for a while?' Robert suggested.

She didn't answer, simply shook her head, her eyes never leaving the road as they hurtled along at top speed.

'We had better stop at the next garage for petrol. Are the coupons in your handbag?'

'The tank is still half-full,' she answered, letting her gaze momentarily flick to the control panel.

'Do you want to stop for a drink . . . or a sandwich?' he asked, looking at his watch.

She shook her head emphatically and her hair fell like a dark curtain between them.

Robert leaned back in his seat, trying to take an interest in the passing landscape since it was useless attempting conversation with Kate. He had hoped she would agree to stop so that he could take over the wheel for a while. She had now been driving non-stop for over three hours and he was sure she must be tired.

'Are you going straight home or to the hospital first?' he asked as they neared Walford Grange.

'I . . . I don't know.'

For the first time since they had left Cornwall he detected a note of uncertainty in her voice. As she pushed her hair to one side, he caught a glimpse of her face and could see the strain she was under and judged she was almost at breaking point.

'We'll go to Walford Grange,' he said decisively. 'Your father may be waiting there for you. If not, Mabel Sharp will be able to tell us which hospital.'

'I just hope we are not too late,' she said in a tight whisper.

'I am sure we are not,' he said and patted her knee reassuringly.

Kate managed a wan smile as she brushed away the tears spilling down her cheeks with the back of her hand. Inside she felt numb. It was as if her whole world was crumbling. Worst of all was the overpowering sense of guilt that she felt. If she had listened to her parents and not insisted on going ahead with her wedding then none of this might have happened.

She had known her mother was perturbed about her marrying but she had not realised just how upset she was. If only she hadn't been so insistent about having her own way, her mother might never have had a heart attack.

She sensed that Robert would not understand her feeling of guilt. He probably thought that now they were married it was her duty to put him first, not her parents, she thought as an apprehensive shiver chased down her back.

As she turned into the drive of Walford Grange, and heard the familiar crunch of gravel beneath her wheels, her stomach felt as if it was in her throat. Her legs were trembling as she climbed out of the car. She ached to see her father, yet dreaded what news he might have for her.

Chapter 11

Lady Dorothea used her heart attack like a weapon, directing it with deadly accuracy against Kate.

At the sight of her mother lying almost lifeless in a hospital bed, propped against a mountain of pillows, her eyes half closed, her waxen cheeks and blue-tinged lips positive proof of the seriousness of her condition, Kate was overcome with remorse. Even her shallow breathing was a reprimand aimed at her daughter who hovered continuously at the bedside, tenderly holding one of her mother's limp hands in her own.

Mabel Sharp lost no time at all in telling Kate that she had been the initial cause of Lady Dorothea's heart attack.

'The shock of you marrying that dreadful man after all she has done to try and persuade you not to,' Mabel scolded. 'And then, on top of that, all the work in getting things ready for your wedding. Lady Dorothea has never been strong, not since that day you were born,' she went on with a loud sniff.

'Mother has never had a day's illness in her life, Nanny,' Kate defended, 'not until now.'

'The worry of Sir Henry being in London and you being away from home all through the war has been bad enough but then your wedding following right on top of it all has just been too much for her,' Mabel Sharp continued undaunted.

'That is utter nonsense,' Kate exploded, her brown eyes hardening. 'Tucked away down here you hardly knew there was a war on.'

'You were such a dear little thing as a child, as good as gold,' Mabel Sharp went on, almost as if talking to herself. 'She was so happy when she knew you were on the way, even though the doctor warned her that she was taking a risk because she wasn't strong. She never dreamed then that things would turn out like this and that she would be harassed to death. None of us did.'

Convinced that her mother would die, Kate haunted the hospital and rarely left her bedside. Lady Dorothea was in a private ward so visiting was not in any way restricted. Kate would arrive there soon after ten o'clock each morning and often it was eight or nine o'clock at night before she left. And by that time she was so exhausted she wanted nothing more than to sleep.

At first Robert felt as concerned as Kate was about Lady Dorothea's health. After three days, when she seemed to neither improve nor deteriorate, he suggested to Kate that perhaps her mother might recover more quickly if she was left to rest. But, because she felt she was to blame for her mother's heart attack, Kate refused to leave Lady Dorothea's bedside.

'We are probably the first people to ever spend our honeymoon in a hospital,' Robert said ruefully on the very last day of his leave.

'I know, but what else can I do?' Kate murmured with a wan smile that tugged at his heart.

'I do understand,' he said gathering her into his arms.

'She looks so frail that I am afraid to leave her bedside in case when I get back it's too late,' Kate said hesitantly.

'Come out tonight,' he urged softly. 'It is our last chance, I go back to Germany tomorrow.'

'I don't know . . .' she demurred.

'Please! I need you too, you know,' Robert said vehemently. 'I had expected you to be coming back to Hanover with me . . .'

'Surely you don't expect that . . . not now,' she exclaimed in a strangled voice, her large eyes dark with surprise.

'Not right away, Kate, of course not. You will come out just as soon as your mother is out of hospital though?'

'I . . . I don't know. It depends on how she is. I may have to wait a few weeks . . . until she is strong enough to stand the parting.'

'That could take several months!' he argued, his voice harsh with dismay.

'Must we go into it now,' Kate shrugged wearily. 'I can't leave her while she is in this state, now can I?'

Robert's jaw was set grimly as he looked down at Kate. It made him angry the way Sir Henry and Mabel Sharp were subtly piling the blame on Kate for Lady Dorothea's illness, and, what was worse, Kate seemed to accept it without argument. It was quite ludicrous to say that all the pressure leading up to the wedding had been the cause, since he knew that Kate herself had done most of the planning and organising.

He suspected the real reason was that Mabel Sharp's constant criticism of him as Kate's husband had worried Lady Dorothea unduly and that the nervous tension had built up and brought on the heart attack.

He felt bitter about the situation but there was very little he could do to change things without causing Kate further distress. Her fixation with her family affronted him yet, deep down, he knew that since his own future security rested on Kate's one day inheriting Walford Grange it would be unwise to raise the issue. He consoled himself with the thought that Sir Henry was now turned sixty, so in another ten years, at the most, he would find running his Estate too much for him and be looking for help. Then, Robert could see his own ambitions being realised. He would be able to retire from the army and take over the running of the Estate, including Home Farm.

Once Lady Dorothea knew that Robert had returned to his regiment in Germany and Kate had remained behind in England, her condition improved rapidly. She became so restless in hospital that her doctor decided she would be much better at home, in her own surroundings.

Kate nursed her assiduously and rarely left her bedside. Lady Dorothea was not a good patient. She was irritable and petulant and needed constant attention. She slept fitfully and after several nights of disturbed sleep Sir Henry moved into one of the guest rooms. And so that she would be close at hand if Lady Dorothea needed her, Kate slept in his dressing-room which opened off the main bedroom.

Sir Henry hated illness of any kind and kept as far away from the sickroom as possible. He had become increasingly involved with running Home Farm and spent most of his time either out walking the fields, or in his study reading technical journals to try and find new ways to improve the soil. He had also begun to take a considerable interest in the livestock and was intent on building up a herd of pedigree cattle. On the rare occasions when Kate left the sickroom, and took her meals with him, this seemed to be the chief subject of their conversation.

By the end of July, Lady Dorothea was well enough to lie out on the terrace on a chaise-longue and Kate's hopes soared. Even her mother's querulous voice constantly demanding attention no longer worried her. She began counting the days to when she could join Robert in Hanover. Robert seemed to be equally optimistic and wrote in glowing details about the married quarters he had arranged. He had some leave due, which he was saving up, and he listed all the places they would visit and the things they would do once she arrived there.

With mounting excitement she began to pack, ready to join him. The doctor confirmed that Lady Dorothea was now sufficiently recovered and, since Mabel Sharp would be there to look after her, he assured Kate that there was no reason at all why she should not be on her way to Germany.

Sir Henry was less confident. He tried to persuade Kate to wait a while longer. 'I agree she is much stronger but she is still very edgy and nervous,' he argued.

'She will have Nanny in constant attendance.'

'There must be someone on call at night.'

'Surely you will move back in with Mother when I leave,' Kate said in astonishment.

'I've become quite used to the room I'm in now,' Sir Henry prevaricated. 'I'm in the habit of rising much earlier than I used to do and it would disturb your mother. If you are determined to go to Germany, you had better talk to Nanny and see if she is prepared to sleep in my dressing-room.'

Kate put off telling her mother that she was going to join Robert until the very last moment. She expected her to make some protest but she was quite unprepared for the dramatic outburst that ensued.

'To desert me like this when I am so weak and helpless,'

Lady Dorothea moaned, reaching for her smelling-salts. 'It's callous, Kate, absolutely selfish. And for that man! I just cannot believe it of you. He is the one who has put this idea in your mind.'

'You are better now, Mother,' Kate protested. 'Doctor Elwell said it would be all right for me to go.'

'What does he know about it,' her mother sniffed scornfully. 'He can tell if my heart is beating as strongly as it should, and if my temperature is right, but he has no idea at all of how I actually feel inside. If you go and leave me here all on my own, Kate, I shall be utterly devastated.'

'You have Nanny here and she is devoted to you. She will look after you just as well as I could. And Father will be here . . .'

'Your father is more interested in his dairy herd than what is happening to me,' her mother said disparagingly. She dabbed at her brow with a tiny lace-edged handkerchief. 'You had better run along and finish your packing, I can see your mind is made up and nothing I say will change your plans.'

'I am going to bring you up a drink and settle you for the night,' Kate said soothingly.

'No, don't go to all that trouble,' Lady Dorothea said in a low voice. 'Let Mabel bring it up. I must try and get used to her looking after me again. It won't be the same but I don't suppose it will be for long . . . then I won't be a burden to anyone.'

Kate hardly slept for worrying about whether she was doing the right thing in going to Hanover. She knew her mother had come to depend on her and that it made her feel more relaxed when she was around, but she also longed to be with Robert. Above all, she wanted to try and make up for the disappointment he must have felt when their honeymoon trip to Cornwall had been cut short by her mother's illness.

Yet, lying there in the dark in her father's dressing-room, listening to the soft whimpering sounds coming from her mother's bed, Kate felt torn in two. She loved each of them so much but it was impossible to be with both of them at the same time. She wondered if her mother would have acted differently if she had approved of Robert. She had never tried to get to know him, Kate thought sadly. Whenever she attempted to talk about him, and what he was doing in Germany, her mother either changed the subject, or pretended to be asleep, so that she would not have to listen.

The night before she was due to leave, Kate had to admit that her mother looked anything but well. Her pathetic grief-stricken eyes seemed sunken into her cheeks.

'Perhaps I should call in Doctor Elwell to have a look at you, Mother,' she said worriedly when Lady Dorothea refused her evening meal and lay back on the pillows, her face chalk-white, her breathing laboured.

'I'll be all right, just leave me,' Lady Dorothea gasped in a weak, breathless tone.

Kate stood hesitantly by the bedside, filled with a deepening despair, knowing that her plans to be with Robert were once more going to be frustrated.

She had hardly settled to sleep before she heard her mother calling her. Slipping on her dressing-gown Kate hurried in to find Lady Dorothea struggling for breath, her face creased with pain. Quickly, Kate summoned Mabel Sharp and asked her to phone the doctor and then rouse Sir Henry.

The rest of the night became a trauma of ambulance, sirens, journeying to the hospital and then many hours of anxious waiting at Lady Dorothea's bedside as she struggled to maintain her tenuous hold on life.

By the time she was once more breathing normally and dozing fitfully, it was mid-morning and there was no chance of Kate catching her plane, even if she had been prepared to tear herself away from her mother's sickbed.

Aching for sleep, she phoned Robert to let him know she would not be arriving as arranged.

'Don't worry, get to the airport as soon as you can and catch the first plane out. I'll be here waiting,' he told her.

'You don't understand ... I haven't just missed the plane ... I won't be coming.'

'Why ever not?'

'Mother has had a relapse ... another heart attack. I've just come from the hospital ... I've been with her all night. She is stable now but she is going to need a lot of nursing. It may take some time.'

The silence that followed was more ominous than an

outburst of anger. Kate held her breath, praying that Robert would understand her predicament.

'When are you going to join me?' His voice was cold, whether with anger or bewilderment she was not sure. Tears filled her eyes. The feeling of being torn in two, tugged between her longing to be with Robert and her duty to her mother returned.

'Just as soon as Mother is off the danger list . . .'

'It's taken three months for her to get over the first attack,' he said in a peeved voice. 'Does this mean you won't be out until Christmas?'

'I don't know, it is too early to say. I'll know more in a day or two. I'll phone you again.'

'And what about my leave? I had a hundred-and-one things planned for us to do.'

'I know, I'm sorry! You could come home . . .'

'And spend it sitting in the hospital like last time! No! Phone me again . . . when you have some good news.'

The anger in Robert's voice cut through her. If only he was just a little more sympathetic she thought despondently. Surely he must understand how anxious she felt about her mother. The tears she had managed to hold in check suddenly welled over. Quickly she pulled herself together, dashing them away angrily. They would be together again soon and then all this would fade like a bad dream. And this time, she resolved, she would make quite sure that her mother really was strong enough to be left before she mentioned to Robert that she was joining him. Then she would make up to him for every moment they had spent apart.

Chapter 12

Propped against the bar in the Schloss Club, a glass of whisky clutched in his hand, Captain Robert Campbell was hazily aware that he was drunk.

He had headed for the Club after Kate's phone call to say she was not coming out to Germany had made his trip to the airport unnecessary. He had intended to have a meal and a drink and find some company. Instead, he had stayed leaning against the bar, downing whisky after whisky, until now the whole room swam before his eyes, a suffusion of colour and noise seen through a haze of cigarette smoke.

Moodily he drained his glass and pushed it across the bar counter demanding a refill.

'Don't you think you've had enough, sir,' the barman said deferentially.

'Fill it up,' Robert ordered sharply.

'Sorry, but I'm afraid we are closed,' the barman told him, spreading a cloth over the beer taps and beginning to mop down the counter.

Muzzily, Robert squinted round the room. A waitress carrying a tray of drinks passed near enough for him to grab her arm and stop her. Triumphantly, he took a drink from the tray.

Fearing trouble, the barman came round the counter to intervene, but when the girl turned to protest the words died on her lips and her face broadened into a smile.

'Ah! it is you, Robert Campbell!'

'You know each other?'

'But yes, the Captain and I met when he was taking a holiday break at Bad Harzburg.'

Robert stared down at her bemused. Very slowly, his mind began to clear. He shook his head, like a dog that has been in water. 'Kate?' he mumbled, peering hard at the girl who was smiling up at him.

He felt bewildered. It was not Kate. Kate was tall and slim not plump. Kate had smooth brown hair and calm brown eyes. This girl's eyes were sea-blue and her hair was as black as coal. And yet he was sure he knew her. Frowning, he struggled to dredge up the memories that were eluding him.

'My name is Maria, not Kate,' the girl bubbled with a high tinkling laugh. 'You must remember me! We went dancing at the Thirty Club.'

In a flash it all came back. The café, the cakes and the waitress who had served him; their evening out, the music and laughter. But most of all he remembered their love-making. His blood stirred at the memory and he lunged out to draw her to him.

'Watch out or I shall be spilling these drinks,' she giggled as she deftly side-stepped out of reach.

'Come here!'

'Let me see to this order, then I'll be back,' she promised.

He leaned back against the bar, watching her make her way between the tables with the loaded tray. Lust stirred within him as he studied her shapely buttocks jiggling beneath her skimpy tight skirt. As she bent over the table to hand out the drinks, his gaze fastened on the cleavage be-tween her plump breasts and he smiled fatuously, recalling the lush feel of their ripeness, eager to hold her again.

Fortified by the sandwiches and coffee Maria brought him, Robert began to sober up. Once the world was back in focus he remembered Kate wasn't coming to Germany after all and felt unbearably depressed.

He had been looking forward so much to them being together at last. He had been allocated a splendid apartment. The rooms were spacious and well furnished and there was a well fitted kitchen and an elegant bathroom. He had thought it would be an excellent start to their life together. A com-pensation for all the many problems they had faced ever since they had decided to marry.

He tried to think dispassionately about Lady Dorothea and her illness. He knew she couldn't fake a heart attack and yet it did seem strange that each time he and Kate planned to do something she was taken ill.

It was all part of the strained relationship between himself and Kate's parents, he thought wryly. Sir Henry was slowly coming to terms with the situation and seemed to be prepared to accept him, as long as he made a satisfactory career of the army. But Lady Dorothea was quite a different matter.

The more Robert thought about it the more he felt sure that Mabel Sharp's influence lay behind Lady Dorothea's intense dislike of him. Kate's old nanny still regarded him as an intruder because he wasn't from the 'county set' and resented the fact that he was taking Kate away from the family.

By the time Maria eventually finished work for the night, Robert was morosely sober.

'But I thought you were taking me home,' she pouted when he told her he was leaving.

'It will be all I can do to take myself,' he observed.

'Perhaps we should see each other home then,' she retorted archly as she linked her arm through his and smiled up into his face.

Once outside in the fresh air, Robert felt decidedly groggy.

'You had better lean on me,' Maria giggled as he staggered down the steps of the Club. 'Tell me where you live and I'll get a cab.'

'Yes, put me in a cab, that is the best thing to do,' he muttered thickly. 'Apartment eight . . . Hanstrasse,' he said hesitantly.

'You don't seem to be too sure about it, perhaps I should come along as well to make sure you have the right address,' Maria suggested slyly.

'I've only just moved in there,' he mumbled, 'but I'll know if it is the right place when I see it.'

'And your wife, she is at this address waiting for you?'

'If she was, I wouldn't be out drinking on my own and getting pissed out of my mind, now would I?' he snarled as he slumped onto the back seat. He lay back, closing his eyes, trying to control the waves of sickness that invaded his throat.

'Then where is she and why *are* you living on your own?'

86

Maria questioned and listened wide-eyed while he explained what had happened.

After they had paid off the taxi, she took his key and helped him into his apartment. Leaving him in the bathroom, and closing the door so that she could no longer hear him retching, she made a quick inspection of the rooms. When he staggered into the living room, white-faced and sweating, she handed him a cup of strong black coffee and steadied his hand while he drank it. Then she mopped away the beads of sweat from his brow before helping him through to the bedroom.

She helped him to remove his shoes, and to take off his jacket and trousers, before he collapsed onto the double bed. Then, she covered him over with the duvet and left him to sleep.

'Well, Captain Campbell, how do you feel this morning?'

Robert groaned and covered his eyes with the back of his hand as someone whisked up the blind and sunshine flooded into the room bringing a promise of a crisp autumn day.

For several minutes he lay perfectly still, wondering where he was and why his eyes and head hurt so much. He was confused because it was a woman's voice that had asked the question and not one of the orderlies.

Cautiously he opened his eyes again, shielding them from the sunshine, and looked around him. At first he didn't recognise the spacious room with its double bed, and floral duvet that matched the frilled drapes at the window.

He levered himself up onto one elbow, groaning as sharp pains shot through his head.

'Here, drink this, it will work wonders.'

Blindly he reached out. It was not coffee as he had expected but something in a small glass that had a sharp acrid smell.

'Drink it!'

Obediently he tipped his head back and swallowed the contents. A shudder ran through him at the bitterness of the concoction. He tried to remember where he was and what had happened. It was not Kate's voice . . . and yet the face seemed to be familiar.

'Is there any coffee?'

'In a minute. Let that do its work first.'

He lay back, eyes closed, trying to remember where he was and how he came to be there. Slowly his brain began to clear.

'What the hell are you doing here?' he asked, sitting up and frowning at Maria.

As she came over and perched on the side of the bed, he noticed that she still had on the skimpy, tight black skirt she had been wearing at the restaurant the evening before.

'Have you been here all night?' he asked suspiciously.

'Of course!' She smiled, lightly running a forefinger down his cheek.

'Where did you sleep?'

'There, with you,' she nodded to the pillow alongside his own and as he turned to look he could see an indentation where a head had rested.

'Do stop worrying, Robert Campbell. Nothing happened. You were out of this world. You fall dead asleep as soon as you lie down and you snore all through the night. After working all evening I, too, was very tired so I lie there and sleep alongside you. This morning I wake early, I shower and dress then wait for you to wake up. It is now lunchtime so I am hungry. We will go somewhere and eat. Yes?'

'I have to get back to Barracks . . .'

'No, that is not so. You told me last night that you had taken some leave to be with your wife when she arrived here from England, only she never came. So, you have much time to spare. You will take me for lunch. Yes?'

'I am not hungry,' Robert scowled.

'Perhaps not, but I am. And since I looked after you last night, when you were so very drunk, I expect you to buy me lunch now,' she told him firmly. 'First though, we go to my place so that I can change my clothes.'

'Just leave me alone, I feel awful,' Robert groaned. He lay back on the pillow, his eyes closed, longing for a drink, yet knowing that if he had one he would probably be sick. If only Maria would just go away and leave him in peace, he thought wearily.

'Come!' Briskly, she yanked the duvet off him. 'Take a

shower. The draught of bitters I gave you will have worked by now.'

Reluctantly, Robert dragged himself out of bed. The stinging jet of water acted like a tonic. By the time he had showered, shaved and dressed he was feeling almost normal. His head had cleared and only a raging thirst was left to remind him of his drinking bout.

Maria had the rest of the day free and she was quite determined that they should spend it together. At first Robert felt guilty about taking her out but by the time they returned to his apartment after lunch not only had he come to accept the situation but was enjoying her company.

'If you are lonely then perhaps I should move in with you,' she smiled provocatively.

'Christ, no! What the hell are you thinking of.'

'Better than for you to be here on your own,' she said with a deprecating little shrug.

'I won't be staying on here in married quarters now that Kate is not joining me.' He looked round the elegant lounge, mentally comparing it with his room back in the Barracks.

'You don't have to give up this wonderful apartment right away though, do you,' Maria whispered persuasively, settling lightly on his knee and sliding her arms around his neck. 'No one knows your wife so why don't we stay here together?' Her breath was warm and soft on his cheek as she raised her mouth temptingly to his. 'Just for a few days . . . to help you get over your disappointment.'

He made to push her away but as his hands came in contact with her body the resolve went out of him.

He never knew how they came to be in bed, naked. One minute they had been in the lounge and the next they were making love with a passion and fervour such as he had never known.

Maria brought such a wealth of sexual experience that he was almost delirious with anticipation. There was no tenderness, no love. It was more like an athletic encounter, but it sent his pulses racing and left him hungry for more. And Maria seemed as eager as he was.

Whereas with Kate their lovemaking had been gentle and almost wordless, Maria was talkative and filled his mind with erotic images. There was an eagerness about every movement of her body, a kind of gutter ecstasy that inflamed him into a savage and fierce taking, as if his body was seeking some sort of carnal vengeance.

Afterwards, although he felt abased by what had happened he was eager for Maria to stay. He had never known such wild sexual pleasure. Her fiery emotions had roused all his pent-up longings and he was filled with tremendous anticipation of what new thrills still awaited him.

His resentment because Kate was not joining him was replaced by the euphoria of almost unbearable excitement. With her glinting sea-blue eyes, lustrous black hair, inviting red lips and curvaceous figure, Maria seemed the most desirable, infatuating creature he had ever known.

In comparison, Kate appeared as timid as a country mouse. Everything about her, from her straight brown hair and big trusting brown eyes to her delicate colouring, soft skin and sensitive mouth, was so gentle and understated.

Her elegant bearing, controlled graceful walk and air of refinement, the things which had initially attracted him to her, now seemed pretentious when compared with Maria's exciting earthiness.

He kept thinking of what Maria had said about not vacating the apartment right away. She was quite right, why shouldn't they stay on there . . . at least for a while. A bizarre sense of excitement welled up inside him. No one had ever seen Kate so how were they to know whether Maria was his wife or not. As long as he never took her to any army functions, and warned her not to talk to anyone else in the apartment block, who would even know they were living together?

And it wouldn't hurt Kate, he argued with himself. It wasn't as if he was in love with Maria. She was simply a diversion because he was lonely. And it was Kate's fault that he was on his own, he reminded himself. If she had arrived as planned he would never have met up with Maria.

He grinned to himself, running a hand through his hair, it was as if Fate was taking a hand again, he thought complacently.

Chapter 13

'Promise me you won't stay away long . . . not more than a couple of days,' Lady Dorothea's voice was faint and two bright spots of colour stood out on her cheekbones like dabs of rouge.

'I'll be back within the week,' Kate promised, gently kissing her mother's damp brow and pushing the strands of lank grey hair back from the raddled face. 'Nanny will take care of you while I'm away, won't you?' She turned with a warm smile to Mabel Sharp who was hovering close by.

'Case of having to, isn't it,' Mabel Sharp sniffed. 'Just you make sure you do come back, that is all,' she added ominously.

'I will, I promise.'

Refusing to be deterred by either of them, Kate walked quickly out of the room. She felt desperately guilty about leaving her mother but it had been almost five months since she had seen Robert and some instinct warned her that all was not well between them even though he wrote regularly.

She tried to explain this to her father while he was driving her to the station but he was less than sympathetic.

'You knew there would be difficulties when you married into the army,' he grunted. 'When you were a child there were times when I was on an overseas tour and didn't see you or your mother for months. I suppose you have forgotten all about that.'

'No, I fully understand that we will be parted from time to time. But we had only just married when Mother was taken ill. It was the very first day of our honeymoon, if you remember. And we haven't seen each other since Robert went back to Germany.'

'He should have had some leave by now,' Sir Henry snapped. 'Check it out when you get over there.'

Her father was right, of course. The same niggling doubt had been festering in her own mind for many weeks now. It was one of her reasons for deciding to make a surprise visit.

She mulled over the problem as she journeyed to London for her flight from Heathrow to Hanover. She still felt she was not to blame for their separation and that under the circumstances her priorities had been the right ones.

When she arrived in Germany it was raining and as she struggled to remember the smattering of German she had picked up from phrase books she wished she had phoned Robert to let him know she was coming.

Finally, she decided there was only one thing to do, phone the Barracks and ask Robert to come out to the airport.

'Captain Campbell? He is not here at the moment. I can give you his home number, you may be able to contact him there.'

Hurriedly, Kate noted down the figures before the line went dead. It was a number she had never heard of before and, as she sorted through her purse for the right coins to make the call, she wondered if the man had made a mistake and confused him with someone else. Still puzzled she dialled. A woman's voice answered in German.

'Do you speak English?'

'Yes. What is it you want?'

'I am not sure if I have the right number . . .'

'This is apartment eight, Hanstrasse.'

'I am sorry to trouble you. I am trying to contact Captain Campbell . . .'

'Captain Robert Campbell? Yes, this is his home . . .'

Kate dropped the receiver back into its cradle. Her hand was shaking, waves of heat sent sweat trickling down the back of her neck.

'Captain Robert Campbell . . . this is his home . . . this is his home,' the words echoed over and over in her head. What could it mean? The only address Robert had ever given her was the Barracks. Utterly bewildered, she reached out for the phone to ring again, then changed her mind. Picking up her suitcase, she went in search of a cab.

'Apartment eight, Hanstrasse.'

She had no idea in which direction they were going and when the cab finally pulled up in front of a block of modern flats she made no move to get out.

'Wir halten sie hier.' The driver spoke to her in German but Kate shook her head, shrugging her shoulders to try and indicate she had no idea what he was saying.

'You English?'

'Yes,' she nodded eagerly.

'This is apartment eight, Hanstrasse. Do you want me to wait?'

'Yes. Yes, wait until I know if it is the right place.'

Leaving her case in the taxi, Kate went up the steps and into the building. It was quite easy to find apartment eight. She hesitated briefly before ringing the bell, hoping she had not made any mistake. Her confusion increased when the door was opened by a plump, black-haired girl.

'I am looking for Captain Robert Campbell . . .'

'You phoned?' The alert sea-blue eyes held hers.

'That is right. I am not sure if I have the right address though . . .'

The girl smiled, her teeth a gleaming white against the bright red of her lipstick. 'He is not here yet but should be soon. You will come in and wait?'

Still wondering what she ought to do, Kate tried to see into the living room beyond. In her smart red velour pant-suit, the girl didn't look like a maid or a cleaner and yet she seemed to have the run of the place.

'I have left my suitcase in the taxi . . .'

'Why don't you go and collect it. I will make you some coffee to drink while you wait for Robert. He will be here any minute.'

Bemused and still unsure who the girl was, Kate nodded her agreement. The taxi driver beamed at her generous tip and pushed a card with his address and telephone number on it into her hand, assuring prompt service night or day.

As she carried her case back to the apartment, Kate heard footsteps behind her. The tall broad-shouldered figure in officer's uniform would have walked right past her had she not said his name. As he came abruptly to a stop, Robert tried to shutter the shock in his green eyes as he recognised her.

'Kate ... it can't be ... what in heaven's name are *you* doing here!'

'Robert! It is the right address, then.'

She was in his arms, conscious of their strength as they clasped her. Nothing else mattered. The surprise that had so nearly turned into a nightmare was over. Then she was suddenly aware that he was frowning as he looked at her.

'I wish you had let me know you were coming,' he said hugging her. 'I am still trying to puzzle out how you managed to find this place.'

He had stopped outside the door of apartment eight, was searching for the keys.

'Your maid said she would leave the door open,' Kate told him and gave it a push so that it swung inwards.

'Aah! So you have found each other.' Maria's sea-blue eyes scrutinised them both questioningly.

There was an uneasy silence as Kate looked from Robert to Maria and back again.

'I'd better introduce you,' Robert said awkwardly. 'Maria, this is my wife, Kate. Maria is using our apartment temporarily,' he added quickly turning back to Kate. 'If I had known you were coming over then, of course, she would have found somewhere else.'

'Yes, I am sure she would,' Kate said drily. 'You never even told me you had taken a flat, Robert.' She began to move around the living room, wandering through to the kitchen and then pushing open the door into the bedroom.

'It was meant to be a surprise. I took it on when you said your mother was better and that you would be joining me. When you didn't arrive, I agreed to sub-let it to Maria.'

'Without even moving in yourself!'

'There was no point in doing so since you were not coming,' he said smoothly. 'It is more convenient for me to stay in Barracks.'

'Yet you keep your clothes here!' Kate said cuttingly.

'My clothes?' A dark flood of colour suffused Robert's face and he frowned fiercely. 'I don't follow you, Kate.'

'Unless your friend Maria is entertaining another Captain

in our apartment, and he is the one hanging up his uniform in *our* wardrobe.' She looked witheringly not at Robert, but at Maria. She pushed wide the bedroom door as she spoke to show Robert's uniform hanging inside the open wardrobe alongside some of Maria's clothes.

'Oh, that is a spare one! In fact, that is what I have come to collect.'

'Well, don't forget to collect your dressing-gown at the same time, will you,' Kate snapped, her chin jutting angrily. 'It is lying over the armchair in the bedroom.'

Maria rolled her eyes dramatically, hunching her shoulders in an expressive gesture. 'I think it is time that I went to work,' she said with a tight little smile at Kate. 'It has been much pleasure to meet you.'

'I bet it has, a most unexpected pleasure at that,' Kate retorted, her brown eyes glittering.

As the door slammed behind Maria, Robert moved to take Kate in his arms but she moved quickly out of reach, her eyes glazed, her lips trembling. She could see that he was upset, a tiny vein throbbed high on his temple and the colour was beginning to creep upward from his collar again. She felt too outraged to think clearly. Undoubtedly, Maria was the reason why Robert had not come home once since they had been married, she thought bitterly. She wanted to hit out, to wound with words, anything to dispel the sense of deep bewildermeant that had taken hold of her.

'Come and sit down and let me try and explain,' Robert said hesitantly.

Kate drew away, feeling disgusted and bitter. She stood looking at him dispassionately, the tall masterful figure, so upright and military in his impeccable uniform, the three gold pips glinting on the shoulders of his jacket. The man who had haunted her thoughts, waking or sleeping, for over three years. The man she had married less than five months ago and who had already taken a mistress. Raising her eyes to look into his face, at the handsome square cut profile beneath the burnished flame of hair that glowed like a halo in the gathering dusk, she saw that his brilliant green eyes were fixed on her in an intense, pleading stare.

It was disturbing to find that her parents had been right. It would seem that her mother had been able to recognise Robert's philandering nature, even though she had been blind to it. She even wondered whether her father's initial dislike of him, his repeated attempts to stop them marrying, had been because he, too, was aware of the type of man Robert Campbell would prove to be.

The thought of going back home and admitting she had been wrong and having to concede that her marriage was a failure, before it had even started, made her cringe inwardly.

Resolutely, refusing to accept defeat, and with an outward calm she was far from feeling, Kate walked over to the settee and sat down.

'I'm waiting to hear your explanation,' she said coolly. 'I only hope it is convincing.'

Robert stared as if unable to believe his ears. The story he had begun to concoct the moment he had realised that Kate and Maria had met, now seemed fatuous in the extreme. As he looked into his wife's candid brown eyes he took a tremendous decision and decided to tell her the truth.

Kate heard him out in complete silence. When he had finished she stood up and walked into the kitchen. 'How would you like your coffee . . . black?'

For a moment Robert was not sure whether he had heard aright. He found it hard to believe that Kate could take the situation so calmly.

He walked over to the kitchen door feeling utterly perplexed by her attitude. He had been expecting tears and recriminations, not this cool acceptance of his misdemeanours. How could Kate take it all so calmly if she really loved him?

In that moment he knew she was the only woman he truly wanted, and that the deep feelings he felt for her were totally different from his lust for Maria. He wouldn't deny that Maria was an exciting lover, but she was just a plaything that he was now ready to discard. Kate's love was something pure and lasting and he felt angry with himself that he had betrayed her trust.

Instinctively he knew that Kate would never betray him and take a lover. Humbled he remembered the suspicions he had once harboured about her and Captain Parkes, until he had met him. Now, instead of feeling relieved that Kate was faithful to him, it suddenly irked him because he had nothing with which to reproach her.

'Is that how much you care?' he frowned angrily, lounging against the kitchen door and glaring at her.

With a light shrug she began to spoon coffee powder into two mugs.

'I thought you loved me!'

'I did . . . and I still do,' she answered in a low voice.

'It is all your fault for not joining me out here, you know that, don't you?'

Her long lashes hid the expression in her dark eyes as she turned to face him. He saw that her lower lip was trembling as she started to speak and watched as her teeth bit down, trying to quell the quivering. She looked so vulnerable that he wanted to sweep her into his arms, shower her face with kisses and beg her forgiveness. Instead he thrust his hands hard into his trouser pockets and averted his eyes.

'May I pass, I want to sit down,' Kate said handing him a mug of steaming coffee and carried her own into the living room.

He followed her and sat at the opposite end of the long settee. He felt as nervous as a schoolboy being hauled before the headmaster.

'How . . . how long are you staying, Kate?'

'Here? Just until I have finished my coffee.'

'I meant in Germany, had you come for good?'

'No, just for a long weekend. I meant it to be a surprise. I seem to have succeeded pretty well!' she added with a brittle laugh.

'Please, don't talk like that, Kate.'

'I should have let you know I was coming and then I would never have walked into this. You could have kept it all quite separate from our life. I did wonder why you had never come home on leave . . . never once in five months!'

'I haven't had any leave, Kate. If you remember I managed to get an extension for our honeymoon and that meant I went right to the bottom of the list for any future leave. I should have some due soon. I intended to write and tell you as soon as I knew the dates.'

'And you'll be home then?' She drained her coffee cup and stood up, looking tall and slim in her tailored blue wool suit and in perfect control of herself.

'Of course I will!'

Before Robert realised what was happening, Kate had picked up her suitcase and was walking towards the door.

'Kate, wait. You can't just walk away like this . . .'

'I'll expect to see you when you get your leave . . . at Walford Grange.'

Head held high, tears streaming unchecked down her cheeks, Kate swept out of the apartment, wishing she had asked the taxi to wait after all.

Chapter 14

September was a golden month. The sun shone from early morning until late afternoon and the entire countryside was bathed in warmth. Everywhere was a medley of yellows, oranges and browns as the leaves turned, the corn ripened and the gleaming hedgerow berries glistened like polished rubies.

Kate sat beside her mother on the terrace, her hands lying idle in her lap. The sewing she had brought out to do was lying untouched on the table beside her. Her mind was blank.

This sense of being suspended in time, as if waiting for something to happen, had stayed with her ever since she had walked away from the apartment in Hanover. She had somehow found her way back to the airport and had sat there for almost four hours, not even bothering to check onto a plane back to England.

It was not until a security guard became suspicious, and stopped to tactfully enquire if he could help, that she remembered where she was and that she wished to return to London as quickly as possible.

Knowing there would be awkward questions if she arrived home several days early she had stayed in London spending the time window shopping and walking aimlessly through streets she had known so well when she had been stationed there.

When she had eventually returned to Walford Grange no one asked how Robert was, or even how she had enjoyed her visit to Germany. Her mother's health had given cause for concern while she had been gone and there was a general air of relief that she was back.

She couldn't bring herself to write to Robert, not even to

let him know she was home. And, in the weeks that followed, any letters that came from him she took straight up to her room and put them away in a drawer unread.

By keeping her mind blank, Kate found she could manage to submerge all thoughts of what had happened in Germany. Even at night she refused to let memories invade her mind. She read copiously, sometimes without comprehension, until her eyelids could stay open no longer and the book dropped from her hand. Often she would wake, many hours later, to find her bedside light still on.

She lost weight. The delicate curves of her cheeks disappeared, her cheekbones became more prominent, and there were deep furrows running down either side of her nose to her mouth giving her a careworn look. Her mouth, permanently set in a firm unyielding line, added to her austere expression. No one at Walford Grange appeared to notice any of these changes. Or if they did they made no comment.

Lady Dorothea was perfectly content as long as Kate was within call. Mabel Sharp walked around with a smug smile, as if delighted that Lady Dorothea's illness was keeping Kate from joining Robert in Germany. As for Sir Henry, he was far too involved with his many new farming projects to give Kate's welfare more than a passing thought.

The only person who did seem concerned was Eleanor. Sublimely happy in her marriage to Ralph Buscombe, she was impatient for Robert to join Kate.

'Just think of the great times we could have going around in a foursome,' she enthused. 'You can't stay at home sitting by your mother's bedside for ever. Life's whizzing past and you are having no fun at all.'

Kate refused to be drawn into either an argument or discussion. She didn't wish to confide in Eleanor any more than she wanted to think about what had happened or what the future held. She nursed a blind optimism that if she put it right out of her mind, and did nothing, then eventually everything would be all right.

It was not in her nature to accept 'second best' so if she rationalised about what had happened she knew the only course open to her was to dismiss Robert from her life. Loving him as she did, that was impossible. Which left her with no alternative but to accept his explanation of how the raven-haired girl came to be in his apartment. Doubts churned deep in the recess of her mind and heart but she was determined not to let them surface. She could not face the truth, not yet.

Kate realised that Robert was not entirely to blame, and that was why she was prepared to make allowances. Her family's opposition to them marrying, the three long years of waiting and all the other obstacles deliberately placed in his way, had been the underlying cause.

She realised now that most men would have openly rebelled at their wife going home to her parents after just one night of their honeymoon! Robert had reconciled himself to the situation. He had, or so she had thought at the time, even understood that she was only doing her duty when at the very last minute she had cancelled her plans to go with him to Germany. And, if she had forewarned him of her visit, instead of trying to surprise him, then the misunderstanding would never have arisen.

She smiled wryly as she realised the truth of this. If he had been pre-warned Robert would probably have sent Maria packing, and removed every trace of her presence. Or else he would have taken her to an hotel and never mentioned the apartment. Either way she would have remained oblivious of what was going on.

Robert sent a picture postcard to let her know he would be on leave over Christmas and the New Year. The view of Hanover stirred up memories but she pushed these resolutely to one side, knowing she must face up to realities. She didn't reply but waited with a kind of fatalism to see what would happen.

As the memories which she had so ruthlessly quelled were gradually allowed to surface so too did the pain and her heart still ached because she loved Robert so desperately. The next few weeks would, she felt, determine the rest of her life.

As Christmas approached, Kate grew increasingly apprehensive. She kept telling herself that if Robert came back to England for his leave, despite her silence, it would signify that she still meant something to him, and that he still cared and wanted her.

Night after night, as she sat by Lady Dorothea's bed, holding her mother's frail hand until she fell asleep, Kate would torture herself wondering whether perhaps she had been wrong in what she had assumed. Was it just possible that Robert had been telling the truth and that he had only rented the flat to Maria? Somewhere in her handbag was the telephone number she had been given when she had phoned the Barracks asking for Robert.

As she waited for her connection Kate's heart was pumping. When the whirrs and clicks died away and a woman's voice answered she swiftly cut off. She felt the colour flooding her cheeks before she went cold and began to shiver. She tried reasoning with herself that it might be some other woman and not Maria who had answered the phone. After this length of time, knowing she was not going to join him in Germany, Robert would surely have given up the flat!

She tried to remember Maria's voice, but her own mind was in such a turmoil that she found this impossible. Then fresh doubts surfaced. Had she phoned the right number?

She paced the room, trying to summon up her nerve to make the call a second time. When she did, she knew for certain that it was Maria. There was a cold hollow inside Kate as she replaced the receiver. She had wanted to ask for Robert, but was afraid to do so in case he was there.

She still wanted to believe that he had been telling the truth when he had said that he had sub-let the flat, and that was why Maria was still there and had answered the phone. Perhaps it was all in his letters, the ones she had put away unopened. As she rushed upstairs to her room to find them, Kate remembered that it was army property so Robert would not be allowed to sub-let and the last shred of hope flickered, guttered and died.

She brooded over the problem, desperate for a solution. In fairness to Robert, perhaps she ought to offer him his freedom. She couldn't expect him to live like a monk when it was not of his choosing. Yet the thought of losing him forever brought a bitterness that was unbearable. The alternative, sharing him with Maria, was equally unpalatable.

Perhaps if they had a child? The idea excited her yet she

was quick to see the disadvantages of that happening while her mother was in such poor health, and Robert living away.

She recalled her own childhood, when her father had been in the army and she had seen him only for brief spells. At times, when she had been quite young, she had resented his intrusion into her well-ordered life. When he was not at home she had been the centre of attention with Lady Dorothea and Nanny dancing attendance. All that changed as soon as her father came on leave. His tall, military figure dominated the scene, everyone scurried to do his bidding and even her mother had spent most of her time with him, making only fleeting visits to the nursery.

As she had grown older, she had come to appreciate him and a deep friendship had developed. She had studied hard, won her way to University and achieved good results because she wanted him to be proud of her. And he had taken an inordinate pride in her ATS record during the war. It was only in her choice of husband that she had failed to come up to his high expectations. Since Robert's promotion to Captain, however, she hoped this was forgotten.

She knew her father would advise on how she should handle the situation but she felt reluctant to confide in him. It was her predicament and if she wanted to hold on to Robert there was no easy or short term answer.

If only he could be posted back to England she thought optimistically. If he was stationed in London or Windsor, or even at the Guards' Depot at Pirbright, he would be able to come home every weekend, or she could visit him. Surely, her mother could learn to live with that arrangement, Kate mused.

Snow was already powdering the ground on the morning of Christmas Eve when Robert arrived in a taxi. Kate had just finished making her mother comfortable for the day and was walking across the hall to see if any help was needed in the kitchen when the doorbell jangled and she paused to answer it.

'Kate!'

Robert was shocked at how drawn she looked and steeled himself, afraid she might turn him away. He noticed that the white jumper and brown tweed skirt she was wearing seemed to hang loosely, as if she had lost weight.

Framed in the doorway, Robert looked immensely tall and masculine in his Guards uniform. The piercing greenness of his eyes startled her as his gaze locked with hers. She heard a thud as the case he was carrying dropped to the floor and then she was in his arms, crushed against his hard chest and his firm mouth was homing in, covering hers in a demanding sensuous hunger.

She responded just as fervently. Those first minutes of his homecoming atoned for everything and wiped out all the months of mounting doubts for both of them. Cheeks flushed, her brown eyes glowing with happiness as she looked up at Robert, Kate felt confident that her fears were groundless and that everything between them was all right.

She ran her fingers through his thick hair, pulling his head down so that she could reach up and press her lips once more against his in a deep and satisfying kiss. As she did so she felt the lean tautness of his body harden against her own communicating his desire.

Knowing that he needed her every bit as much as she wanted him was all that mattered, she decided. It would be the bedrock on which they would build their marriage no matter what other difficulties they had to face.

'Let's go upstairs ... before anyone else knows that you have arrived,' she whispered invitingly.

Grinning broadly, Robert picked up his case and followed her. After what had happened in Germany, and Kate's persistent silence ever since, he had certainly not expected his homecoming to be quite so welcoming.

Chapter 15

Robert's Christmas leave set the pattern for the ensuing years. When they were together, they were ecstatically happy, nothing else mattered, and with every leave their love for each other seemed to deepen.

Kate still considered Robert to be the most handsome man she had ever set eyes on. Everything from his burnished shock of hair to his swaggering military stride, spelled perfection in her eyes. As he matured, his figure with its wide shoulders, slim hips and long muscular legs became more powerful, even more masculine. She felt proud to be seen with him.

Her heart still quickened when his brilliant green eyes lit up with enthusiasm, or darkened when his emotions were stirred. She even approved of the moustache he decided to grow when he was promoted to Major.

'You'll be twirling the ends of it in no time, just like my father,' she teased the first time she saw it.

'Mm! By the time I get my promotion to Colonel it might well be long enough to do that,' he replied, taking her remark seriously.

And for his part, Robert found Kate more captivating at each homecoming. Her satin smooth skin with its delicate peaches-and-cream colouring, her deep brown eyes that so often became dark mysterious pools when they looked into his, the perfect oval face with its delicate bones and express-ive inviting mouth, never failed to fill him with desire. Whether she was wearing tweeds, a twinset and pearls, or one of the latest 'New Look' outfits with their nipped-in waists and full skirts to mid-calf, her long, shapely legs and firm breasts ensured an elegance that he found highly pleasing.

They were so attuned to each other's needs that it seemed hard to believe that in effect, they led separate lives. Robert's promotion to the rank of Major satisfied her that his army career was still going well so she didn't question how he spent his leisure time.

Lady Dorothea's health continued to give rise to concern but once Kate had managed to convince her that she had no intention of leaving her she became less clinging. She even accepted that Kate needed interests of her own and raised no objections when Kate participated in local events or, occasionally, went on a shopping trip with Eleanor to Taunton or Bristol.

It was only if she stayed away overnight, that Lady Dorothea became agitated. When Kate told her that she and Eleanor were planning a few days in London, so that they could be outside Westminster Abbey when Princess Elizabeth married Prince Philip, Lady Dorothea made a great fuss and became extremely upset.

'Waste of time I call it,' Mabel Sharp sniffed disapprovingly. 'There's far too much fuss being made about this wedding. And letting her have all those extra coupons for her dress, unfair I call it.'

'Well, Eleanor and I will let you know if Princess Elizabeth's dress really was worth three hundred coupons,' Kate laughed.

'It will be so dreadfully crowded, my dear, do you think it is wise to go?' Sir Henry demurred. He rarely interfered in the domestic scene but seeing how distressed Lady Dorothea had become, he feared it might bring on another heart attack.

'I was in London on VE Day and I doubt if there could be a crowd bigger than the one that was outside the Palace then,' Kate reminded him.

In spite of everyone's protests, Kate and Eleanor went ahead with their plan to go up to London for three days. On the morning they were to leave, Lady Dorothea complained of pains in her chest. She certainly looked ill so Kate phoned Eleanor and said she thought they had better call off the trip.

'Nonsense, she's playing up. Phone Doctor Elwell, you know what she is like,' Eleanor said cheerfully. 'We'll take a later train.'

Like Eleanor, Doctor Elwell thought there was very little cause for concern and urged Kate to go ahead with her plans. 'The break will do you good, and I don't think your mother will come to much harm,' he assured her. 'Anyway, if it makes you any easier in your mind I will call in each morning while you are away and check that she is all right.'

Kate was glad she had taken his advice because it was to be their last major outing. Eleanor was pregnant and when Geoffrey was born, their lifestyle changed considerably.

Watching Eleanor with her new baby, a tiny replica of Ralph with his jet hair and dark blue eyes, Kate felt envious and longed for the day when she would have a baby of her own.

Once, but only once in all the years she remained at home nursing her mother, did Kate ring the Hanover number. The same woman's voice, the voice she was quite convinced was Maria's, answered. Unnerved, her hand trembling, Kate quickly replaced the receiver. The incident haunted her for weeks. It was like picking the scab from an old wound and feeling the smarting pain afresh.

When Robert next came on leave, Kate tried to bring the matter up but he had quickly turned away.

That night, his passion had been intense, almost brutal, as if he was determined to master her completely with a callous intimacy. When she protested that his violent lovemaking was hurting her, he became overwhelmingly gentle and tender until she was the demanding one. Wild with pent up longings, and the need to establish that their love was something special, she was determined to push him across the emotional brink. Every movement, every touch took on a new significance as she demonstrated her needs as never before.

When Lady Dorothea died suddenly and peacefully in her sleep, Robert was on leave prior to going to Cyprus. His long spell in Germany had finally ended. A few years earlier, when the Korean war had broken out, Kate had been worried in case he was sent to the Far East. Then, later, when George VI had died and Queen Elizabeth had come to the throne, there had been rumours that his regiment would be returning from Germany to serve 'in waiting'.

They did return to London but only for the Coronation. Eleanor and Kate were not amongst the two million people who crammed the capital to see the golden State Coach, drawn by eight greys, carry Princess Elizabeth in regal splendour from Buckingham Palace to Westminster Abbey and bring her back as Queen Elizabeth II.

'Why don't you come to Cyprus with me,' Robert suggested after they returned to Walford Grange after Lady Dorothea's funeral.

He held her close, tenderly pushing back her dark hair from her high brow. 'Come on, you'll be thirty-two in October, life's slipping by. It really is time you lived a little and saw something of the world.'

'I don't know . . .' Although her voice was hesitant there was eagerness in her deep brown eyes.

'It is what you need after eight years of caring for your mother. It will be like starting a new life . . . our life together at last,' Robert persisted.

'What about my father?'

'Sir Henry would be the first to agree with me. He is so wrapped up in his farming projects that he will probably never even notice that you are not here. Ask him, I am sure he will agree,' he added confidently.

Sir Henry did.

'Of course you must go with him, my dear,' he affirmed, twirling the spiked ends of his moustache. 'It has been difficult for both of you having to live apart all these years.'

'But it means you will be left here all on your own . . .'

'Nonsense! This place has so many staff that I will never have a moment to myself.'

The thought of exchanging the cold and damp of the coming British winter for the sunshine of Cyprus was a temptation in itself and she was easily persuaded.

'You will be back home again next Spring,' her father pointed out. 'Just think of it as a long overdue holiday and enjoy yourself. I may even fly out and join you for a week after Christmas.'

Kate felt nervous about meeting Robert's fellow officers and their wives. It seemed incredible, even to her, that she and Robert had been married for over eight years and she had never met any of them and never attended any of the functions to which wives were regularly invited.

Her greatest concern was in case those who had been in Hanover with the regiment might have met Maria. She desperately wanted to ask Robert about this but each time she tried to do so her courage failed. In the end, she convinced herself that since Maria would not be in Cyprus, there was nothing to worry about.

Kate found Cyprus was far more agreeable than she had imagined it would be. Their house in Nicosia was high on a hill, looking out over the Mediterranean. The climate, the companionship, the galaxy of events to which wives were invited, ensured a charmed existence. The months rolled by, a long delightful holiday, just as her father had predicted.

'You look wonderful,' Sir Henry enthused when he came to visit them just after Christmas. He couldn't remember when she had looked better, he thought, admiring her sun-tanned figure, her carefree wind-blown look and happy laughing face.

'Thank you!'

'You are enjoying life out here?'

'Very much. I've never felt so well, or so happy.'

Robert went to great lengths to ensure that when they were in the Mess he always referred to Kate's father as General Sir Henry Russell. He also stressed to all concerned the fact that Sir Henry had once served in their regiment, so as to ensure that he was always treated with the correct deference.

The visit was such a success that instead of returning to Walford Grange at the end of the week, as planned, Sir Henry stayed on for a further ten days. Kate was overjoyed that the two men had come to terms with each other. It was easy to see that her father was proud of the way Robert had forged ahead in the army and carved out a worthwhile career for himself.

'You should be a Colonel by the time you are ready to retire,' Sir Henry told him confidently during his stay.

'I would like to think so,' Robert agreed, 'but the nearer the top you get the harder it becomes to get promotion. There's not even "dead men's shoes" in peace time. It is a question of waiting for one of the top brass to retire.'

'Mmm! You will get there, my boy,' Sir Henry affirmed, tapping the side of his nose with a forefinger.

Kate was secretly relieved to see her father leave. Although the build up of tension before his arrival had been quite groundless since there had been an excellent rapport between him and Robert, it was now taking its toll. She felt completely enervated, and was looking forward to some early nights and less strenuous days.

At first, Robert thought she was missing her father when she appeared slightly off-colour. Then, when she began to complain of feeling sick when she woke each morning and to refuse breakfast he became more concerned and insisted she saw the doctor.

'When are you planning to return to England, Mrs Campbell?' the army medico enquired.

'I haven't a date as yet. I think my husband's tour of duty ends in August.'

'I see.' He pursed his lips and doodled on the pad in front of him for a moment. 'I think you should return towards the end of May, certainly no later than June, because, if my calculations are correct, your baby is due towards the end of July and I don't recommend flying after seven months.'

'Baby . . . what are you talking about?'

'You are pregnant, Mrs Campbell. Didn't you recognise the symptoms?'

'No!' Kate shook her head bemused. Her mind went back to the early days of Eleanor's pregnancy, the bouts of early morning sickness, the way certain foods and smells made her feel queasy. She should have known, the symptoms were exactly the same.

At first Robert was dazed by the news, then incredibly jubilant. He wanted to phone her father right away but she restrained him.

'I can tell him when I go home,' she protested.

'No! Your father should be told right away so that he can make any necessary changes to his Will. This baby could make all the difference to his plans for the future of Walford Grange. Don't you see, it will stop him selling out!'

His remark staggered Kate. Although her father had now turned seventy she didn't regard him as ready for retirement. He certainly didn't look old. His hair, though thinning, was still brown except at the temples, his bearing still imposing and his voice as commanding as ever.

The only significant deterioration was that he now suffered from arthritis which sometimes made walking difficult, something he went to great lengths to disguise.

Robert's inference that her father was contemplating retirement, and his obvious concern over the future of Walford Grange, made her acutely uneasy. It was her home, and it had been the home of the Russells, for generations. He couldn't possibly be thinking of leaving there.

As she lay on the shaded verandah, looking out at the Mediterranean, a sparkling blue under a cloudless sky, Kate tried to piece together what her father's plans might be. She remembered the way he had refused to consider Robert running Home Farm. She thought of how involved her father had become since his retirement in improving the land and expanding both crops and cattle. It had never, at any time, entered her head that he might be doing all this with a view to selling.

Kate returned to England in late May. The Mediterranean heat left her feeling exhausted most of the time and she was looking forward to the cool greenness of Somerset. She had written telling her father she was coming home but made no mention of the baby, apart from telling him she had a 'surprise' for him.

He was so overjoyed when he heard her news that the words 'an heir to Walford Grange' escaped her lips before she could stop them. He frowned, but his hooded eyes concealed his full reaction to her words.

Later, when she again broached the subject he was evasive. So much so, that in order to allay her own fears, she forced herself to ask him outright if he was contemplating selling up.

'It is getting rather too much for me,' he confessed guardedly.

'But you can't sell. It has been in the family for almost five hundred years,' she exclaimed aghast.

'I wouldn't want to burden you with the place,' he told her.

'It wouldn't be a burden . . . its my home!'

'It is not as simple as that, Kate, my dear. The upkeep is enormous. You must retain servants for the house and grounds . . .'

'But all that is offset by Home Farm,' she interrupted.

'If only that were so. I've done a great deal to increase the profitability of the place but it still operates on a knife edge.'

'Then let Robert help you . . . he has farming experience.'

Sir Henry's expression hardened and a wall of silence came between the two of them.

'It is the perfect solution,' Kate persisted. 'He will be leaving the army soon so what better future could he have but to run Home Farm. Then our son could be raised here. Please, you can't deny me that,' she pleaded wistfully.

Chapter 16

The sun was already high in the sky, promising another sweltering hot day, when Russell Campbell entered the world at eight o'clock on the morning of 26th July 1956. A bouncing eight-pounder he had none of the wrinkled prune-like appearance of so many newborn babies. He was as chubby as a cherub, with a shock of red-gold hair.

Her brown eyes shining with pride, Kate counted his ten tiny toes and his long slender fingers, relieved to find that he was perfect in every respect. Her face flushed with mother-love, as she held him in the crook of her arm for Robert to admire, she felt he was worth every moment of the arduous ten-hour labour she had endured.

Robert was equally impressed with his son. The baby rekindled all his earlier enthusiasm and hopes about Walford Grange. 'Russell, the future heir,' he enthused, his green eyes glinting with satisfaction as he took the baby from Kate's arms and held him out to Sir Henry.

'You can't name him "Russell", it's like putting a label round his neck!' Sir Henry commented cryptically as he looked down at his grandson.

'We thought you would be pleased that we were keeping the family name alive,' Robert replied.

Sir Henry didn't answer but his shoulders drooped as if he was very tired and Kate was suddenly aware of how much he had aged in the past few months. His hair was liberally sprinkled with grey and there were lines around his eyes she hadn't noticed before.

'It was Robert's idea . . . he thought it would be a nice tribute to you!'

'He did, did he. To please me . . . not you.'

'I thought it a splendid idea, too. As Robert said, it is one way of making sure there would always be a Russell at Walford Grange.'

'And did he go as far as to predict when the changeover would be?' Sir Henry asked cynically.

'No, of course not,' Kate said in a shocked voice, looking down at her baby. 'I shouldn't think this little chap will be interested in running the place for at least twenty years!'

'I'm hardly likely to hold on that long,' Sir Henry said harshly.

'Well, perhaps baby Russell will turn out to be a child prodigy and be ready to take over by the time he is ten,' Kate joked, smiling at her father.

'If not, then doubtless Robert will act as regent.'

'Let us stop speculating about the future, it's making you morbid,' Kate exclaimed, aware of the sharpness of her father's tone. 'One way or another we will make sure there are Russells at Walford Grange.'

'Here, Nanny,' she held the baby out to Mabel Sharp who was hovering nearby, 'I think this little Russell is ready for sleep.'

Restored to her favourite role, Mabel Sharp was once again in her element. She had secretly begun to wonder if there would ever be a baby entrusted to her care. Now her days, and nights, were fully occupied. Robert was full of praise for the way she looked after his son, and even went as far as to tell her so before he went back to his unit.

With such a competent nanny, Kate found she had plenty of time on her hands. When she had first come home from Cyprus, in the weeks before Russell was born, Robert had written almost every day. His letters had been full of tender messages, and sweet reminders of the things they had done together. She had kept them all and now, from time to time, when the separation became almost unbearable, she read and re-read them, trying to recapture the wonderful sense of unity with Robert that she had known in Cyprus.

Now, the letters they exchanged were mostly about Russell. Much as she adored her baby, Kate longed for the old closeness between herself and Robert. She frequently felt as if there was an immense gulf dividing them, the same as there had been during her mother's illness when Robert had been in Germany and she had been at home in England. When she woke in the early hours of the morning to feed Russell, vague doubts cluttered Kate's mind. Afterwards, when she had changed him and laid him down to sleep again, replete and rosy, she would find herself remembering Maria and wondering where Robert was and what he was doing.

And yet, she knew such doubts were unfounded and that she had only to read her daily paper to know that the crisis brewing in the Middle East was the reason for Robert's preoccupation. Ever since August, there had been problems with Egypt's President Nasser over the Suez Canal and Robert had been involved in a full-scale military alert with no possible hope of any leave.

When Russell was four months old, Kate decided that perhaps it was time she returned to Cyprus. The thought of a bungalow on the beach at Akrotiri was certainly tempting since, in England, it was already proving to be a cold, wet winter. She even suggested to Mabel Sharp that she might like to go with her.

'You would love it out there, Nanny. Plenty of sunshine! Do you good, you've worked so hard looking after Russell.'

'All that heat and flies and foreigners everywhere won't do a young baby any good at all,' Mabel Sharp protested. 'Much better for him to be brought up here. Why don't you go and leave him here with me.'

'Leave my baby behind!' Kate was aghast at the thought.

When she mentioned to her father that she was planning to join Robert, he looked just as doubtful as Mabel Sharp had done. The arthritis in his hips had become progressively worse so that now he found it difficult to walk any distance and the baby had become an important part of his life. Kate could see that the idea of being separated from Russell did not meet with approval.

'You could come as well,' she suggested.

'I am too old to travel that far in my state of health,' he said firmly.

'The warm sunshine would ease those aching joints,' Kate persisted. 'You could more or less shut this place up. Someone could come up from Home Farm a couple of times a week to check everything was all right . . .'

'No!' The old note of authority was back in his voice as he straightened up, towering over her, his brows knitted angrily. 'This is my home and I'll see my days out here.'

'I'm not asking you to leave here permanently,' Kate snapped, 'only to take an extended holiday. As I see it, it would make sense if we all went out to Cyprus for the rest of the winter instead of sitting here shivering. It would give Robert a chance to see something of Russell now that he is beginning to sit up and notice people. Do you realise, Robert has only seen Russell once since he was born!'

But Sir Henry stubbornly refused and so too did Mabel Sharp. Kate felt torn between pleasing them by staying where she was at Walford Grange or taking Russell to Cyprus and joining Robert.

When she finally made up her mind and told her father that she intended joining Robert, immediately after Christmas, he was aghast.

'You can't be serious, not with things the way they are out there,' he told her sternly. 'Haven't you read your paper or listened to the radio?'

'Of course I have, but it will soon calm down again.'

'You can't possibly travel out to Cyprus now,' Sir Henry said firmly.

Kate's mind was made up and she fully intended to go. When she made her application, however, it was turned down. EOKA, the underground Greek terrorist movement, had stepped up their campaign of violence on the island in an attempt to force the British into giving them independence. And, in addition, there was war between the Israelis and Arabs along Egypt's Sinai peninsula.

Kate said nothing to her father but read the newspapers assiduously in the hope that things would sort themselves out and her application would be reconsidered. She wrote frantically to Robert for news but he was not very reassuring.

As Christmas drew nearer, Kate became more and more restless.

'I've decided to stay in England until the New Year,' she told her father, 'but then I intend to join Robert.'

'Impossible! There's a war going on out there.' His arthritis was decidedly worse and his nerves were frayed and his temper extremely short.

'If you mean the Suez Crisis well that is all settled now,' Kate argued.

'Settled! Anything but settled, I can assure you.'

And, of course, he was right. The strategy behind Anthony Eden's thinking had been considered wrong right from the start, and in December, following a cease-fire, the British troops pulled out, the Suez Canal was closed, and the Russians took over. There was now no question of her joining Robert in Cyprus and she could only hope that it wouldn't be too long before he was home on leave again.

Not only did she feel that her place was out there with him but she was missing him acutely. The months she had been in Cyprus before Russell was born had been filled with fun and laughter and nights of loving and now, although she had the most wonderful baby in the world, it wasn't enough. She needed Robert as well. Without him life was incomplete.

By the time Robert returned from Cyprus, Russell was almost two years old. A sturdy miniature replica of his father, with a shock of burnished gold hair and brilliant green eyes. Already, he sat his pony confidently and chattered volubly, and was in danger of becoming the kingpin around which the entire family and staff at Walford Grange revolved.

Russell idolised his father from the moment they were re-united. And for his part, Robert seemed to want to spend every minute of his time with him. Just watching them together, so very much alike, even to the way they walked, brought a lump to Kate's throat and tears to her eyes. She had been rather afraid that after so many years of leading almost a bachelor existence, Robert would resent the intrusion of a child, but in that she had been quite wrong. He was so inordinately proud of his son, and so eager to comply with the child's slightest whim, that she was sometimes worried in case Russell became spoiled.

Kate's fears proved unfounded and as Russell got older, the closer he and Robert became. When Robert was away, Russell missed him sorely. Too brave to cry, because he was a 'soldier's son', Russell would be silent and withdrawn, shunning Kate as if he blamed her for his father's absence.

'It's a pity you didn't have a daughter,' Eleanor consoled. 'I know I find Melany far more amenable than Geoffrey. Already we share so many of the same interests that I am quite looking forward to her being in her teens. A girl would have been more company for you. It is still not too late', she added speculatively.

For a long time, Kate hoped much the same thing but it seemed it was not to be. She talked to Doctor Elwell about it but his only advice to her was to let nature take its course. So there was nothing she could do but sit back and watch as Robert tried to mould Russell more and more into his own image and the magic slowly went out of their own relationship. All his energies and love seemed to be concentrated on Russell.

Sir Henry also idolised Russell but, because of his ever increasing arthritic disability, he was frequently crabbed and tetchy. When he was in pain he preferred to keep to his own room. Russell had surprising patience with his grandfather and was often to be found with him playing chess, backgammon or dominoes.

As Sir Henry became more and more crippled, Robert talked incessantly about leaving the army and helping with the running of Home Farm but Sir Henry continued to resist the idea violently. Kate, caught in the middle, watched with growing dismay as the old feud was rekindled.

Robert flung himself into local activities on every possible occasion. He became an enthusiastic patron of a variety of events and she noticed that these days he seemed to be able to take leave almost to order.

He began to show a keen interest in equestrian events, whether it was riding to hounds, or organising a gymkhana. He encouraged Russell to join the local pony club and take part in competitions. He insisted that they should be the ones to provide Cups that could be awarded annually not only at the various equestrian shows but also at the annual Flower Show.

'As one of the largest landowners around here it is our duty to give people as much encouragement as we can,' he maintained. And because Sir Henry was now too incapacitated to attend such events, it fell to Robert to present these trophies, a task he undertook enthusiastically, almost as if he was the 'lord of the manor', Kate thought angrily.

When such thoughts came into her mind she tried hard to dismiss them, reminding herself that since Robert was at home more frequently it was only natural that he should want to involve himself in local affairs. In her heart she knew the real reason behind his interest and found it increasingly difficult to watch in silence as he went out of his way to cultivate the friendship of anyone he thought might be useful in promoting his image locally.

Even though he had now been promoted to Lieutenant-Colonel, Robert still talked of resigning. In his new post, his time was divided between Chelsea Barracks or Wellington Barracks, in London, or at the Guards' HQ at Pirbright. This meant he was at home most weekends and often for the odd day, or evening, during the week as well. And to make his travelling easier, Robert had bought himself a stylish black and grey high-powered Riley motor car.

Although Robert was leading a much more flexible life, Kate found herself more and more confined to Walford Grange. Her father suffered a series of strokes which left him frail and partially paralysed. She felt so worn out with nursing him that she barely noticed the cooling off between Robert and herself. A brief kiss and he would be snoring peacefully while she lay there half-awake, listening in case her father needed her.

Chapter 17

General Sir Henry Russell died in his sleep in April 1966. He was eighty-one and for the last five years of his life had been confined to a wheelchair.

In spite of his physical disabilities, he had held on to the reins of Walford Grange right up until a few days before his death. Greg Paxton, his Farm Manager, called each morning to discuss what needed attention. At five-thirty each evening he came back again to report progress and Sir Henry's mind was so astute that nothing was ever overlooked.

As Kate sat in the morning room, filled with bright spring sunshine, reading her father's obituary, tears blurred her eyes. It was the sort of day he had loved, the garden bright with daffodils and tulips, against a background of magnificent pink and white blossom trees.

His funeral had been a very impressive occasion, with full military honours. The village church had been packed to capacity. General Sir Henry Russell's coffin, draped with a Union flag, his cap lying on top of it, had been carried by six high-ranking Guards officers, led by Lieutenant-Colonel Robert Campbell. Guardsmen had lined the path from the church to the cemetery and a trumpeter had played the 'Last Post' as the coffin was being lowered into the family vault.

That was more than a week ago but Kate still missed him sorely. Although he had been demanding and irascible during his declining years, the great house seemed empty without him and she wondered what the future held in store.

She sighed as she looked out over the flower-filled garden to the rolling fields beyond. Robert had been so obviously disappointed by her father's Will. She had known for years that Robert dreamed of the time when he would be in sole charge at Walford Grange. In recent years he had put a great deal of effort into preparing for his forthcoming role. Whenever he was home on leave, he had taken an active interest in local events, building up a rapport with neighbouring landowners, determined to become an integral part of the local community.

At times his behaviour irked her, since when they had first been married, Robert had shunned not only her close friends, but most of her own set and had openly mocked what he termed their narrow conservative ways. Now, it seemed, he couldn't get enough of their company and for the most part they seemed to reciprocate readily enough. Kate wondered if their attitude towards Robert would change when they learned that Walford Grange had been left solely to her in trust for Russell.

As if to offset this, a few months after the General's death Robert plunged into a round of entertaining that left her both exhausted and bewildered.

'If you find it too much for you then we must get in some more staff,' he told her when she complained that it left her more tired than nursing her father had done.

'But do we need to offer hospitality on such a scale?' she asked bemused.

'Of course we do. You've had hardly any social life since we've been married! I want to make up to you for all the years when you've been shut away down here with so little happening. All those years of looking after your mother and then, almost immediately afterwards, having to nurse your father, have been very trying for you.'

'It's not been much fun for you either,' she smiled apologetically as she reached up and stroked the side of his face.

He pulled her close with a fierce savagery that startled her. The emerald glint in his eyes stirred her senses. As their lips met, they were both transported back to those early days when their passion for each other had been so great that it had surmounted all obstacles.

They made love with such intensity that she was filled with a momentary dizziness. Robert was as exciting a lover as ever and she felt as light-spirited as a young girl.

Kate wished she could hold on to this precious moment

forever. All too soon it passed and Robert was back on his hobby-horse, planning events that could be staged at Walford Grange and would bring them into the limelight.

His striving for local recognition was coupled with his intention to leave the army. The more she thought about his retirement the more apprehensive she became. It would mean that he would be at home all the time and with his boundless energy and organising ability she was concerned what changes this might make to her own lifestyle.

She didn't agree with Robert that she led a dull, uninteresting life. She was able to fill her days with as much social activity as she needed. Eleanor had persuaded her to become involved with various local charities and so she now sat on several committees.

Robert's appointment to Colonel, far from reviving his interest in the army, seemed only to make him all the more determined to retire.

'This place needs me here all the time,' he told Kate. 'It is not practical to leave the running of the entire Estate to a manager.'

'Greg Paxton does a wonderful job,' she argued.

'Gregory Paxton is way behind the times. The whole place needs to be reorganised. Most of the machinery ought to be updated and the methods we employ need to be streamlined.'

'Sounds rather a tall order. I am not sure that it will meet with Greg's approval.'

'Since he is only an employee he can either do as he is told or leave,' Robert said firmly.

'But Robert, he has been at Home Farm all his life. His father was Bailiff here. Greg was actually born at Home Farm,' Kate argued.

'Then it probably is high time there was some new blood around the place,' Robert answered sharply.

'You are not suggesting that Greg should be dismissed, are you?' Kate asked in astonishment.

'He has the choice. Either he does things the way he is told or he must go,' Robert told her decisively.

'My father would turn in his grave if he thought Greg was no longer in charge of the Estate,' she said shocked.

'Perhaps if Sir Henry had run things more efficiently

than they are today the place would not need an urgent programme of revitalisation.'

'How can you say that?' Kate blanched. 'My father devoted himself to improving the land and the herd. It was his pride and joy . . .'

'His methods of farming were archaic, very little different from ones your grandfather used. He still believed in old-fashioned principles. He discouraged the use of insecticides and refused to try out any of the more recent innovations.'

'When he made me trustee I am sure he didn't intend that I should make such radical changes,' Kate argued.

'It's the only way to preserve Russell's heritage,' Robert told her sternly. 'Look,' he went on persuasively, 'why don't you take care of the domestic side and leave me to run the Estate? And talking of the domestic side,' he added firmly, 'the way I shall be running things here in future will mean that there will be money to spare for improvements to the house. The entire place needs refurbishing and smartening up. It's time we spent some money on it.'

'You are probably right about the house,' Kate smiled. 'Things do grow shabby over the years but when you are living in the midst of them you don't really notice it happening.'

'And much the same happens to us. We could probably both do with smartening up,' Robert laughed heartily. 'It is time we started spending some money and having a good time, neither of us is getting any younger.'

'You talk as if we were both in our sixties,' Kate remonstrated.

'You are turned forty, my dear, and I am almost fifty,' Robert reminded her.

'I know. And before we know what's happened we'll have a son in his teens!'

'That reminds me,' Robert said quickly. 'I have managed to reserve a place for Russell at Danebury Prep School, in Windsor. He will be starting there next term. It's a first class training school, for Eton . . .'

'You have done what!' Kate stared at Robert in disbelief. Her mind was racing ahead, wondering what Nanny's reaction would be to such a revolutionary step.

'If he stays where he is now he doesn't stand a chance of passing the entrance exam for Eton,' Robert said blandly.

'What on earth are you talking about. He is already attending one of the finest private day schools in this part of Somerset,' Kate exploded.

'Their curriculum might be excellent for Marlborough or Winchester but not for Eton,' Robert informed her. 'I've looked into the matter very carefully and, believe me, I know what I am talking about.'

'I am quite sure you do, but why on earth has he got to go to Eton?'

'Much the best grounding for him. And after that, to Oxford or Cambridge and then into the army.'

'Russell may not want to go in the army.'

'Rubbish! He will be given a commission automatically if he has a degree, which means he will go straight to Sandhurst . . . He will be proud to serve in the same regiment as his father and grandfather.'

'Well, you may be right but I think we should ask him what he feels about it.'

'Nonsense! I have already made the decision, and I am sure Russell will thank me for it when he is older.'

Knowing that Robert's mind was made up, Kate didn't argue further. Nevertheless, she was determined to have a talk with Russell at the first opportunity she could and see how he felt about it all. It was all very well for Robert to decide for him but she had reservations about the army being right for Russell. He might take after Robert in looks but he was more like her when it came to temperament and she was not at all sure that being a peace-time soldier was the perfect outlet for him. There were so many other careers available that he might enjoy much more.

In this, as with so many other changes Robert made at Walford Grange, Kate was the loser. Robert built up such a glowing picture of what life would be like at boarding school and at Eton, that Russell was eager to go. The only person who seemed to side with Kate was Mabel Sharp who realised that once Russell went away to school then she would no longer be needed as a nanny.

Kate hesitated to tell her that since she was now in her late sixties the time had come for her to retire but Robert had no such qualms.

'I would say the time has come for you to be pensioned off, Nanny,' he told her bluntly when she confronted him about his decision to send Russell away to school.

'Give up!' Her voice was filled with scorn, her hooded eyes bright beads of anger. 'What would I want to do that for, eh? This is my home and always will be . . . thanks to Sir Henry!'

Robert frowned. He knew Sir Henry had stipulated in his Will that in recognition of her long years of service, Mabel Sharp was to consider Walford Grange her home for as long as she lived.

'Wouldn't you like a little place of your own, Nanny,' Robert persisted. 'A cottage, or a flat, where you would be free to do just as you chose. I'm sure we could fix you up with something suitable.'

'I'm sure you could . . . and you would like to,' she told him sharply. 'Walford Grange is my home, always has been and always will be. There's no cause for you to try and fix me up with anything else. Sir Henry said I could see my days out here and that's what I intend to do. And I'll tell you something else,' she went on, her mouth a tight line of determination, 'the only thing that would make me change my mind would be if Miss Kate was to turn me out. Then, of course, I'd have no choice.'

'Nanny, stop it! There's no question of you being asked to leave. Robert was only trying to be helpful. He just thought you might like your own place, that's all.'

'Well, he's got my answer and he was wrong, wasn't he,' the old woman answered belligerently.

Within a year, the whole lifestyle at Walford Grange seemed to have changed. With Russell away at school all term, Kate had plenty of time to enter into all the activities Robert proposed. She was glad of any distraction that helped to deaden the overwhelming sense of loss she felt.

She went on shopping sprees for new clothes with Eleanor. In the past, because she had rarely gone out, and seldom entertained, she had shown little interest in fashions, but now she began to take stock of her clothes and decided that most of them were dull and did little for her. Not satisfied with bringing her wardrobe up to date, Kate also had her hair re-styled so that even Robert was quite impressed with her new, elegant image.

Robert was determined that Russell should also establish his rightful place in local society. With this in mind, he planned a gymkhana and invited not just their immediate friends and neighbours but opened it up on a grand scale to riders for miles around. The specially engraved Cup that was to be presented aroused considerable interest and Robert was in his element organising it all. It proved to be so successful that after he and Russell had presented the Cup and the other prizes, Robert promised competitors that it would become a regular annual event.

Two years later, Russell, who was now at Eton, begged to be allowed to hold a pop festival in the grounds. Several of his new school friends had already staged one at their ancestral homes and they were now looking for somewhere to hold one in July to coincide with Prince Charles being installed at Caernarvon Castle as Prince of Wales.

Robert was in complete agreement that Walford Grange should be the venue. A large meadow, with easy access from the main road, was made ready. An enormous marquee was erected and draped with red, white and blue bunting, the Union Flag and the Welsh dragon.

The event caused so much interest that even the National newspapers sent reporters along and there was coverage on local radio and television news.

Robert and Russell were elated by it all. And even Kate found herself walking round humming some of the tunes that had thundered out from the rock bands that had played non-stop for forty-eight hours to an assembled gathering that ran into thousands.

Russell returned to Eton as a hero, cheered by those who had attended and envied by those who had not been able to be there. It had changed his entire personality. From being rather shy and nervous he was suddenly full of self-confidence. His place in the school hierarchy was firmly established. Everyone was eager to be invited to Walford

Grange and the range of events staged there during the long summer holidays grew rapidly. Robert was always willing to help with any scheme suggested and parents, too, gravitated towards the Somerset mansion when it was learned that the entertainment there was always of the best.

Chapter 18

Kate was proud of Russell's achievements at Oxford. He was an excellent scholar and his prowess at sports was equally rewarding. He had grown tall and filled out so that he now stood shoulder to shoulder with Robert and was almost as broad.

Seeing them side by side, the one a younger replica of the other, with their burnished hair and green eyes, brought misgivings to Kate's heart. She was afraid that Robert was moulding Russell too close to his own image. She sometimes thought that it was almost as if Robert was trying to relive, through Russell, the sort of childhood and adolescence he would have liked to have had himself. Robert was such an accomplished organiser, and cajoled Russell into doing whatever he wanted him to do so skilfully, that often Russell believed it to be of his own choice. She secretly hoped that just for once Russell would not take his father's advice, and go straight into the army when he left Oxford, but follow a career of his own choosing.

Her prayers went unanswered. There was never any doubt in the minds of either Robert or Russell that Russell would go into the Guards. He applied for a commission even before sitting his finals and as soon as his degree was confirmed he went straight to Sandhurst.

Kate's one great fear was that once Russell's initial training was over he would be sent to Northern Ireland. Ever since Bloody Sunday, three years earlier, the news from the war-torn North grew daily more disturbing. Terrorist activities were even being extended to the mainland with soldiers and civilians in Aldershot, and Birmingham, as well as in London, being killed by IRA bombs.

The sight of him, looking so resplendent in his Second-

Lieutenant's uniform, brought a lump to Kate's throat the first time he came home on leave. He seemed to be a reincarnation of Robert when she had first known him. The same brilliant eyes, decisive mouth, prominent nose and firm square chin with a cleft in the centre. The only real facial difference was that Robert sported a bristling moustache, and the colour of their hair. Robert's, though now fading and streaked with grey, had been curly and a deep rich glowing red when he was in his twenties, whereas Russell's was straight and sandy.

Not only were they alike in looks and build but in their mannerisms and attitudes to life also. The only dissimilarity was that Russell's self-assuredness seemed to stem naturally from within whereas Robert's manner remained slightly pompous and self-imposed.

Robert did everything possible to make sure that Russell's first leave was something of an occasion. The entertaining was lavish. Friends and wealthy neighbours for miles around were invited over for drinks, or to dine. Even though it was rather late in the year for tennis, the courts were tidied up and matches arranged.

On Russell's last night at home they staged a splendid dinner for a select number of close friends and afterwards ten times that number were invited to a dance that went on until the early hours of the morning.

Around midnight, as she sat sipping champagne and watching the whirling crowd of dancers, Kate caught sight of Russell and Melany Buscombe dancing together, Melany's head resting on Russell's shoulder. It made Kate feel suddenly old. It was hard to believe that Russell was now twenty-two and that he was old enough to marry.

'Watching the love-birds? They make a handsome pair, don't they?' Eleanor commented as she appeared at Kate's side. 'I didn't know that they were quite so close though, I must say.'

'Are they close?' A tremor of fear ran through Kate as she asked the question. She didn't want to lose Russell yet, not even to her dearest friend's daughter.

'I believe they have been writing to each other.'

'You mean while Russell has been at University?'

'I'm not sure about that but certainly since he has been at Sandhurst.'

'I had no idea . . .'

'Well, Mother is always the last one to hear these things.'

Kate turned her attention back to the dancers, looking for Melany or Russell, but she could no longer see either of them. She felt uneasy. It was impossible to overlook Melany for she was so tall, her long, dark hair piled up on top of her slender neck, revealing her fine aristocratic features, and making her look even more willowy. Where were they, she wondered.

Questions boiled inside Kate's head. Just how serious was Russell about her and would she make him a good wife. She could hardly wait to find Robert and have his reassurance.

'I can't think of a finer match,' he enthused, his green eyes glittering, when she confided in him. 'Just think what it would mean . . . the Buscombes' lands joined on to those of Walford Grange, Russell would be the most powerful landowner in the whole county.'

Kate turned away, her heart heavy with shock; aching with disappointment. He had not said one word about whether Russell and Melany were suitable for each other, only the resultant wealth and power such a liaison would bring. It sent her thoughts hurtling back to when she had said she wanted to marry Robert and her father's opposition. Had he recognised, even then, Robert's innate desire for power, and the ruthlessness with which he was prepared to pursue his aims? She wondered if Russell's interest in Melany was just as mercenary.

Her unease lessened over the next few months. Once Russell returned to his unit, Melany seemed to spread her favours amongst a number of eligible young men. When she mentioned this fact to Eleanor, her friend frowned and looked rather worried.

'I am beginning to think she is a born flirt,' Eleanor admitted. 'She never seems to be with the same young man two days' running. The latest seems to be Carlile Randell.'

'I don't think I have even heard of him,' Kate frowned.

'Probably because he is quite new on the scene. He has just bought Wherwell House.'

'Oh!' Kate looked suitably impressed. 'Is Carlile the son?'

'No, he's the chap who has bought it. Made his money in oil, I believe. They say he is a multi-millionaire.'

'How old is he for heaven's sake?' Kate asked in surprise.

'Late thirties, early forties. Rather old for Melany, I suppose.'

'Mm, I agree. Still, Melany is almost twenty so he can hardly be accused of cradle-snatching, I suppose. What is he like?'

'Quite devastating. Tall, dark and handsome, looks a rogue but very dashing. He has impeccable manners and oozes charm. I can see why she is attracted to him.'

'And is he serious or just playing around?'

'It is very hard to tell. I don't know very much about his background. He's obviously well-educated but ...' she shrugged rather helplessly.

'Let's hope he doesn't break Melany's heart,' Kate said thoughtfully.

'I agree. Like all young girls she is pretty headstrong, so there is not much point in talking to her.' She giggled. 'Remember what we were like at that age?'

'We were both in the forces, it was all so different in those days.'

'Well, we were probably the same when it came to marrying. Neither of us married the men our parents thought suitable.'

'You did, Eleanor ... eventually.'

'Yes, I suppose so. My first escapade though must have turned my mother's hair white. And your parents didn't exactly approve of your choice, now did they?'

'They didn't mind once Robert had his commission,' Kate answered, her mouth tightening.

'No, it automatically made him a gentleman when he became an officer, I suppose,' Eleanor agreed drily. 'He has certainly picked up the lifestyle without any problems.'

'Robert's an excellent farmer and a very good business-man,' Kate defended.

'Yes, and Russell has probably inherited those qualities as well as breeding and background so he has the best of both worlds. I would like to see him and Melany marry. Somehow seeing our Estate merge with yours would make me far happier than seeing them taken over by a newcomer like Carlile Randell.'

Kate smiled non-committally. She knew that it was what Robert hoped for but for very different reasons. He wanted to see Walford Grange expand while he still had some control over it and she wondered how Eleanor would react if that happened.

Russell seemed oblivious to the turmoil going on in the minds of the people around him. His interests lay solely in furthering his career in the army. And, at that, he was already making good progress. He was now a full Lieutenant and scheduled for a course at the end of which he would be promoted to Captain.

Robert was elated by the news and never tired of telling Kate how right he had been to insist on Russell joining the army.

'It has made a man of him,' he boomed, twirling the stiffened ends of his bristling moustache. 'Finest career in the world! And since he comes from a long line of soldiers it was only fitting that he should follow.'

Since she knew there was no arguing with such facts, Kate kept her own counsel but she still hoped that in the not too distant future Russell would tire of the army and come home to Walford Grange. She knew in her heart that Robert would discourage such a decision because, just like her father, as long as he was fit he wanted to be in control.

Although she had to admit that Robert did an admirable job in organising and running the Estate she wished he were not quite such a tyrant. He had made such sweeping changes, that her father would hardly recognise Home Farm and the surrounding farmland, she thought wistfully. Most of the changes were beneficial and all of them were cost effective. He planned everything in much the same way as if he were fighting a battle. Cleanliness and orderliness were top priority and everything was done strictly to the rule book.

She had been deeply grieved to see Greg Paxton leave Home Farm since she knew he loved the place almost as much as she did.

'I never in all my life expected to be doing something like

this, but I'm afraid the new Master's ways are not mine,' he told her bluntly when they parted. 'I just can't bring myself to change, not at my time of life.'

'Then why not think it over again,' she urged.

'I have done nothing else but think about it ever since the Colonel took over. His ways are not mine and that's all there is to it. No, it will be better for both of us if I go.'

'Have you managed to find another farming job?' Kate asked, her brown eyes dark with concern.

Greg Paxton shook his grey head. 'No one wants a man of my age. My eldest boy and me are taking on a small-holding. Sheep and steers, we thought. He's got another job so we will manage all right. I hope, in time, to build the place up ready for him to take over. Not afraid of hard work, you know, Miss Kate.'

'I know you are not, Greg.' She smiled into the weather-beaten face as she held out her hand. 'Good luck. Come and see me sometime and let me know how you are getting on.'

'I shall look forward to doing that,' he told her as his gnarled hand closed over her soft smooth one. 'We've known each other a long time. I remember you when you were a tiny girl with your first pony. I used to be that proud when Sir Henry allowed me to take you out on a leading rein . . .' His rheumy eyes filled with tears and Kate found herself turning away, afraid he would see that her own eyes were also moist at the memory of those far off days.

In her heart Kate felt angry that Robert was making such dramatic changes. She didn't want them to be commercialised, couldn't see the necessity of being the biggest or the most modern farm in the county. Anger flooded her when she recalled their most recent argument, that they should open up Walford Grange to the public.

The thought of having hordes of gawping strangers invading her privacy appalled her.

'Lord Bath does it down at Longleat and makes a killing from it, and so do most other titled landowners,' Robert had argued.

'Walford Grange hasn't that kind of appeal,' she protested.

'Not quite the same historic interest, I grant you,' Robert agreed, 'but we could make our model farm the attraction.

Lord Montagu shows off his collection of vintage cars when people visit Beaulieu, but here they would view our dairy herd and farming methods. Where else could the public see stabling and byres as clean and methodically run, such streamlined sheep-shearing facilities or such perfect piggeries?'

'Show them those by all means,' she told him, 'but I don't want the public anywhere near the house. Now that you've turned Greg Paxton and his family out of Home Farm you can organise everything from there . . . just leave our home out of your plans.'

Robert had been both surprised and offended by her outburst. She wondered afterwards if she had been too forthright but stubbornly refused to amend her statement.

Robert, she decided, had got away with running things his way for far too long. It was time she took a stand. After all, she was the one who was custodian of Walford Grange, not Robert. And she didn't intend that Russell's heritage should be ruined before he took it over.

Chapter 19

Colonel Robert Campbell strode out from Walford Grange, and across the Home Paddock heading in the direction of the small wood on the far side. He was dressed as though for a day's shooting in moleskin breeches, a thorn-proof tweed jacket, matching deer-stalker hat and high-legged brown leather boots. He carried a double-barrelled shotgun, the barrel resting along his forearm at just the same angle as General Sir Henry Russell had always carried his gun when he strode the same paths.

Like his late father-in-law, Robert used the excuse of a day's shooting in Badger's Wood as a means to soothe his nerves and to escape from other company. It was just another of the countless ways in which he aped Sir Henry.

His mind was churning with anger, hate and frustration as he stalked across the meadow. When Sir Henry's Will had been read out after the funeral it had taken every ounce of Robert's highly-trained self-control not to cause a scene and denounce him as a two-timing bastard to anyone who cared to listen.

He had heard the expression 'revenge beyond the grave' but never before attributed to it any particular circumstance. Now he knew precisely what it meant. He felt cheated, robbed of his rightful place and, not for the first time since Sir Henry had out-manoeuvred him, needed to be alone in order to work out his future moves with military precision.

Reaching Badger Wood he made for a small clearing and raising his gun to his shoulder, fired a volley at random. As the blast shattered the sweet stillness, sending birds squawking into the air from the surrounding trees, he expelled a deep breath, giving relief to his pent-up feelings.

He sat down on a fallen tree, propped his gun against it and took a little-used briar pipe from his pocket and lit it. As he contemplated the blue smoke that rose in a spiral, he began thinking about the events in his life and to wonder if he could have changed them in any way.

He had known right from the moment he had asked for permission to marry Kate that General Sir Henry Russell didn't approve of him. The obstacles he had placed in their way had been positive proof of that, Robert thought grimly.

He had worked hard to surmount them all. He had made a career in the army, and when he had finally achieved the rank of Colonel, Robert assumed that he had managed, at last, to find complete favour in the General's eyes. Certainly in the last years of his life, Sir Henry had been affable enough towards him, he reflected.

'And so he bloody well should have been,' Robert muttered aloud as he knocked the ash from his half-smoked pipe and stood up. He had modelled himself on Sir Henry, and done everything in his power to prove that he was the right person to be in charge at Walford Grange when the time came.

Yet, if Sir Henry's Will was anything to go by, then obviously he certainly hadn't convinced his father-in-law, he thought gloomily. Leaving Walford Grange to Kate for her lifetime use and then to pass on to Russell, instead of leaving it jointly to him and Kate was a direct snub. 'It's almost as if he was afraid I would sell up once I got hold of it,' Robert muttered defiantly, kicking angrily at a fallen branch.

He had expected Kate to understand how hurt he felt at being passed over but she had merely smiled coolly and said it was her home and she was, after all, next-of-kin.

Her calm assurance infuriated him. She'd never even hinted to him in all the years they had been married that eventually she would be the sole owner even though she must have known how much being Lord of the Manor meant to him.

As he strode deeper into the woods his thoughts went back to the first time he had met Kate. Even in her ATS uniform, her patrician manner, and cool unruffled self-assurance, had impressed him. It had been that, almost as much as anything else, that had made him determined to get to know her, just to breach her self-complacent air. He had never considered, not even in his wildest fantasies, that eventually she would fall in love with him or that they would be married.

Summoning up the courage to speak to her had taken a lot of nerve. If she had objected violently, or reported him to her father, he could have ended up on a charge. Not only was she an officer in her own right but the General's daughter to boot. Of course he had been virile and handsome in those days but, even so, he had found it flattering that she should be so susceptible to his charms. That she had also fallen in love with him had been an added bonus.

Sir Henry had been the stumbling block. But then, Robert thought smugly, what General would be happy to see his only daughter marrying his driver? If he had been a civilian, and not a soldier, it would have been comparable to Kate marrying the chauffeur!

Lady Dorothea, of course, had been quite unapproachable. She had not even tried to disguise her feelings. Robert knew right from their first meeting that she despised him, and saw through him. He had taken the precaution of avoiding her as much as possible. She had wrought her revenge though, he thought darkly, remembering how he and Kate had been forced to live apart because Lady Dorothea had demanded Kate's presence throughout her long illness. He had only accepted the situation because of the long-term benefits he expected to gain if he was amenable.

Indirectly, Lady Dorothea had triumphed even there, he thought cynically. He had put up with being separated from Kate all those years and yet Lady Dorothea hadn't even mentioned him in her Will. Sir Henry had also ignored his existence completely even when he had drawn up a new Will to ensure that Walford Grange would eventually go to Russell.

A smile twisted his lips as he remembered the years he had spent in Germany ... and Maria. Funny how Kate had reacted to that, almost as if by ignoring the incident it wasn't happening. He let out a guffaw as his memories welled up. Maria had been so uncomplicated, so raw, earthy, and shallow. She had been fun to be with and tremendous in bed. Nothing prim and proper about her!

It had been Kate's own fault that he had taken up with

Maria, he thought defensively. What red-blooded man wouldn't have turned elsewhere for solace if his wife left him on the first day of their honeymoon to go back home to nurse her mother. The only thing he regretted was that day Kate had come out to Germany, without a word of warning.

He often wondered if Kate knew there had been other women as well as Maria. After Russell was born, when Kate had stayed home to nurse her father, the girls had been legion; he didn't remember half of them.

Kate had probably guessed he was being unfaithful but she was too ladylike to discuss it or even reproach him. Which in some ways, he reflected dourly, made him feel all the more guilty. He wondered if the General had ever found out about his casual affairs. Cutting him out of his Will could have been his way of getting back at him, he reflected.

He still couldn't reconcile himself to the fact that after all the work he had put into making Walford Grange a show-piece he had no stake in its ownership. It put him in such an invidious position. If Kate wanted to, she could probably turn him out at a moment's notice and even have the law on her side.

Not that such a situation was likely to arise, he thought smugly. She allowed him a pretty free hand and accepted his decision on most issues, but there was always the possibility that she might decide to change the way things were done. It was the uncertainty that gnawed at him.

It was fortunate that Russell had taken to army life so well. If he ever decided to come back home then there could be insurmountable problems for all of them. Kate might even decide to let him run things. Still, that was a long way off, for now there were other more pressing matters to be contested. Like opening up Walford Grange to the public and having his Model Farm as the main attraction.

But would Kate agree? He very much doubted it! She had already made it clear that she valued her privacy far too much. She didn't mind entertaining when it was her own friends. Charity galas, balls, fêtes, all those sort of things, were all right but when it came to actually making money out of entertaining that was much too mercenary! It made his blood boil. First Sir Henry had held the purse strings, now it was Kate and soon it would be Russell.

Not that he was doing it just for the money. They had plenty of that. Home Farm more than paid for the upkeep of Walford Grange. He also had his army pension and Kate had money left to her by her mother, as well as a personal nest-egg from her father. It was the sense of achievement and prominence in the local community that such a venture would bring that fired his determination to go ahead with his scheme.

He lashed out angrily at the undergrowth. In the army he had been someone with authority, a man of standing that others looked up to. Now he was a nonentity! He didn't own his own home, the horses he rode, or even the cars he drove round in. His wife owned all the clothes, fur coats and inherited jewellery she was ever likely to need. If there was anything at all she desired then she could buy it out of her own money without even mentioning the fact to him. Sir Henry had made sure of that and Robert was quite certain it had been intentional. Being such a dominant character himself, Sir Henry would realise how emasculating being beholden to a woman for even the roof over his head would prove to be. The more Robert thought about it, the more certain he became that the terms of the Will had been calculated deliberately.

He pulled out his pipe and lit up again. He wondered how many of their friends knew the truth about the situation. Lawyers were sworn to secrecy but someone had to type up the letters and documents.

The role that he had been playing for so long was far too enjoyable to lose, Robert decided. Somehow he must ensure that his status remained unchanged. He slammed his fist into the palm of his hand. If only Kate could be persuaded to make the property over to him by Deed of Gift. Even joint ownership would be a welcome concession.

The trouble was that Kate didn't seem to attach the importance to legal ownership that he did. She never had to assert herself, people took it for granted that she was the 'lady from Walford Grange' and acted accordingly.

He had worked hard to establish his place in the local

hierarchy. Now he was a Magistrate, a member of the Parish Council, Master of Foxhounds, Chairman of the local Conservative Association, and a school Governor. If his peers found out he had no ownership rights whatsoever to Walford Grange, their attitude towards him might well change. People could be such snobs.

He would talk to Russell about it, he decided. He was sure he would be able to make him understand the situation. Army life would have taught him the importance of rank and position.

Thinking of Russell brought a warm glow to his heart. He was proud of the way he had already begun to ascend the promotional ladder. Being top cadet of his year at Sandhurst had given him a flying start and he would be a Captain any day now.

It pleased him, too, that Russell was establishing a close relationship with Melany Buscombe. If they married, and the land she inherited was amalgamated with Walford Grange it would make Russell the largest landowner in the county.

In some ways, that sort of power was more important than wealth. The knowledge that your ancestors had farmed the same fields for hundreds of years gave you a special sort of standing. 'The King is dead long live the King' syndrome, he thought contemptuously. It was why wars were fought, the true meaning of patriotism. And the trouble was, Robert thought gloomily, those who inherited such benefits rarely seemed to appreciate it, they took it for granted.

As he returned home later in the day, his mind was made up. He'd organise a family conference and suggest to both Russell and Kate that they should form a limited company. And if Russell agreed then eventually Kate would have to go along with his scheme to admit the public to view the farm. It would be a start . . . His mind wandered off as he visualised how successful it could be and by the time he reached the gun room he was whistling.

Chapter 20

Russell Campbell was fully aware that he led a charmed life. Ever since his first day at prep school, Fate had smiled kindly on him. Lessons had never been any problem and, unlike some of his academically inclined classmates, he was also good on the sports field. He had thoroughly enjoyed his time at Eton and found University even more fulfilling.

He had not raised any objections to his father's idea that he should go into the army straight from University because there was nothing else that he particularly wanted to do. He had always thought his father looked rather splendid in his Guards uniform and quite fancied following in his footsteps. He sensed that his mother was not very keen on the idea but, since she was always over-protective where he was concerned, he imagined she was afraid he might find the rigours of army life rather daunting.

As it had turned out her fears had been groundless. Mabel Sharp had been a stickler for obedience so he had been used to discipline right from the nursery. And his years at boarding school and University had accustomed him to mixing and living with people other than his immediate family.

After he completed his training at Sandhurst, Russell was sent to Wellington Barracks in London and spent most of the next six months either on Guard duty at Buckingham Palace or taking part in ceremonial parades.

Being stationed in London had distinct advantages. There was always plenty going on and a wide variety of things to do, both in and out of Barracks, during off-duty hours. He welcomed the opportunity of being able to go to the theatre and the cinema and see all the latest shows.

It also meant that he was within travelling distance of Walford Grange for weekend leave and Russell made the most of such occasions since it was rumoured that they would be going to Ireland in the very near future for an indefinite tour of duty. Hostilities out there were reaching a new peak as the struggle between Protestants and Catholics heated up. The campaign was spreading and terrorists were once again attacking mainland targets. At the end of March, a bomb placed underneath an MP's car had gone off just as he was driving away from the House of Commons. And in August, the boat on which Earl Mountbatten was taking a fishing trip off the coast of Ireland was blown up by the IRA, killing him, his grandson and one of the boat boys.

Such wanton destruction of human life incensed Russell. It left him feeling that he should be out there, helping to control the area, not merely parading in London, even though guarding the Queen and the royal palaces was equally important. He sensed that the men serving under him felt much the same way. Gary Collins, his Platoon Sergeant, openly voiced agreement with his sentiments.

He admired Gary Collins. He was in his mid-thirties, a broad-shouldered handsome man with vivid blue eyes, a square face and strong chin. An outspoken cockney, he was invariably good humoured and had a strong infectious laugh.

A professional soldier, Gary Collins was always ready to face trouble squarely. Yet he would never ask any of the men under him to do anything he was not prepared to do himself.

He and Sergeant Hugh Edwards were inseparable. They were about the same age and had joined the army straight from school at about the same time and served together for most of their army life.

The bond of friendship between the two men intrigued Russell because they were such exact opposites in both looks and demeanour. Hugh Edwards was dark-haired, handsome, and self-possessed and with alert dark eyes and an authoritative manner. Whereas Gary was friendly to the point of impudence, Hugh Edwards was reserved and spoke only when addressed.

The families of both men lived in Married Quarters and when he had met Gary Collins' wife, Russell had been amused to see how well she fitted Gary's description of her. Gary had once told him that he had been brought up by his grandmother who had a pub in the East End and Russell could easily imagine Sheila, a plumpish, faded blonde with a rich cockney accent and a ready wit, in the role of barmaid.

Hugh Edwards' wife, Ruth, was quite different. He had never spoken to her but with her dark hair and intelligent brown eyes she reminded him very much of Kate. Like her husband, she appeared to be very quiet and reserved.

He might never even have noticed her at all, had it not been for her younger sister, Lucy Woodley. The moment Lucy's vivid blue eyes locked with his there had been a magnetic attraction that stayed with him. He couldn't put her out of his mind and he was eager to get to know her. When he went home for the weekend, Lucy Woodley was in his thoughts even when he was out riding with Melany Buscombe.

He and Melany were friends of such long standing that he didn't have to explain his preoccupation. She assumed that something to do with his work was troubling him and cheerfully ignored the slight tension between them.

If she was aware that he was comparing her with a girl he hardly knew, but who filled his thoughts night and day, she would be a lot less tolerant, he thought ruefully.

Perturbed, he considered his relationship with Melany. They had grown up together and there had always been a close affinity between the two of them, even to the point of enjoying the same type of caustic humour. They shared a great many similar interests, and were both fond of horses and riding. Ever since he could remember he had preferred Melany's company to that of her brother, Geoffrey.

He was aware that his parents hoped they would marry. He knew she would make an excellent wife and, as his father was always pointing out in none too subtle a way, she would bring with her a dowry of land that would make Walford Grange into one of the largest Estates in south-west England. In his heart he knew that such a liaison was impossible; his affection for Melany was the same as he would have felt for a sister.

He'd teased fellow officers about 'falling in love' and being unable to think about anything except the girl who filled their thoughts. It had never been like that with him and

Melany. He was always pleased to see her, enjoyed being with her and regarded her as an exceptionally close friend. She was someone he could talk to on any subject under the sun and who understood his moods, but thoughts of her certainly didn't fill his every waking moment.

Now that he had met Lucy, he knew that his feelings for Melany were certainly not love. Lucy had turned his whole world upside-down and he was unable to put her out of his mind for a single moment. He was avidly curious about her background as well as everything she did. He was constantly watching out for her around the Barracks on the off-chance she might be invited along to the Sergeants' Mess by either Gary Collins or her brother-in-law, Hugh Edwards.

When Gary Collins formally suggested that he might like to look in at the Sergeants' Ball, Russell accepted with an inward sense of Fate once again taking a hand.

'Of course, Sergeant, if I'm Duty Officer,' he conceded.

'It's going to be very well attended, sir,' Gary told him, his eyes glinting. 'Hope you can make it.'

'Does that mean that delectable little blonde is going to be there?' Russell asked nonchalantly, raising an eyebrow.

'You mean Sergeant Edwards' sister-in-law, sir?' Gary Collins asked and added with a wide grin, 'We won't be able to keep her away if she knows you are coming, sir.'

Russell walked away quickly, his heart thumping. What the hell had made him do such a stupid thing? Being on friendly terms with one's Platoon Sergeant was one thing but openly showing interest in his family and friends was damned foolhardy.

Although he was careful not to enter into any further discussion about the matter with Gary Collins he was sure there was an amused gleam in the Sergeant's blue eyes when he repeated the invitation on the morning of the Ball. It worried Russell and throughout the rest of the day he found himself debating the rights and wrongs of his decision.

As he shaved and dressed ready to go on duty that evening, Russell felt as though he was preparing for his first date. He had never felt so excited in his life even though he kept telling himself that he was probably only imagining Lucy Woodley's fascinating and attractive personality.

She might appear to be a diminutive blonde beauty with petal-soft skin, delicate features and forget-me-not blue eyes but what if she had a rasping cockney accent, or a strident laugh?

Remembering the gentle pressure of her tiny hand when Gary had introduced her, the sweetly pouting lips and the shy smile he was convinced that she really was everything he had imagined. He looked at his watch, he would soon know.

The Ball was already under way as he entered the Mess. He was acutely aware that he had never felt so keyed up. His nerves were more tense than when he had sat exams at University or when he had been dressing for his passing-out parade at Sandhurst.

The ballroom was packed. There was a sprinkling of officers, but most of the men present were Sergeants, all resplendent in sparkling white frilled shirts, contrasting against the red of their jackets and the gleaming buttons, buckles and insignia. Many were campaign veterans, proudly displaying their medals.

For a moment Russell was filled with dismay as he stared round the crowded room at the sea of faces. He would never find Lucy Woodley in such a throng. There were so many glamorous women, all so magnificently gowned and groomed, that pin-pointing just one was going to be an almost impossible task.

He walked over to the bar and ordered a drink. Just as he was lifting the glass to his lips someone touched his elbow and there was no mistaking the cockney voice.

'Nice to see you here, sir.'

As Russell turned he found himself looking into Gary Collins' twinkling blue eyes.

'Good evening, Sergeant. Would you like a drink?'

'No thank you, sir. I just wanted to let you know that a certain young lady is here tonight. I'm just going to ask her to dance. If you should decide to cut-in while I'm on the floor with her, I would quite understand.'

'Really, Sergeant?' Russell tried to keep his tone in-different but wasn't sure he had managed it. He could hardly believe his luck that Lucy was there, in the same room. He turned away quickly, leaning with both elbows on the bar counter so that Gary Collins could not see the expression of joy that he knew must be on his face.

He downed the rest of his drink in a gulp, hoping it would steady his nerves, then looked round, trying to locate Gary Collins.

The moment he caught sight of him with Lucy his heart began to pound. Visually, at any rate, she was just as he remembered. Her long blonde hair flowed over her shoulders like a glittering shawl, framing her face and giving her delicate features an ethereal look.

He had never seen anyone quite so beautiful. He wanted to gather her in his arms, protect her, shield her from the rest of the world. He understood now why sheiks kept their womenfolk hidden from other men's eyes. He would like to do that with Lucy. Carry her off to a high tower somewhere and surround the place with fierce dogs so that no one could enter.

'My brain needs servicing,' he muttered and he felt a sense of soaring anticipation as he saw Gary Collins escort her out onto the dance floor.

'Evening, sir,' Gary Collins said formally, greeting him as though it was the first time they had met that evening.

Russell's heart hammered against his rib-cage as he nodded and tried to formulate the right words of greeting. He had eyes only for Lucy. She looked entrancing in a low-necked black dress, the bodice trimmed with shimmering coloured sequins in the shape of a flower.

'I think you have met Sergeant Edwards' sister-in-law once before, sir. Lucy, this is Lieutenant Campbell, I'm sure you remember him. Would you like to dance, sir?'

'Thank you.' Russell accepted the invitation with alacrity, aware Lucy's forget-me-not blue gaze was fixed on him wide-eyed, her pouting lips parted in a shy smile, as he took Gary's place.

As they moved into the circling dancers he was once more aware of how petite she was. Her golden head barely reached his shoulder, his arm completely encompassed her waist. Although she was small, she was shapely. He could feel the firm round mounds of her breasts pressing against him as they swayed in unison to the music.

146

When he looked down, past the golden crown of her head, he caught sight of the tantalising cleavage revealed by the low-cut neck of her dress and his pulse raced. As he held her a shade tighter, the material of her dress felt as soft and slippery beneath his hand as if he was holding her naked body and the intoxicating fragrance of her perfume excited his senses.

The music stopped and he knew he ought to take her back to her table, and let her rejoin her family but parting from her was out of the question. He was afraid that if he let her out of his sight for a second she might disappear and he would never see her again.

Normally he was level-headed and cautious, but she had bewitched him utterly. Common sense told him that to become involved with a Sergeant's sister-in-law was not only contrary to Guards' rules but would create all kinds of difficulties. He could imagine his own family's reaction. His father would be outraged by the breach of military protocol. His mother, too, would be dismayed by his choice when she learned that Lucy was not 'county' and even Mabel Sharp would think it her place to scold. He sometimes thought she still regarded him as a small boy.

Yet, undaunted by these adverse prospects, at the end of the evening Russell's mind was made up.

'You really don't have to see me home,' Lucy told him wide-eyed. 'I am staying with my sister and her husband, I can go with them.'

'I think I should . . . I want to meet your mother and you said she is there looking after your sister's children.'

'You do . . . why?' she looked up at him wide-eyed and mystified.

'Can't you really guess why?' he breathed as he bent and gently kissed her on the lips.

As she shook her head, he felt a tinge of apprehension. He had never felt for anyone the way he did about Lucy. It seemed madness, even to him, that he should find himself in the grip of such illogical sensations. He hardly knew Lucy and yet he had this tremendous inner conviction that they were destined for each other. He felt an overwhelming tenderness towards her and a fierce desire to protect her as well as a burning need for her physically.

'I want to ask her if she will let me marry you, Lucy,' he told her softly. 'You do want to, don't you?'

Her wide-eyed silence unnerved him. The startled innocence on her face touched his heart, and for a moment he wondered if he was rushing things too much. He didn't want to frighten her into refusal by declaring his love too soon but the uncertainty was unbearable.

He kissed her again, fiercely, possessively, holding her face trapped between his two hands. When he finally released her mouth, her breathless whisper, 'Yes, I do want to marry you, Russell,' was joy to his ears.

Filled with confidence, he escorted her back to where the rest of her party were sitting and told them the news. Even their stunned silence failed to disconcert him.

'I think perhaps you should be the one to tell Mum, Ruth,' Lucy whispered cautiously.

'Not tonight!' Ruth exclaimed aghast. 'She'll be in bed. Asleep, probably. Can't it wait?'

'I would like to settle things immediately,' Russell said firmly.

Ruth looked enquiringly at her husband, a worried frown knitting her brow.

'Very well, sir,' Hugh Edwards said coldly, his face impassive. 'We will leave now, so if you could give us ten minutes or so, and then bring Lucy home, we will do our best to try and explain the situation to Mrs Woodley.'

Chapter 21

Russell and Lucy were married with almost unseemly haste, in Kate's opinion. However, remembering the long delay she had experienced, she said nothing. Even now it was still agony to recall the frustration she had endured all those years ago.

She was still stunned by the idea of Russell marrying. Although he was almost twenty-five, he seemed so young, so very unworldly, that she wondered if he really knew what he was doing. He had lived away from home since he was ten yet in many ways he had led a very sheltered life. He had experienced so few of life's harsh realities. He had never had to stand on his own feet, or compete for a livelihood. Since childhood, his every wish had been satisfied. Bicycle, motor-bike, car, sports equipment, holidays; he had only to show an interest in something and it was his to keep. Robert had always been eager to gratify his slightest demand.

His pocket-money had been liberally increased at regular intervals. Even now, his army pay was supplemented by a more than generous allowance.

'It belongs to him, it comes out of the Estate,' Robert had pointed out when she had protested. 'He needs it, his salary will barely cover his Messing bills. I know!'

Strangely enough, or possibly because of the very fact that he had never been short of money, Russell was not extravagant. He took it for granted, of course, that there was always a horse in the stables for him to ride, and dogs to accompany him, walking or shooting. His taste in clothes was expensive but not over indulgent so that there was always a healthy balance in his bank account.

'We will make all arrangements for your wedding and hold

the reception here,' Robert declared the moment he had recovered from the shock that Russell was marrying a complete stranger and not Melany Buscombe as he had hoped. 'That means there is no problem about the number of people you invite, but I'm afraid you may have to limit it to "family only" at the church. Unless, of course, I am able to arrange loud-speakers and relay the service to the village hall. If that is possible, then we could accommodate the overflow in there.' He produced a notebook and began writing down the points as he spoke.

'Hold it, we are planning on being married at the Guards' Chapel in Wellington Barracks,' Russell told him firmly. 'It is what Lucy wants.'

'That poses a few problems,' Robert frowned, stroking his moustache thoughtfully.' It will be a long way to drive home after the reception, my boy! Most people will be over the limit, remember. Much better to hold it here . . . where they are known, if you get my meaning.'

'The Guards' Chapel sounds wonderful. Why don't we hire a coach to take our guests up to London and bring them back afterwards,' Kate suggested.

'Splendid idea! We must make a guest list as soon as possible. Important to have the numbers right so that we book a suitable size vehicle,' Robert enthused.

'Now don't give it another thought, Russell.' He tapped his notebook. 'I will organise everything. Understand? Just let me have a guest list from the bride's family and then leave everything to me.'

'I think Lucy's family want a quiet wedding. Mrs Woodley is a widow . . .'

'Don't worry about it, my boy,' Robert boomed. 'Tell her I will pick up the tab. It won't cost her a penny-piece. All she needs to do is buy herself a new hat! Send Lucy along to Harrods for her wedding dress and charge it to our account . . .'

'I don't think *that* will be necessary!' Russell protested. 'Lucy did intend having a white wedding . . . just not too many guests.'

'I will be funding the reception, tell her, so she can invite as many people as she likes.' He laughed jovially, slapping

Russell on the shoulder. 'I'll organise that side of things completely, just leave everything to me.'

'Let your father get on with it, he's enjoying every moment,' Kate told Russell when, just before he returned to London, he protested about his father's intervention in his plans.

'I know, but how are Lucy's family going to take it?'

'I am sure they will understand. Mrs Woodley will probably be quite relieved to discover she won't have to pay out for the reception.'

'I just hope she doesn't mind,' Russell frowned. 'Maybe I should leave it to Lucy to tell her, she can probably handle it better than I can.'

Robert threw himself into organising Russell's wedding with a fervour and verve that left Kate bewildered. Absolutely everything was done on the grandest scale possible. Two large coaches were hired to transport the many friends they had invited from Somerset to Wellington Barracks. A London florist was instructed to bedeck the Guards' Chapel. There was to be a full choir, a guard of honour, and the Guards' Band as well as an organist. A battery of professional photographers was hired to record, for posterity, every moment of the spectacular service, including cine-cameras positioned high up in the gallery.

As the wedding day approached, Kate felt vaguely apprehensive, afraid that Lucy's family would feel overwhelmed by so much opulence. When Russell arranged for her to meet Mrs Woodley for luncheon, Kate was struck by the sadness in the other woman's eyes as well as the resignation in her voice as they discussed the forthcoming wedding. Kate had expected her to be elated that her younger daughter was marrying into a wealthy family but she seemed quite unimpressed. Her genuine concern as to whether Russell and Lucy were right for each other and her wish that they would postpone their wedding until they knew each other better, struck an echoing chord in Kate's own mind.

But then, neither Lucy nor her mother had been anything like she had expected. Helen Woodley was a tall, slim woman in her mid-fifties, her dark hair liberally streaked with grey, her face, a network of fine lines, especially around her expressive grey eyes. Quiet and reserved she looked tired, as if she had found life an immense burden. They were about the same age, Kate guessed, but compared to Helen Woodley's dispirited manner she felt positively spritely. Lucy's mother had the air of someone who had given up trying to make the most of herself. The style of her navy dress and jacket was dated and looked as if it had been worn on a good many occasions and her navy shoes and handbag were neat but nondescript.

Kate decided she quite liked Helen Woodley. She had probably once been very attractive, Kate thought, studying her profile and she wondered what life had done to her to make her look so utterly dejected and weary. It seemed unbelievable that Lucy, so diminutive, and bubbly, should be her daughter, and for some inexplicable reason Kate felt perturbed that Russell should be so enamoured of the girl. She was extremely pretty, of course, but Kate suspected that behind her Dresden-doll looks there was a sharp shrewd mind and that she would be able to twist Russell around her little finger.

Over lunch, Kate's concern seemed justified when she learned there was a considerable age gap between Lucy and Mrs Woodley's other two children. Ruth had been fourteen when Lucy was born and Mark twelve, and they had both spoiled Lucy and so she was used to getting her own way.

Helen Woodley's husband, Kate was shocked to learn, had been killed on a training exercise just weeks before he was due to retire. Russell had told her that he had been a Sergeant in the Guards, but she had no idea until now that Mrs Woodley had been a widow since before Lucy had been born.

Helen Woodley accepted Robert's proposal that the Campbells should pay for the wedding with quiet dignity. Her only stipulation was that her two grandchildren, Ruth's daughters Sally and Anna, should be bridesmaids.

'That shouldn't present any problem,' Kate assured her. 'We have no small children in our family. In fact, I hadn't given any thought to attendants.'

'They've talked of nothing else since the first moment they heard that Lucy was getting married,' Helen Woodley commented. 'They have even chosen their dresses!'

Lucy's wedding dress and the bridesmaids' dresses were, in fact, the only things Robert didn't contrive to stage-manage. He organised everything else on a grand scale, pulling rank whenever it was something that had to be ratified by the Guards. The result was fairytale splendour, the kind of wedding most brides dream of having, but seldom achieve.

The magnificence of the Guards' Chapel made the perfect backdrop, and when the two coaches Robert had hired to transport their own guests arrived the place was packed to capacity.

Kate had remonstrated with Robert about the numbers, afraid there wouldn't be room for Lucy's family and friends, but her fears had been groundless. There were so few of them that they occupied only the first three pews on the bride's side and judging by their age it seemed that they were mostly Lucy's friends.

Russell was being married in uniform, but owing to the difference in rank, Lucy's brother-in-law, Sergeant Hugh Edwards, was wearing civilian clothes and so, too, was his friend Sergeant Gary Collins.

Lucy looked breathtakingly lovely when she arrived on the arm of her brother, Mark, who had elected to give her away. He was so very tall and broad that Lucy, in her floating white silk gown, looked almost ethereal beside him. As she moved down the aisle, the soft murmur of voices from the people waiting for the service to begin gave way to gasps of admiration. She carried a posy of white rosebuds, and the filmy lace veil that covered her golden hair was held in place with a matching circlet of rosebuds.

Sally and Anna walked sedately behind Lucy. Sally was wearing an ankle-length dress of dusky pink which contrasted attractively with her dark hair. Anna was dressed in wedgwood blue, which made her shoulder length fair hair appear almost silver. Both of them wore tiny circlets of white rosebuds on their heads and carried matching posies.

The entire ceremony went so smoothly that it could have been a TV spectacular, Kate thought. Afterwards, they all posed outside in the brilliant sunshine, standing on the steps of the Guards' Chapel while countless cameras whirred and clicked. Lucy, her veil now thrown back, looked radiant as she clung to Russell's arm.

It was inevitable, that at the reception Lucy's family were isolated into a small group on their own. Robert made several forays into their midst, jovially exhorting them to enjoy the lavish feast he had organised and insisting their glasses should be kept filled up with the vintage champagne.

Kate cringed inwardly at Robert's speech. She looked across at Helen Woodley and saw her mouth tighten resentfully when his voice boomed out, 'Now, we want you all to enjoy yourselves to the full. We can't take it with us so we may as well spend some of it now. Russell's our only child dammit, so we want to do him proud and give him the very best send-off we possibly can! Fill up your glasses. If you don't like champagne then ask for whatever you do like.'

Kate sighed. Robert was so insensitive! It must be difficult enough for Helen Woodley, knowing that her daughter was marrying out of her class, without being patronised by Robert.

It was a long time since she had thought about such matters but Kate now remembered vividly how shocked her own parents had been when she had said she wanted to marry Robert because he had come from a background that was quite different from her own.

She had felt then, and still did, that such things as social position and breeding were not the real issue and that it was the character of the individual that mattered. She was fully aware that other people thought differently and remembered the problems Robert had encountered when he had first become a Guards officer.

She made a mental note to go across and have a few discreet words with Helen Woodley after Russell and Lucy left for their honeymoon in Paris. She would hate for the day to be ruined for her because of Robert's overpowering condescension. The Guards were particularly class-conscious; and none more than those who had themselves been elevated from the ranks, she thought ruefully, as she watched Robert bombastically fulfilling his role as host.

Chapter 22

'Captain and Mrs Russell Campbell.'

Lucy felt a tingle of excitement snake down her spine as all eyes in the enormous ballroom turned to watch their entrance. She had taken the utmost care with her appearance and knew she looked a picture of perfection from head to toe.

She paused dramatically, fully aware of the stunning picture she presented in her black lace dress with its billowing skirt flouncing to mid-calf. With deliberate casualness, she moved her head so that her hair danced on her shoulders, catching the light of the chandeliers which made it glisten like molten gold.

The delicate black lace clung to her plump curves invitingly, the low neckline enhancing the soft creamy-whiteness of her arms and throat and exposing a fascinating glimpse of cleavage.

Even in her spiky-heeled black patent sandals her head barely reached Russell's shoulder. It made other women seem clumsy by comparison.

Russell, resplendent in his red and black Mess dress, gilded with heavy gold braid, stiffened proudly, his sandy head held high, his green eyes arrogant. He, too, was conscious of the impression they were making and, as his arm went round Lucy's waist possessively, aware that every red-blooded man in the room envied him.

At times like this he felt delighted that he had taken the momentous decision to marry. Lucy could be an enchanting companion and he loved her deeply. It was only when the bills piled up, and Lucy's demands exceeded what he could afford to provide, that the exhilaration dimmed.

They had been married less than six months, yet already

he'd been to his father twice to ask for a loan over and above the allowance he already received.

'Expensive business being married these days, isn't it,' his father guffawed on the second occasion. 'Never mind, I can't take it with me!' he quipped reaching for his cheque book. 'I've added on another couple of hundred. Buy the little lady something from me,' he added as he signed with a flourish of his gold topped pen. 'I can see I'll have to talk to your mother about increasing your allowance, Russell. Utter rubbish, y'know, saying that two can live as cheaply as one! Don't you agree?'

Russell had taken the cheque with mixed feelings. Relief that he could now pay their bills tinged with a feeling of umbrage that he should need his father's help in order to support a wife. It wasn't as if he was extravagant, he thought resentfully. He didn't gamble, or even bet on the horses.

In the past, of course, there had been only his Mess account to contend with and his army pay had covered that leaving his personal allowance as spending money. Now, he had a place of his own to maintain as well as his Messing bills and he had no idea where all the money went. Lucy seemed to run up enormous bills at Harrods, Heals and Selfridges each month. He hoped that once their home was furnished to her taste then these would ease off. Luckily, they had no mortgage, their flat in Belgravia had been a wedding present from his parents.

There would still be Lucy's clothes, of course, but as she kept telling him, they did socialise a great deal and to wear the same outfits over and over again would be letting him down.

'I want you to be proud of me, Russ,' she pouted, when he had brought the matter up.

Her enormous blue eyes misting with tears, she had looked up into his face contritely and immediately he had felt conscience-stricken. She was so young, so unworldly and so very lovely. Gathering her into his arms, and kissing away her tears, he found himself succumbing to her charms.

When it came to love-making, Lucy was complete fulfilment. And afterwards, if she wanted to go out and buy a whole houseful of new furniture, or half a dozen dresses, he wouldn't have stopped her. Keeping her happy with material things, in return for the breathtaking satisfaction she brought into his life, was a small price to pay.

Watching her now, as she moved forward gracefully to mingle with his fellow officers, their wives and guests at the New Year's Eve Ball, Russell felt that 1982 was going to be a momentous year for him. It was certainly starting out well. His promotion to Captain had been confirmed that morning and he could hardly wait to tell his father. He would do so at midnight, when he phoned to wish them a Happy New Year.

Only one thing troubled him. Lucy was not yet nineteen, so was she going to be able to cope with her position as a Captain's wife?

Although her father had been a regular soldier he had died before she was born so she had no practical experience of what army life entailed. He frowned, remembering the scene just a few weeks earlier when they had invited some of his fellow officers in for pre-Christmas drinks. Lucy had been wildly excited by the prospects of giving a party and it was sheer good fortune that he'd thought to check whose names she'd included on the guest list.

Tears and recriminations had followed when he had told her that under no circumstances could she invite Sergeant Hugh Edwards, her brother-in-law, or Sergeant Gary Collins.

'You don't seem to understand, Russ,' she had pouted. 'If they don't come, how can I have my sister Ruth along?'

'You can't,' he told her firmly.

'What are they going to think,' she stormed. 'They're bound to find out we have had a party.'

'They won't expect to be included, they know the rules, and so does your sister,' he added cuttingly.

'Sheer snobbery,' she stormed but he had remained immovable. Protocol simply had to be observed.

'Do you mean we're never going to be able to ask them to our parties?' she had sobbed.

'Not if there are officers amongst our guests,' he told her resolutely. 'If it's a family get-together then that is another matter.'

Right up until an hour before the party started, Lucy tried to persuade him, even threatening she wouldn't put in an appearance unless he allowed her to phone Ruth and tell them to come over. When he adamantly refused she dissolved into tears but he had gritted his teeth, hardened his heart, and gone downstairs without her.

Miraculously, by the time the first guests arrived, she had been at his side, looking radiant and showing no traces at all of their traumatic argument.

He had anticipated an outburst after everyone left but Lucy had simply kicked off her shoes and collapsed onto the sofa.

'I'm much too excited to sleep,' she breathed. 'Shall we have a nightcap?'

When he handed her a brandy, she had patted the cushion invitingly and looked up lovingly into his eyes, clinking her glass against his and breathing triumphantly, 'To the success of our first party.'

'And the prettiest hostess in London,' he responded gallantly as they sipped their drinks.

Neither of them had mentioned the matter since and, as he gathered her tenderly in his arms at midnight to welcome in 1982, Russell fervently hoped she now clearly understood the situation and that there would be no more unpleasantness.

He had realised before he married that having a brother-in-law who was merely a sergeant, and in his own Regiment to boot, could be embarrassing. As a highly-trained, seasoned soldier, Hugh Edwards had been equally concerned and had realised that it would be impossible to openly fraternise.

Mrs Woodley, too, had expressed reservations when he had asked if he might marry Lucy, knowing how strict the army could be about such matters.

His own father had bluntly denounced the idea as preposterous when he learned about Lucy's brother-in-law.

'A sergeant in your own Regiment, my boy!' he exclaimed aghast. 'You'll find that dashed awkward, won't you? I know things are a lot more relaxed than they were when I was serving, but all the same there's discipline to consider, y'know.'

'I can handle it.'

Even when he had assured his father, Colonel Campbell looked worried and related numerous harrowing anecdotes of fellow officers he had known who'd 'breached the gap' and married actresses or shop-girls. But even he had never heard of an officer marrying the sister-in-law of a sergeant in his own Regiment!

Colonel Campbell's opposition, however, was overcome the moment he met his future daughter-in-law. As Lucy rested her tiny hand in his massive one, and raised her big blue eyes trustingly, it seemed his heart had softened and he couldn't do enough to smooth their path, buying them a flat in Mayfair as well as paying for their wedding.

And his father was still spoiling her, Russell reflected, as he caught the scintillating glint of the gold and crystal necklet and earrings Lucy was wearing which his parents had sent her for Christmas.

The Ball ended at four in the morning and after enjoying a hearty champagne breakfast they made their way home. As he closed the front door, shutting out the crisp clear dawn that was heralding the first day of the New Year, Russell drew Lucy into his arms, and found her warm and responsive.

His hands slid down over the soft lace of her dress, he could feel the tantalising warmth of her body through the seductive material, and his overwhelming desire for her wiped everything else completely from his mind.

'I love you, my darling, more than anything in this world,' he murmured softly into her ear. His lips moved slowly over the peachy softness of her cheek to find the generous sweetness of her mouth.

Her breathy moan of pleasure fired his loins. Fumbling in his eagerness, he slid her lace dress off her satin-smooth shoulders, burying his face in the creamy fullness of her breasts.

While he saluted each rose-tipped nipple, she wriggled off her dress, and the black lace panties she was wearing under it, kicking them aside. Then, with nimble fingers she began undoing the pearl buttons on his frilled white shirt. When she slipped her small cool hands inside it to tease the sandy mat of hair that covered his chest, he was filled with a frenzy of desire.

Still clasping her body to his, Russell began feverishly to shed his shirt and shoes and remove his trousers, before urgently lowering her onto the carpet. His lips found hers again and as the moist tip of her tongue crept into his mouth Russell felt a surging passion, a fierce desperate urgency to possess her completely.

They responded to each other's touch in perfect accord. As her arms reached up and circled his neck, his entire body was aflame. He could feel her nipples hardening with desire as they pressed into his chest. A tremendous heat burned inside him, building up greater and greater, until his nerve ends were so sensitive that he almost cried out with the pain. He could restrain himself no longer. His excitement mounting to fever pitch, he entered her with an exultant cry, discovering a strange, wondrous rhythm that united them as never before. And the last delicious shuddering moments came on them simultaneously. Utterly spent, he rolled onto his side completely exhausted.

With a small sigh of contentment, Lucy snuggled even deeper into his arms. He reached out for her fur coat, which she had slung down on one of the armchairs when they had come in, and pulled it over them. Satiated and warmly cocooned, they slept.

Chapter 23

They had been married for almost nine months before Russell took Lucy to visit his parents. It was his first leave since their honeymoon. Immediately after being made up to Captain, at the end of December, he had been sent on a course which had lasted well into February. On his return he had been assigned to a new unit and his leave postponed.

'You'll love Walford Grange in the springtime,' Russell assured her 'and we'll be there all over Easter.'

'I had planned to go and see my mother over Easter weekend,' Lucy protested plaintively.

'You spent three weeks with her while I was away on my course,' Russell reminded her. 'It's time you visited my parents,' he added firmly.

Lucy had mixed feelings about what lay ahead. She had met Colonel Campbell twice since their wedding day. On the first occasion he had looked over their new home as if carrying out an inspection. The second meeting had been for a drink in the Mess before he'd gone off to a Regimental Dinner.

With his ramrod back, and bristling ginger moustache, he was an older version of Russell and she had already discovered she could twist him round her little finger with just one of her winsome smiles.

Russell's mother, however, was an unknown quantity and remembering the elegant designer outfit she had worn to their wedding, and knowing that she came from a titled family, Lucy felt very much in awe of her and anxious about what clothes she ought to take on holiday.

'You've lived in the country most of your life, my love, so you must know the sort of clothes to pack,' Russell told her when she had questioned him as to what she should take.

'I usually wore jeans and sweaters,' she told him. 'I'm sure that's not how your mother will expect me to dress, not now that you are a Captain.'

'I understand Captain Mark Phillips' wife often wears jeans,' he told her with a roguish grin.

'She might, after all no one can criticise her,' Lucy said crossly. 'You might try and be more helpful, Russ, I shall be meeting all your friends for the very first time and on their ground, not mine. If I'm not dressed right then I shall feel awful,' she pouted and her blue eyes misted over.

'They will love you whatever you're wearing,' he assured her, pulling her into his arms and silencing her protests with his lips.

But Lucy was not to be pacified. Her background was so different from Russell's that she felt it was important to have the right clothes. She bought a new suit in cream tweed, then worried whether it would be warm enough for late March so added a cashmere sweater, the exact shade of blue as her eyes, and an enormous cream and blue mohair scarf.

It was all very well Russ saying that jeans and a sweater would do, but she only had his word for it. She toyed with the idea of buying some really expensive jodhpurs and a black velvet jacket. There was something so dashing about the cut of riding clothes that she couldn't resist trying them on when she went on her final shopping spree, even though she couldn't ride.

As she was leaving the Sloane Square store, an outfit on one of the display models caught her attention. With trembling fingers she eased the skin tight tawny leather trousers over her legs and hips. They fitted as sleekly and smoothly as a second skin. The matching top was trimmed and deeply fringed with the softest of cream leather that moved sensuously over her hips and thighs, seductively concealing yet, at the same time revealing, the skin tight trousers. As her fingers slid down over the doe-soft material she knew she must have it.

The assistant smiled approvingly and handed her a matching cowboy-style hat, rakishly caught up at one side with an ornate silver clasp, and Lucy recognised it as the final touch. Without any hesitation she handed over her charge card.

Her own extravagances paled into insignificance when she saw Walford Grange. As they entered the courtyard through the porticoed gateway, and walked across to the magnificent Elizabethan house, Lucy caught her breath in wonder.

She marvelled at the enormous stone fireplace that dominated one end of the great entrance hall and at the minstrel gallery facing it, and the collection of life-size family portraits painted in oils and framed in massive gilt frames that adorned the walls of the wide staircase.

Russell walked past them as if they were not there, through an elegant dining room, dominated by a massive rosewood table and spoon-backed rosewood chairs, and on into a comfortable chintzy sitting room where a crackling log fire provided welcoming warmth.

'I'm sure you are gasping for a cup of tea after your journey,' Mrs Campbell sympathised, as she greeted them, pecking Lucy on both cheeks and permitting Russell to give her a restrained hug.

She sat very upright in one of the big armchairs, elegant in her red silk dress with its pleated skirt. Sitting beside Russell, on a settee facing Mrs Campbell, Lucy sipped her tea and nibbled at the cucumber sandwiches, awestruck by her mother-in-law's cool self-assurance. She had no idea how to address her. Russell called her 'Mater' but she couldn't bring herself to even say the word, it sounded so pompous, almost ludicrous.

As soon as she and Russell were on their own, she asked his advice.

'I've no idea,' he frowned, shaking his sandy head in bewilderment. 'What do you call your own mother?'

'"Mum", usually.'

He repeated the word as though it was something strange and foreign and his frown deepened.

'It doesn't really fit your mother, does it,' Lucy said tentatively.

'No, you're quite right. Perhaps you should call them both by their first names. My father's is Robert, and my mother's is Kate. Mind you,' he grinned, 'I rather think my father would prefer "Colonel".'

'I'm sure he would! And since that is how I always think of

163

him I shall go on calling him that. It's how I should address your mother that bothers me.'

'Don't worry, you'll find the answer,' he told her. 'I'm sure the two of you are going to get on terribly well. Come on,' he took her arm, 'I want to show you around.'

For the first few days, Lucy felt nervous and ill at ease. The Campbells' lavish life-style was quite different from anything she had ever experienced.

Her own mother had always been busy, helping out on the farm, from the moment she got up in the morning until she sat down after supper in the evenings, and she'd had hardly any time for her own interests.

Mrs Campbell's days were a complete contrast. She was organiser for numerous Charities, a member of the Parish Council, a magistrate and a school Governor. In addition, she seemed to lead a very busy social life. She was constantly talking on the phone, and her cool decisive manner, and the authority in her voice, left Lucy feeling quite over-awed.

Each morning, immediately after breakfast, Colonel Campbell insisted that Russell should accompany him on his morning ride. After that, either they went to Home Farm so that the Colonel could show him the latest improvements and inspect the stock or into the Colonel's study to discuss future plans for the Estate. As a result, for the greater part of each day, Lucy found herself either left to her own devices or with no alternative but to accompany Mrs Campbell.

Although she didn't really enjoy these occasions she found that at least they provided her with an opportunity to wear all the new clothes she had bought for her visit. And, she was gratified to find that she had chosen well and that everything she wore seemed to meet with her mother-in-law's approval.

Russell had grown up at Walford Grange so people were eager to meet his new wife and Lucy felt delighted by the impression she was creating. The evenings, in particular, were exciting and she greatly enjoyed dressing up and looking her most glamorous for the whirlwind of dinners and parties. She enjoyed being the centre of attention and the envy of most of the women present.

She also found her feelings for Russell deepening. When they had first met she had been attracted by the glamour of his uniform, and the thrill of knowing that he was an officer. She had given hardly any thought to his character or personality, except that he was fun to be with and she felt happy in his company.

Since they had been at Walford Grange, she had discovered that there was a serious side to his nature. Listening to his erudite discussions with the Colonel she was astounded by his knowledge on farming matters. Seeing him striding across a meadow in tweed jacket, jeans and wellingtons or looking debonair in evening dress, she felt proud to be his wife.

The second Friday that they were at Walford Grange, Colonel Campbell announced that he'd arranged a Meet for the following day. He'd invited all the most prominent families in the county and his enthusiasm was infectious.

'Your wife shall be the first to be blooded,' he told Russell, as they finalised details over dinner that evening.

Lucy looked agonisingly at Russell, hoping he would help her out of her predicament, and was dumbfounded when she saw the gleam of pleasure in his green eyes at the honour his father was conferring on her.

Haltingly, she explained that she didn't ride, then sat staring down at her plate, wishing the floor would open as her admission was met by stunned disbelief.

Hesitantly, she looked across the table and saw the mixture of consternation and chagrin on Russell's face. His mouth was set in a grim line and his eyes, as they met hers, were emerald hard.

'Lucy and I will see you off and afterwards we will drive over to The Pheasant and meet you there for luncheon,' Mrs Campbell said coolly, breaking the agonising silence.

'But surely you'll be riding with us, my dear?' The Colonel boomed. He looked perplexed, his neck flushed angrily and his sandy brows pulled together in bewilderment.

Lucy's gaze darted between them, then to Russell, but he remained tight-lipped. She opened her mouth to protest that it was unnecessary for Mrs Campbell to spoil her day's sport on her account but found herself unable to speak.

Later, lying in the huge four-poster bed, she tried to

explain to Russell that, unlike him, she had never had the opportunity to learn to ride.

'You grew up on a farm, so why on earth not!' he exclaimed in disbelief, turning away and hunching the bedclothes round his shoulders.

Miserably, she tried to explain that it had been a working farm and that the animals they had kept were mostly milking cows, and heifers which they fattened up for market, but he'd made no response.

Lucy was still asleep next morning when the Colonel banged on their bedroom door, calling out that they were almost ready to leave.

'You are going to come down and see us off,' Russell said curtly as he fastened his stock.

'Must I, Russell?'

'It's the least you can do! Father arranged this event for your benefit . . . before we all learned you couldn't ride!'

Lucy looked at him imploringly, tears welling up in her eyes, longing for him to take her in his arms. Instead Russell looked at his watch and let out an impatient whistle. 'You'd better get dressed,' he ordered, as he crossed to the window and looked out.

'What shall I wear?'

'Just slip on your jeans and a sweater, they're already starting to assemble in the courtyard.'

It was a bright, crisp morning and the horses' breath hung like mist on the frosty air as they champed, tossed their heads and pawed the ground impatient to be off. The Colonel, and half a dozen other men in scarlet hunting coats, looked tremendously impressive as they sat their horses. The air was charged with excitement as the pack of liver-and-white hounds, tails erect, milled around their feet.

Mrs Campbell, wearing a smart green tweed trouser suit, and a white polo-necked sweater, dispensed glasses of hot punch to all the riders. Standing in the shelter of the doorway, Lucy felt very insignificant and out of things.

From the moment he'd mounted his lively black stallion, Russell had ignored her. At first she had thought it was because he was having so much trouble controlling his horse but even after he had calmed the handsome beast he had not returned to talk to her. Instead he had drawn rein on the far side of the courtyard and was in animated conversation with a slim dark-haired girl with a long thin face and wide-spaced dark eyes, mounted on a grey gelding.

'That's Melany Buscombe. They live about ten miles from here,' Mrs Campbell told her crisply. 'Melany and Russell grew up together and have always been close friends. In fact, until quite recently, they did most things together. Everyone always thought . . .' she hesitated, her mouth tightened and she gave a little shrug before moving away and busying herself collecting up the glasses.

Lucy sensed the implication and she felt too choked to speak. The strange turbulent sensation tearing at her heart could be only one thing . . . jealousy!

Miserably she stared across at Russell. It was the first time she had ever seen him in riding habit. The close-fitting black jacket emphasised his broad shoulders and slim hips, and as she lovingly studied his strong jawline, prominent cheek-bones and firm decisive mouth, she was left in no doubt that he was the most handsome man present. She felt desolate. It was bad enough that she had let him down by not being able to ride alongside him, but to see him so engrossed with Melany Buscombe, and so obviously enjoying her company, added to her humiliation.

The huntsman's horn sounded and they all surged towards the porticoed gateway, horses and riders jostling each other in their eagerness, hounds barking and whining as they, too, struggled to take up the lead.

Lucy watched them cantering away into the distance, the red coats leading the field, Russell and Melany galloping side by side. She turned away, feeling inwardly bruised and betrayed. She sensed her mother-in-law was watching her and angrily brushed away her tears with the back of her hand.

'We can leave whenever you are ready,' Mrs Campbell said briskly. 'I'll take you on a tour round some of the local beauty spots, a much better idea than moping around here until lunchtime.'

'I . . . I would like to get changed first.'

'Good!' There was an understanding gleam in Mrs Campbell's eyes.

'I . . . I won't take long?'

'Ten minutes do?'

Head high, Lucy went up to her room. With trembling fingers she unpacked the expensive leather outfit that so far she had not even shown to Russell. It was every bit as flattering as when she had tried it on in the shop and the hard core of uncertainty inside her began to dissolve.

Mrs Campbell regarded her with an expression of mild astonishment when she rejoined her.

'I'm ready!' Lucy said and her chin went up defiantly.

'Yes, I can see that. Very stunning! It should prove sensational . . . quite a winner,' Mrs Campbell commented drily as she picked up her car keys.

Their eyes levelled.

'It will be *the* winner . . . Kate,' Lucy said with spirit as she followed her mother-in-law out to the car.

Chapter 24

The Lounge Bar of The Pheasant was soon packed to capacity as the Hunt arrived, muddy and sweaty, all talking vociferously about their own particular exploits.

While several of them were sympathising with Kate because she had missed all the excitement, Lucy looked round for Russell. He was not amongst the early arrivals and as the room became more and more crowded she realised he was not there at all. Nor was Melany Buscombe!

A mixture of anger and fear welled up inside her. How could Russell do this to her, treat her in such a cavalier fashion in front of all these people? She stood there feeling bitterly hurt, hating him, and unsure of what to do. She wanted desperately to run out of the place but knew that would only fuel the fire.

By the time Kate turned to her and said, 'Have you heard about the accident?' she had herself under control.

'No?' she looked enquiringly at her mother-in-law.

'Melany's horse fell. She is not badly hurt but she has had to go to the hospital for a couple of stitches. Russell has gone with her. We will have to start lunch without them.'

'Do you want me to save him a seat?'

'I don't think that will be possible. I'm sure more people have turned up than we estimated. Probably the best thing is for you to sit with Carlile Randell since he will be on his own if Melany is missing.'

'Who?' Lucy looked at her blankly.

'Come on, I'll introduce you,' Kate told her, taking her arm and steering her towards a darkly handsome man in his late thirties. Unlike everyone else in the room, he did not look as if he had been out with the Hunt, but was impeccably dressed in fawn slacks and a brown jacket.

After she had introduced them, and commiserated with Carlile about Melany's accident, Kate left them together.

'I must go and join the Colonel,' she explained. 'Lucy knows hardly anyone here, so will you look after her, Carlile.'

'My pleasure!' he replied without looking at Kate.

His dark blue eyes studied Lucy speculatively and he decided he liked what he saw. She was the complete opposite of Melany and he was intrigued by her attractive figure, the peaches and cream complexion and the kissable, pouty red lips.

Melany might be far more elegant, with her willowy figure and classic features, but she was always so serious that sometimes he longed for a more frivolous companion. Now this delicious little filly, he thought approvingly, giving Lucy a winning smile, looked fun-loving and frisky. And, he thought shrewdly, like him, she didn't appear to be enamoured by the rigours of the hunting field.

'Well,' he breathed, taking her small soft hand in his, 'this could be quite a challenge. What are we going to talk about? If we make "Hunting, Melany and Russell" taboo subjects, what is left?'

Lucy's forget-me-not eyes widened innocently as she gazed up at the lean face with its hawkish nose, so prominent that it made an already weak chin look positively receding. 'I suppose we could talk about you,' she murmured, with a cheeky smile.

'I can't think of a better subject,' Carlile agreed, with a roar of laughter that had heads turning in their direction.

With the ice broken, Lucy found Carlile a highly entertaining escort. He was a fount of information about everyone present, and was able to add an entertaining anecdote about each of them. By the time they were halfway through the meal, Lucy felt she knew most of the people present as intimately as if she had lived amongst them for years.

Carlile also had a clever way of making her tell more about herself than she meant to do. Within a very short space of time he knew all about her background, and that her sister was married to a sergeant in the same Regiment as Russell.

The information amused him greatly and he stored it away

in his fertile mind for future use. Although not an army man himself, he knew enough about such matters to appreciate the problems such a relationship could bring. Looking at Lucy's smiling, open face, he shrewdly assumed that she did not.

Russell and Melany arrived a little later. Everyone made a great fuss of them both, especially of Melany who had her arm in a sling. The Colonel insisted that they both sat at his table so Lucy remained where she was with Carlile Randell until the meal was over.

She was both surprised and hurt when she finally managed to be with Russell to find him in a black mood and claiming that she had been flirting with Carlile.

'Flirting with him!' she exclaimed in genuine astonishment. 'Your mother introduced us and asked him to sit next to me because you had disappeared with Melany Buscombe.'

'I felt it was my duty to take her to hospital,' he said stiffly.

'And how was I to know that? You didn't even bother to leave a message to let me know where you had gone. I only found out by hearing other people talking about it,' she exclaimed struggling to keep her voice steady.

A dull flush crept up from Russell's neck and darkened his face. His lips tightened angrily but he refused to be drawn. Instead, he returned to his attack about her behaviour with Carlile.

'I know what I'm talking about, Lucy, I could see you both quite clearly from where I was sitting,' Russell growled.

'We were only chatting,' Lucy exclaimed indignantly.

'From where I was it didn't look quite as innocent as that. I would say you were openly flirting with him.'

'I most certainly was not!'

'I can't recall you looking so attentively into my eyes when we've been "just chatting",' Russell said sardonically.

'Perhaps you are not as scintillating,' she said, tossing her head defiantly.

'Other people noticed as well,' Russell muttered irritably.

'Really! I suppose by that you mean Melany . . .'

'Yes, Melany for one. In fact, I dread to think what she must have been thinking.'

'If she doesn't like her boyfriend talking to other girls then she should stay with him herself.'

'Carlile doesn't hunt.'

'Oh dear, how very remiss of him!' Lucy retorted with affected concern. 'Probably he tries to keep it secret so that people don't ostracise him.'

'Don't be childish, Lucy,' Russell snapped, biting his lips in annoyance. 'No one is ostracising you.'

'We were talking about Carlile Randell, not me,' she retorted.

'Carlile does ride, he's a superb horseman. He just doesn't hunt . . . except other men's wives.'

'*Touché!* That was not very gentlemanly, Russell,' Lucy giggled, hysterically. 'Anyway,' she added demurely, 'he didn't need to be a predator on this occasion. As I told you, your mother asked him to be my escort. She probably felt sorry for me, knowing you had gone off with Melany.'

'Utter rubbish. I've partnered Melany on the hunting field for the past ten years and since you weren't with us, she would expect me to do so today.'

'She might, but I don't,' Lucy flared.

'Look, let's discuss this later, people are looking at us,' Russell muttered.

'All right. Then you had better take me home,' Lucy stated, 'or do you have to escort Melany Buscombe home first?'

'You'd better go back in my mother's car. I have a horse,' Russell said stiffly.

Lucy burned with humiliation all the way home. By the time Russell arrived she had worked herself up into a towering rage and even before he had time to pull off his riding boots she attacked.

'Next time you find it necessary to go off with someone else and leave me marooned with strangers, at least leave a message,' she stormed.

'We've been over all this once,' Russell protested. 'Anyway, you must have heard about the accident.'

'Yes, by listening to the gossip going on,' she snapped, 'and it didn't stop there!'

'What are you talking about?'

'As if you didn't know! Everyone was agog about you and Melany Buscombe being together again. Some were even betting how long it would be before it was permanent.'

'That's absolute rubbish! I'm a married man, or had you forgotten.'

'*I* hadn't, but I thought perhaps you had . . . and so did a lot of other people,' Lucy said sweetly.

'Melany is practically engaged to Carlile Randell, something he probably forgot to tell you,' Russell retorted.

They stood glaring angrily at each other, Russell's green eyes emerald chips under furrowed sandy brows as he towered over her.

She looked up at him defiantly, standing her ground, still furious because he had been so inattentive, and refusing to accept his criticism of her behaviour.

Their altercation was abruptly ended by the Colonel bursting into the room.

'Your Commanding Officer is on the phone, Russell. Some sort of emergency to do with this Falklands business.'

By the time Russell returned, Lucy's anger had subsided. She loved him too deeply to be able to remain on bad terms with him for very long. It frightened her when they quarrelled. Russell could be so unbending, so obdurate.

She saw from his face, the moment he came back into the room, that something was wrong.

'I've got to leave at once,' Russell announced. 'My Company is being sent to the Falklands. I must get back to London. Are you coming with me, Lucy or staying here?'

'I'll come with you, of course.'

'Pack your things then, while I get changed and fetch the car round.'

Their squabble forgotten, they took their leave of the Colonel and Kate. The Colonel was visibly proud that Russell was to play a part in 'putting the Argies in their place'.

Ever since the disturbance had come to public notice, the Colonel had been vociferously detailing the tactics he would use if he was in charge. No one had paid too much attention, since most of them believed that the threat of war would blow over without a single shot being fired.

On the drive back to London, Russell expressed his concern about what Lucy would do during his absence.

'I shall probably stay on at the flat. I have plenty to do there to keep me busy,' she said evasively.

'I may be gone for several months,' he said in a worried voice.

'Surely it will all be over in a couple of weeks!'

'It will take longer than that to even get there,' he told her, dropping a hand from the wheel to squeeze her knee. 'It's over eight thousand miles from here to Port Stanley!'

'Two days' flying time.'

'They won't fly us there! We'll have to go by ship.'

'That will take months!' Lucy exclaimed in shocked surprise.

'About five or six weeks. That is why I'm concerned about you staying in London on your own.'

Lucy was silent, suddenly afraid. The Falklands War was no longer a vague encounter somewhere out in the South Atlantic but something that was going to affect her life for quite some time to come.

'Will Hugh be going? If so, I could stay with Ruth.'

'I don't know until I see Orders,' Russell told her crisply. 'Whether he is or not, I don't think you should be seen staying in Married Quarters with the wife of one of my Sergeants!'

Tears blurred Lucy's vision. The three-lane M3 motorway became a never-ending, yet ever-narrowing, grey speedtrack, rushing her to eternity. Why was it that whenever she mentioned her family it raised a question of protocol and her loyalty to Russell and his career. Why couldn't officers mix freely when they were off duty. How could it possibly undermine discipline.

If Hugh went to the Falklands, he would be sharing the same rigours of war as Russell. They would be living in close proximity to each other night and day, eating the same food, fighting the same enemy, breathing the same air, and facing the same dangers. So what was wrong with their wives sharing their worries and fears and comforting each other in their loneliness.

'Don't worry about it, darling,' Russell consoled, taking her silence for apprehension because she would be alone in their flat. 'You could always have a friend to stay.'

'Yes, of course. As long as she is the wife of someone who is an officer and a gentleman,' she added softly.

Russell glanced at her briefly, frowning slightly. 'Sorry, I didn't quite catch what you said?'

'Nothing. I was thinking aloud.' She gave a deep sigh. 'Perhaps I will ask my mother to come and stay. The change might do her good. She said in her last letter that she was feeling very lonely now that Mark has gone to New Zealand and she is on her own . . .'

Russell's frown deepened and Lucy saw his hands grip the steering wheel a little more tightly.

'You wouldn't mind her coming to stay at the flat, would you?' she asked in astonishment.

'No. No, of course not. Not as long as Ruth, and her children, don't visit her there.'

Chapter 25

The quayside at Southampton Dock was jammed with people. Mothers, fathers, wives and children, from every part of Britain, all come to wave off their menfolk. Standing there amongst them, Lucy felt as if she was in some sort of dream. The light breeze, still carrying a March bite, sent a shiver through her as it chased wispy white clouds across the early April sky.

The 45,000-ton luxury liner *Canberra* had been requisitioned as a troopship and now it stood in Berth 106 dominating the scene. *Hermes* and *Invincible*, the latter with Prince Andrew amongst the thousand men crammed on board, had already sailed down the Portsmouth Channel and now the television crews and reporters were turning their full attention on the *Canberra*.

Lucy couldn't visualise the Falklands. She had barely known where the remote islands in the South Atlantic were when Russell and the Colonel had been discussing the imminent invasion and the military tactics that would be involved. Even now, when she knew it would probably take Russell five or even six weeks to reach there, she still felt the whole thing was something of a nightmare and beyond her comprehension.

A great sense of loneliness swept over her as she saw Russell's tall straight figure walking up the gangplank. It was almost as if he was going out of her life for ever. As she remembered the bittersweet hours they had spent in each other's arms, after they had arrived back from Somerset, she wanted to shout out and stop him, attract his attention in some way and bring him back to her side. She couldn't bear to think of the empty lonely nights ahead.

Tears gathered and stung behind her eyes and she blinked

them away rapidly, refusing to give way in public. Russell would be so ashamed of her if she did.

Last night, with his strong arms around her, it had been so easy to promise not to become despondent. His lips had been brushing over her cheeks, caressing her eyes, nuzzling the lobes of her ears, as he had urged her to be brave.

She had even felt strong and courageous and confident about facing life on her own. As their lips had met she had responded to the demands of his hungry mouth with matching fervour.

His strength had communicated itself to her as his long, sensitive fingers moved down the length of her body, exploring and caressing with infinite tenderness until they aroused a fiery passion in her. As the glow of her body grew to a burning heat, a fire that he alone could appease, she had shuddered with agony knowing that soon they must part.

Much as he loved her, Russell could not conceive her anguish. At that moment, physical consummation of their love had been uppermost in his mind. Skilfully, he brought her to a tumultuous climax, fulfilling his own needs with each deep penetration, until satiated and expended he slept, his body still entwined with hers.

While he slept, she cradled him, gently stroking the back of his head, conscious of the waves of warm breath that fanned over her breasts from his parted lips as he breathed deeply and regularly. She carefully timed her own breathing to match his, so that the rise and fall of their bodies was as one.

Indulgently, her hands moved lightly over the nape of his neck, travelling down across his broad shoulders to the defined waist and tight round buttocks. As her fingers skimmed their hardness, his muscles tightened and she felt again the stirring of his penis against her as it hardened into life.

A groan of desire escaped her as her fingers gently manipulated it into position. Then she lay perfectly submissive, receptive to every tiny tremulous movement, deriving blissful pleasure from the swell within her. She found it so thrillingly sensuous, that she wanted the sensations that were building up to last for ever. The tiny throbbing stabs, that rippled out to reach every nerve end; the slow mounting pulse that grew fuller and bigger until she thought she would expire from sheer ecstasy; the deep sweet sensations, like waves lapping up the shore, dribbling back and then returning with a thunderous crash.

Her entire body seemed united with Russell's. Their breath mingled. Wherever their skin touched it adhered, one to the other, as though glued together. Their very bones seemed to be entwined, and even their senses were in absolute harmony.

Although she had no signal that he was awake, he was suddenly there right with her, his body demanding, giving, taking, fulfilling; joining hers in a rhythm as old as time itself, a breathless aching struggle for unity and Utopia that transported them both into limbo.

Breakfast had been a desultory affair, their passion of the previous night forgotten in the rush for Russell to report back on time. Listening to the controlled excitement in his voice as he detailed what his programme was likely to be, her stomach knotted. It was hard to believe that he was looking forward to it, actually relishing action on such a scale. He discounted his tour of duty in Northern Ireland as 'skirmishes' and in Zimbabwe as a mere 'training exercise'.

It was the first time she had fully realised that Russell was trained to kill . . . or be killed. Panic rose like bile in her throat. What sort of man was this she had married who could become ecstatic at the thought of fighting, of being an integral part of the war machine, who was prepared to travel halfway round the world to kill his fellow man.

A hysterical giggle bubbled up as she wondered if protocol was involved when it came to dealing with the enemy. Would Russell only kill officers, or were officers exempt and only Other Ranks killed?

Ashamed of her flippancy, Lucy concentrated on being as supportive as possible. After he'd left the flat, she remained at home, waiting for his call to tell her exactly when he'd be leaving for the Falklands. She kept the volume low on the television so that she would hear the very first bleep of the phone. She slept fitfully, snapping back to consciousness at the slightest sound. When Ruth phoned, to let her know that

Hugh was also going to the Falklands, Lucy was so anxious to clear the line, in case Russell was trying to get through to her, that she didn't even ask when, or which ship he'd be on.

Now the actual moment for Russell's departure had arrived, Lucy felt an overwhelming sense of loss. Almost blinded by tears, she turned to Kate and the Colonel for comfort and support. They had travelled up from Walford Grange and come straight to the dockside, the Colonel bursting with pride at the sight of Russell ready to go on board the *Canberra*, Kate stoically controlling her feelings behind dark glasses.

Kate's gaze remained fastened on her son as he walked up the gangplank. The Colonel, too, was intently following the progress of the straight-backed, square-shouldered figure, a look almost of envy on his fierce face. Feeling only desolation, Lucy raised a hand in a farewell wave as Russell, having reached the deck, paused to turn and salute before disappearing from their sight.

'The Guards will sort out the Argentinians in next to no time, you just wait and see,' the Colonel boomed confidently, as they turned away.

'It will take them over five weeks to get there,' Lucy said wistfully.

'Once they land and attack it will all be over.'

'It still means Russell may be away for months!' Lucy gulped.

'Hmm. You do have a point. Perhaps you should come and stay with us for a while. You don't want to be on your own in London at a time like this.'

'My sister is in London,' Lucy said. 'Her husband is going to the Falklands as well.'

'Let's see, he's a sergeant though, isn't he?' The Colonel frowned, pulling at the ends of his moustache.

'Ruth is still my sister. She will miss Hugh just as much as I will miss Russell,' Lucy said defiantly.

Kate patted her hand kindly. 'Why don't we leave all these decisions until later. Phone us in a day or so, when you have had time to decide what you want to do. Don't stay on in London and be lonely.'

'Thank you. Perhaps in a couple of weeks' time.'

Kate kissed her coolly, almost impersonally. The Colonel simply patted her shoulder and echoed his wife's invitation as they walked away to where he had parked his car.

Determined to be self-sufficient, Lucy remained alone in her Mayfair flat. With each passing day she felt more and more nervy as she scanned the newspapers, listened to the radio reports and watched the graphic developments shown on television. She was so edgy that she found it hard to keep to any routine, or to concentrate. Sleep was impossible, her mind worked overtime.

Each night, as she went to bed, Lucy remembered the last night she and Russell had spent together and her feeling of desolation increased. Her need of him was a continuous ache, sapping her interest and energy for even routine activities.

When Sheila Collins called on her unexpectedly, she was shocked to find Lucy looking thin and haggard, her blonde hair lank and dull, her face devoid of makeup.

'For heaven's sake, Lucy, pull yourself together,' she told her sharply. 'Put the kettle on and make a coffee.'

As she followed Lucy through to the ultra-modern kitchen, Sheila gasped in despair at the chaos that met her eyes. It looked as if Lucy hadn't cleaned up or washed a single cup since Russell had left over three weeks earlier.

While the kettle boiled, Sheila stacked the dirty dishes, filled the sink with hot suds and began washing up.

'Here,' she tossed a teacloth towards Lucy, 'start drying up.'

Listlessly, Lucy picked up one of the cups and stood staring down at it until Sheila finished washing the others and took it from her.

'Sit down, Lucy, out of the way. I'd ask you to make the coffee but you'd probably forget to put any powder in the cups,' she said exasperatedly.

Over coffee Sheila told her that Gary had also left for the Falklands. They had been away on holiday when he had been recalled from leave and although he was supposed to sail on the *Canberra* she wasn't sure whether he had made it to Southampton in time or not.

Lucy took some comfort from knowing that Gary and

Russell would be together. Ever since Gary had been made Platoon Sergeant there had always been a degree of rapport between him and Russell and she would never forget that it had been Gary who had introduced her to Russell.

After Sheila had gone home, Lucy found herself worrying much less about Russell. She still felt desperately lonely but whereas before she had been listless and apathetic she was now restless. In the end, she could stand the isolation no longer and phoned Kate to ask if she could take up her invitation.

'Of course, you are always welcome.'

'Would it be all right if I came right away?'

'Russell's room is always ready so come whenever you wish,' Kate told her.

Chapter 26

As the *Canberra* slipped anchor and headed down the Solent, Captain Russell Campbell stood on deck, peering down at the quayside trying to detect his wife and parents amongst the many hundreds of people grouped there, but from where he stood they looked like figures in a Lowry painting.

Parting from Lucy had been heartrending. Seeing her forget-me-not blue eyes mist over with tears, her mouth tremble as she tried to control her feelings, had been like a knife turning in his heart.

He would have felt so much happier if she had agreed to go and stay at Walford Grange. He would have known she was safe, protected, taken care of and looked after properly. Staying on her own in London was madness. She had never lived on her own before so she would be lonely and probably frightened. And half-starved into the bargain, he thought grimly, since shopping and cooking were certainly not Lucy's strong points, as he had quickly discovered.

A feeling of panic welled up inside him as once more he scanned the upturned faces on the quayside, wondering if he could pick her out from the crowd. Maybe if he made one last appeal, now that he was on the point of departure, she would listen to reason.

As he edged along the deck, peering over the rail, it seemed the crowds below were becoming even thicker, and realising how futile it was to try and spot them he turned away and went below deck to find out if anyone else from his own Company was on board.

The summons back to duty, coming as it did in the middle of his leave, left him in something of a quandary. When he reported to HQ he found that those in his Platoon not on leave had already set out for the Falklands, some on the

Invincible, others on the *Hermes*. Gary Collins, his Platoon Sergeant, who had started his leave when he did, had not even been located and Russell wondered if he would make the *Canberra* before she sailed.

The huge liner was packed to capacity with over three thousand personnel aboard. Flight decks for helicopters, and fittings for refuelling at sea, had been hastily added and Russell wondered what conditions were going to be like once they sailed. Since it was an eight thousand mile journey, it was imperative that drills and exercises were maintained right up to the moment of landing if they were to be in peak physical condition for whatever awaited them.

After just one day at sea, Russell knew to his dismay that he was not a 'born sailor'. The iron grey swell, with a sky to match, added to his discomfort.

'You need fresh air,' someone told him. 'Go up on deck for an hour.'

The activity up there certainly did take his mind off his own physical discomforts. Sea King helicopters, looking like enormous buzzing hornets, were landing on the forward flight deck every few minutes bringing or collecting stores and mail. The huge loaded nets, which they lowered in by winch, swung precariously as they were caught and twisted by strong cross-winds.

By the end of the first week, however, not only were they into calmer waters and the cold dull days forgotten, but a working routine had been established. Physical fitness became the cult and exercises of some kind or another seemed to occupy almost every waking hour.

Whenever he had any free time, however, Russell usually joined fellow officers in the Crow's Nest bar. He was there, playing one of the interminable games of Scrabble, when the cry went up that someone had sighted land.

'It can't possibly be the Falklands but it could be Freetown,' Russell commented as he joined in the rush to the fo'c'sle which provided a splendid view out over the ship's bows.

'It is quite unbelievable, like a floating market!' he exclaimed, as fascinated he watched the tiny bumboats circling the liner and offering their wares.

'Does anyone want any skins or ornaments to send home as souvenirs?' someone called out.

'Yes! if we can go ashore for them,' another voice replied.

But they were not allowed ashore. Land remained temptingly in the distance. Russell remained at his vantage point in the Crow's Nest, watching a second flight deck for helicopters being installed. Before they sailed again, the interlaced scaffolding had been extended so much that it infiltrated the Crow's Nest, spoiling even that pleasant retreat. He was glad when they once again put to sea.

When news came through that *Hermes* was less than 3,000 miles from the Falklands then, like many of the others, he began to fret in case all the action was over before they reached their destination. And this feeling became even more acute when the *Canberra* dropped anchor off Ascension island and no one seemed to know just how long they would remain there.

Looking out at the enormous heap of rocks, with their backdrop of red volcanic dust, Russell found himself longing for Somerset where the fields would now be yellow with buttercups. Or even the leafy squares around his Mayfair flat where at night, after the rush-hour traffic abated, the air would be sweet with lilac.

Although training and discipline, physical exercise and practised landings still took up the greater part of the day, Russell sensed that everyone was as restless as he was. Top brass, closeted in tiny cabins that had been turned into strategic command posts, argued and plotted over large scale maps to try and decide the best landing tactics to employ when once they reached the Falklands. The delay was made all the more galling because they knew that the Argentinians had landed and were already well established.

'Don't worry, your turn will come soon enough!'

Russell looked up quickly. He had been enviously watching as a small detachment of tanks, manned by the Blues and Royals, was being put ashore for practice. Now his interest shifted to the party of newcomers who arrived on board headed by Lt-Col 'H' Jones, commanding officer of 2nd Paras. It was one of his accompanying officers, Tony Rice, who had spoken. He grinned encouragingly at Russell as he and his fellow officer, Alan Coulson, followed 'H' Jones below deck.

Russell saw that also in the party was Major Mike Norman who, or so rumour had it, had actually been in the Falklands only four days before they had been invaded. The arrivals and departures in the *Canberra* were matched by a parade of ships coming in to the anchorage at Ascension and then leaving for the south.

When the *Canberra* finally sailed, under cover of darkness to avoid underwater attack, Russell breathed a sigh of relief. News had already reached them that Port Stanley had been attacked, and that the Argentinian ship, the *General Belgrano*, had been torpedoed and sunk, and he was impatient to be there and actively doing something.

Within days, the sea and air bombardment of the Falklands had increased and *HMS Sheffield*, one of the British destroyers, had been sunk by Exocet missiles. Lt-Col 'H' Jones' battalion arrived in the *Norland* and he was transferred to it. The *Canberra*, too, was once more heading straight for the Falklands and all talk was centred on how, when and where the landings would take place.

No matter how much speculation went on, there were still a great many nautical miles to cover, and nothing but a great expanse of sea to stare out at so, in an effort to overcome the boredom that threatened to dishearten the men on board, a Sports Day was organised. The chief event, the 10,000 metres, entailed running twenty-four times round the promenade deck. This exhausting marathon, to everyone's amazement and amusement, was won by the *Canberra's* leading laundry hand.

Tension grew as the daily lectures included not only how to land but how to survive afterwards. These covered gruesome details such as killing, and skinning rabbits, sheep and cattle, as well as how to capture, kill and use the flesh of penguins for soups, and stew.

Gloom and depression followed as the *Canberra* entered rougher waters and was caught up in a major storm but Russell hardly noticed the discomfort. He had been told that he was to rejoin his own Company which had already landed.

As soon as they entered San Carlos Water, he was transferred to the *Norland*, which served as a ferry. Conditions on board were even more cramped than they had been on the *Canberra* but even that couldn't dampen Russell's good spirits. 'H' Jones and his officers were already on board and 'H' was the decision maker.

To Russell, of even greater importance was finding Gary Collins, his Platoon Sergeant, also on board. Their reunion was like that of old friends. One of the first questions Russell put to him was whether he had any news of Lucy.

'Lucy has never written a letter to me in her life,' Gary laughed. 'I shouldn't worry about her, she is well able to take care of herself.'

'I am not so sure,' Russell told him. 'Lucy is a country girl and living in London on her own, she could run into all sorts of problems.'

'She can always turn to Ruth if she needs help.'

'Except that I have warned her that she must not visit her sister.' Russell paused, embarrassed at the way the conversation was going. 'Damn it all, you know what the situation is!' he exclaimed exasperatedly.

'I still think she would go to Ruth ... or to my wife, Sheila, if she needed any help,' Gary answered, his blue eyes narrowing.

'Yes, you are probably right,' Russell agreed heavily. 'I wish I knew whether she was still in London or not. My parents asked her to stay with them when they were at the quayside in Southampton. She said something about considering it and perhaps going there later.'

'Well, there you are. Stop worrying. There are plenty of people she can turn to. She doesn't have to stay on in London on her own if she feels nervous or lonely. When the mail gets here there will be a bundle of letters from her and you will find you have been uptight about nothing after all. Once we land and the fighting starts you won't have time to worry about anything or anybody except yourself.'

'Yes, I suppose you could be right,' Russell admitted reluctantly. He knew Gary Collins was talking sense and that it was futile to worry about Lucy.

'As soon as I heard that you would be joining us I made

it my business to acquire the right kit and equipment for you, sir,' Gary told him, dragging his thoughts back to the present. 'It includes a full stock of Field Rations since I didn't think those would be available on the *Canberra* for general issue,' he added with a knowing grin.

'I see.'

'And I've even managed to get you some puttees.'

'Really!' Russell looked at him in bewilderment. 'What do I need those for, Sergeant?'

'To make sure your trousers are held in tight to the ankle, not left flapping in the mud and water.'

On the 20th May, when orders to land finally came, it was a grey misty day with threatening rain clouds and the headland was just an indiscernible mass. Then it was all happening and everyone was slithering down the short ladder into the landing craft that was bobbing alongside.

The *Norland* and *Fearless* seemed to loom over them in the dusk as they moved down San Carlos Water and Russell felt the stirrings of fear churn inside him. This was his first encounter with real warfare and he wondered if he was ready for it. The months of preparation, the field exercise and drills, bombarded his mind. He felt dazed, his brain an inferno of knowledge.

It was the kind of sensation he had experienced just before sitting an exam. A feeling of panic in case he was unable to sort out the jumble in his head and find the right answers in time. Now, it was coupled with a stark sense of danger that gripped him like an icy band.

He breathed deeply, determined to quieten the racing of his heart and the pounding of blood in his ears. He fought back the sour taste in his throat though his mind still swam with ugly visions.

Then the ramp was down and everyone, men and officers alike, scrambling and stumbling, wading through the shallows and floundering over the soft, peaty soil towards land.

As he breathed in the salty air, Russell's nerves steadied, the frenzy inside his head calmed. He quickened his step as the entire body of men pushed forward towards a huddle of small houses. He felt alert, aware of every sound around him, and ready for action.

Chapter 27

As Lucy left London's busy grey streets behind her and headed west on the motorway, her mood lightened.

Once she crossed the county border into Somerset, she wound down the window and let the warm April sunshine stream into the car. The air smelled crisp and refreshing and the hedgerows glittered with celandines, shining like bright new pennies amongst the sharp spikes of green grass. In the fields on either side of the road, young lambs frisked along-side their mothers, and cattle newly turned out into the lush fields grazed contentedly.

Spring at its best, she thought, as she sped through the rolling sunlit countryside and Russell was missing it all. It would be high summer, at the earliest, before he returned home. By then the headgerows would be pink and white with red campions and cow parsley, the lambs would be full grown and the corn ripening.

She still couldn't understand why she had found living on her own in London so desperately lonely. She had been looking forward to her freedom and the chance to shop whenever she wanted to, entertain her own friends and even visit Ruth without the fear that someone might see her and report the fact to Russell. Yet she had done none of these things.

Perhaps I really am a country-girl at heart, she sighed. It had certainly made things worse when she had phoned home to her mother and discovered that Ruth and her two girls were staying there.

'The weather here is glorious,' Ruth enthused when she came to the phone. 'Anna and Sally are thoroughly enjoying themselves. We've been to Furze Copse today picking daffodils. I've never seen such a carpet of yellow, it's an absolute picture. There are primroses and violets there as well, if you know where to look for them.'

'I expected to see you at Southampton when I went to see Russell off,' Lucy said plaintively. 'I was sure you would be there since the girls are on holiday from school.'

'Hugh left on the *Invincible*,' Ruth told her. 'We did go to wave him off. The girls were thrilled skinny when they caught sight of Prince Andrew. He really is rather gorgeous. I think they were more impressed because he was going to the Falklands than by the fact their dad was going there.'

Neither her mother nor Ruth had suggested she could join them, probably because she couldn't bring herself to admit how lonely she was on her own in London. Instead, she had let them think she was enjoying herself and full of plans on how she was going to spend her time while Russell was away.

So she stayed on at the flat, becoming more and more despondent. Although she had been on her own there at night, when Russell was on duty, the fact that there was no possibility of him being back for weeks, or even months, seemed to cast an air of gloom over the place.

She lost all interest in the decorating schemes she had planned. Without Russell's opinion she found it impossible to make up her mind about colours or anything else. She had no real enthusiasm even for shopping sprees at Heals or Harrods; they suddenly seemed quite purposeless.

By the middle of the week she felt suicidal. She couldn't even be bothered cooking but lived off snacks and coffee, piling the dirty dishes into the sink afterwards. Sheila Collins' surprise visit had made her realise just how sluttish she had become which was why, as soon as Sheila had gone home, she had phoned Russell's parents to ask if she could visit them.

Walford Grange was basking in the mid-afternoon sunshine when she arrived. She found Kate pottering in the garden, planting out geraniums in the massive stone urns that flanked the patio.

'You've arrived at just the right moment to make me stop for a break,' Kate greeted her. 'The trouble is, I get so involved out there I forget the time and even though I'm dying for a cup of tea and a rest I refuse to give in.' She smiled as she peeled off her gardening gloves.

Relaxed in wicker chairs on the terrace, drinking tea, nibbling biscuits and making small talk, neither woman mentioned the person who was uppermost in their minds.

They sat there until the Colonel rode up on an enormous black gelding, both horse and rider steaming after an energetic ride. He held it on a tight rein while he greeted Lucy enthusiastically, pulling at the ends of his moustache, his green eyes bright with obvious pleasure.

When he moved off towards the stables, Kate went to put away her gardening tools and Lucy went out to her car to collect her cases.

'I'm so pleased you managed to get here early,' Kate told her when she came back into the house. 'We've friends coming for dinner.'

Lucy's heart lifted. She had made the right decision. This was going to be much better than staying in the flat on her own. Perhaps later, when she tired of the country, she could persuade Kate to come back to London with her for a shopping spree. She would keep it in mind. For the moment, though, she intended to enjoy whatever hospitality her in-laws had to offer.

The dinner party was a splendid affair. Kate had invited nine other people and Lucy found herself sitting between her father-in-law and Carlile Randell.

Carlile's undisguised delight at seeing her again gave an added zest to the evening for Lucy and her scintillating talk kept both men entranced. The only time she felt out of her element was when they talked about horses and then she kept her eyes demurely fixed on her plate.

'How long are you staying down here this time, Lucy?' Carlile asked at the end of a lengthy discussion comparing the merits of his horses with those the Colonel owned.

Lucy gave a tiny shrug of her bare shoulders as she looked questioningly at the Colonel.

'Lucy can stay with us just as long as she likes,' he said heartily, patting her hand affectionately. 'Why do you ask, Carlile. Had you something special in mind?'

'Actually, I had two things in mind,' Carlile said, his eyes gleaming mysteriously.

'You are trying to tease me,' Lucy pouted, fluttering her eyelashes at him.

'Come on, come on,' the Colonel boomed. 'I am as curious as she is.'

'Well, there is a race meeting next week at Wincanton and I wondered if Lucy might like to attend. Secondly, if she is staying down here for a while then it might be a good opportunity for her to learn to ride.'

'Hmm! I see! And what do you have to say to those suggestions, Lucy?' the Colonel asked with a twinkle in his green eyes.

'Well,' Lucy gave a little pout, 'yes, to the first offer, but I'm not sure about the second.'

'Hmm!' The Colonel looked at her appraisingly. 'It would be a pleasant surprise for Russell to come back and find you were as accomplished on horseback as you are in every other way,' he remarked thoughtfully.

'I'm not sure I ever would be,' Lucy said in a crestfallen little voice, fluttering her lashes as she looked from one to the other.

'Nonsense!' boomed the Colonel. 'Give it a try.'

'Excellent,' Carlile said quickly. 'I've got the perfect horse, a mare that is as docile as a lamb, so how about trying her out?'

'Well . . . I am not really sure . . .' Desperately, Lucy tried to think of an adequate reason for not doing so. 'I . . . I haven't any suitable clothes,' she said lamely.

'Jeans and a pair of wellingtons will do for a start,' Carlile told her. 'I can provide you with a hard riding hat. Do you want me to bring the horse here or will you come over to my stables?'

'Might be better if you went over to Carlile's place,' the Colonel said thoughtfully. 'The horse will feel more comfortable on home ground.'

Miserably, Lucy took up the challenge. She hated the idea of riding. Horses were all right as long as there was someone else on their back, or a fence between her and the animal, otherwise they scared her stiff. For a moment she wished she had stayed in London after all. Even the thought of one day being able to ride alongside Russell didn't make her enthusiastic.

Eleven o'clock the next morning she drove to Carlile Randell's home. It was a clean refreshing morning when her heart should have been singing with the birds but instead was lodged deep down inside her green wellingtons as she thought of the trauma that lay ahead. She had always hated being in close contact with animals. She remembered the countless rows with her brother, Mark, because he was always grumbling that she never pulled her weight. He could never understand that she was scared stiff of the cows and anything else to do with the farm. Even the chickens, with their pecking and clucking, alarmed her. She had never been able to summon up the courage to push a sitting hen to one side and fumble underneath it for the eggs, like Ruth could. Even now, young Anna had more nerve than she did when it came to helping around the farm.

Carlile was waiting with the horse already saddled. He led it out to the mounting block in the courtyard in front of the stables, and held it steady until she was on its back. Then, holding the leading rein, he began to walk it slowly round the yard with Lucy balancing nervously in the saddle.

After a few minutes, when she seemed slightly more confident, he led the horse into the adjoining paddock and walked it around the edge of the field. As they moved he instructed Lucy on how to sit, and how to hold the reins. By the end of half an hour she felt less nervous but still not completely confident.

'Is that it?' she asked in surprise when he led the horse back to the stables and helped her dismount.

'That is all for today. I don't want you feeling so stiff you won't want to ride again,' Carlile told her. 'Now that you have got the feel of things we can really start training you. Same time tomorrow?'

Lucy began to look forward to her daily lessons although she still felt nervous of the animal when she was on the ground. She hated it when the horse pushed its face into her shoulder, or tried to nuzzle at her pocket for the lump of sugar provided by Carlile so that she could reward it after each riding session.

At the end of the second week, Carlile insisted she attempt to saddle the horse herself. With his help she managed to do so, although reaching under its belly to adjust the girth terrified her even more than slipping the bit into its mouth.

'You will soon get used to it,' Carlile assured her, at the end of the day's ride as he encouraged her to unsaddle before stabling the horse.

Perhaps it was because she was feeling tired after her ride, but she found this procedure even more unnerving and her uncertain handling made the horse jumpy. When she went to slip the harness over its head it jerked sideways, sending her spinning against the wall, momentarily stunning her. Carlile was at her side almost before she touched the ground.

'Keep quite still,' he breathed, 'otherwise you will frighten the horse even more.'

He spoke to the startled animal in soothing tones as he opened the stall door and guided it inside. Then he turned back to comfort Lucy.

She was still trembling and so obviously shocked that he gathered her into his arms. Removing her riding hat, he began stroking her hair to try and calm her. As she looked up into his face, her blue eyes wide with terror, he involuntarily held her tighter and before Lucy realised what was happening his mouth was covering hers in a long, lingering kiss that left her breathless.

As she struggled to pull free, Carlile only increased his hold. His dark eyes were fever bright.

Before Lucy knew what was happening Carlile had kicked shut the outer door and pushed her backwards onto a pile of sweet-smelling hay. She struggled to break free but he had fallen across her, pinioning her arms to her side so that she found it impossible to move.

As she struggled ineffectually to free herself from Carlile's embrace she tried to quell the panic inside her that threatened to sap her strength and leave her powerless.

His breathing was heavy and laboured so she knew it was useless to plead with him to release her, yet she couldn't bring herself to submit. She managed to free her arms. As her nails raked down his face he grabbed her, twisting her wrist savagely. Her struggles were short-lived, she was no match for his strength as he began tearing off her clothes in a frenzy of desire.

She tried to remain impassive, ashamed of her mounting sensations of pleasures as he made love to her. Tears of despair dampening her cheeks, she lay there inert, paralysed by what had happened.

Chapter 28

At dawn, as Russell looked out at the white cottages tucked into rolling green pastures, and the sheep grazing contentedly, everything looked so peaceful that he wondered why it had been thought necessary for them to come all these thousand of miles.

An hour later, when the air attack started, he had his answer. The raids went on all day. At first it was small Pucara bombers in a ground attack and almost instantaneously the defending ships out in San Carlos Bay filled the sky with missiles. Wave after wave of air attacks followed.

Russell watched as Mirages dodged Harriers, and heard the bombs exploding on the hilltops as they dropped their load before disappearing out over the channel with a roar of engine power. Almost immediately came the resounding explosion of guns and missiles from the defending ships.

As the day advanced, Skyhawk fighter-bombers dived down on the ships that lay at anchor, producing a barrage of fire from the ships as well as from the anti-aircraft batteries that were being hastily constructed on the shore to secure the beachhead.

From his vantage point, a rise in the ground overlooking San Carlos Bay, Russell saw the frigate *Antelope* come limping in, shrouded in smoke, the main mast buckled where it had been hit by an Argentinian plane. And on each side of her hull was a gaping hole where a bomb had gone in. Even as he watched, the helicopters flew in to make an orderly rescue, searching low over the water for survivors, despite the risk of explosions from the damaged *Antelope*.

A week later, he was at Goose Green, and experienced a different aspect of the war. For almost a month the 114 inhabitants had been imprisoned in their own Community

Hall by the Argentinians. Now free, they returned to their desecrated houses and his heart bled for them as he witnessed the bleakness in their eyes as they found their few possessions were ruined.

Even so, they were eager to offer hospitality to their liberators, and not wishing to offend, Russell accepted the tea and cakes they managed to provide.

The place was alive with reporters. Patrick Bishop of the *Observer*, John Witherow of *The Times*, Brian Hanrahan and Robert Fox from the BBC, were no longer anonymous names but men like himself doing a job in an unusual situation.

Colonel 'H' Jones, Commanding Officer of No. 2 Paras who had liberated the settlement, had been killed. As they brought his body down from the hillside where he had fallen, Russell felt even more despondent. A soldier walked in front, his weapon pointed to the ground. A tribute to 'H' stated that he had carried out the liberation of Goose Green with dash and heroism, a verve not seen since World War II.

Afterwards came the grim clean up. Russell's gorge rose as he directed his company of men to bury those British soldiers who had died in the assault.

'What about the Argies, sir?' a young Lieutenant asked, his face green as the last of the dead were lowered into the ground.

'Bury the whole damn lot of them,' a voice muttered thickly.

'Arrange for any who are injured to be moved to one of the field hospitals,' Russell ordered, 'and see that the helmets and packs of any Argentinians who have surrendered are laid out in neat lines on the recreation ground.'

By the time the clearing up was completed, the centre of the square was a huge mound of ammunition, everything from hand-grenades, anti-tank rockets and mortar bombs to several thousand rounds of rifle bullets.

'And what are we supposed to do with all the prisoners, sir?' Gary Collins asked as tired and dirty he stood alongside Russell at the end of an arduous day. 'There must be hundreds of them housed in the sheep-shearing sheds at the end of the village.'

Russell sighed wearily. He felt so utterly exhausted that it was difficult to think clearly. He longed for a hot bath, clean clothes and, above all, a stiff drink. It had been one of the most gruelling days of his life.

'I suppose we will have to fly them back to San Carlos as soon as there are any helicopters available.'

'We could put them on board one of the landing ships that are still lying at anchor in the Bay.'

'Possibly. Do something about these supplies first, though,' Russell told him.

And that was when the accident happened. One minute Russell was directing Gary on where he wanted the ammunition stored and the next minute he heard a shout as Gary Collins gave him a violent push that sent him stumbling backwards before a massive explosion shook the ground.

Apart from being momentarily stunned and covered in debris, Russell was all right, but Gary Collins was lying a few hundred yards away, covered in blood and groaning.

Russell feared the worst. He gave orders for him to be taken to the field hospital that had been set up in an abandoned refrigeration plant and waited with growing anxiety for a report on his condition.

As he paced up and down he kept remembering the horrifying stories that were circulating about men who had been injured. Flesh wounds from high-velocity missiles quickly became gangrenous. In the past ten days, most of the 200 men who had been treated at the hospital had needed limbs amputating.

When he heard that Gary was not to be treated there but was being sent back to England on the hospital ship *Uganda*, he wondered if he dared ask him to take a message to Lucy. It would be breaking all the rules of protocol but he was sure he could rely on Gary to be discreet. She was always uppermost in his mind. He worried about her being on her own in London far more than he did about his own predicament and discomfort. If he could be sure that she would stay with his parents at Walford Grange he would stop feeling so anxious.

He had only a few minutes with Gary before he was taken away. As he looked down at the crumpled figure covered by a blanket, he knew it was pointless asking him to convey any message to Lucy. Heavily bandaged and sedated, Gary was barely conscious.

Almost immediately, Russell was ordered to Bluff Cove to join a Guards battalion which had left England on the QE2. Their arrival was heralded as one of the turning points of the war. It would give the British command a chance to regroup and, for the first time, outnumber the Argentinians. His instructions were to 'Advance forward, over the troops already holding the ground there.'

He felt keyed up by the magnitude of the operation, yet in some ways glad to be plunged into a major assault since it helped to keep him from worrying about Lucy. It was hard going. So many troops and supplies had come ashore that the beach, and the tracks from it, were a morass of mud.

By Sunday, 6th June, tired out but triumphant, his men had captured the tiny settlement and gained control of what was a vital bottleneck on the road to Port Stanley, without a shot being fired.

But, the 3000 men who made up the bulk of the Fifth Infantry Brigade, were still behind the mountain in San Carlos Bay, together with their stores and ammunition.

'Surely, the best way to move them across the island is to put them on ships and sail them round the coast,' Russell suggested. 'That way we will save days of cross-country marching as well as the need for airlifts. There will not only be a saving on time but the men will be less tired.'

It should have been a four-hour trip but because of high seas, driving wind and heavy rain it took much longer. Six hours later they were still being buffeted off the coast and Russell wondered about the wisdom of his suggestion.

The following night, when another battalion made the same crossing, they had to contend with an additional hazard. The Argentinians had been alerted and attacked the landing craft with a tremendous air offensive, by far the heaviest of the campaign.

Later that day at the Fitzroy settlement, while the two landing support ships, *Sir Galahad* and *Sir Tristram*, were being unloaded, Skyhawks struck.

There were only seconds' warning before bombs hit the accommodation quarters. One landed on the main cargo deck of *Sir Galahad*. Confusion reigned. Their flat bottoms made them roll like an elephant on wet grass. Within a matter of minutes, smoke and flames choked the corridors, making it impossible to see what was happening or what damage had been done. The dense smoke also impeded the helicopters and boats as they swarmed alongside, trying to take off the injured and survivors and get them ashore.

In next to no time, flames from the *Sir Galahad* had spread to the *Sir Tristram*. With both ships ablaze, rescue operations became even more perilous. Helicopters returned again and again swooping low down and hovering precariously before coming in as close as possible to try and pick up the injured. And all the time, black smoke poured out as the ammunition on board both vessels ignited with a horrendous cacophony of noise.

Doctors and medical assistants worked feverishly at the first-aid posts, without thought for their own safety, struggling to free those trapped and render temporary assistance to the injured until they could receive full-scale treatment.

On the cliff tops, doctors and nurses watched the blazing inferno as they waited for the helicopters to arrive with the casualties. The vast majority of the injuries were burns, some so horrific that it seemed unlikely the victims would ever recover. And throughout the whole rescue operation, everyone was conscious of the constant crack of ammunition, the sudden spurts of flames that rose above the pall of smoke and the sounds of even bigger explosions coming from the *Sir Galahad*.

Russell was one of those badly hurt. He was taken away strapped to an armoured car. As it climbed up the hillside, he was able to look back and, through a haze of pain, he saw that there was a huge pall of black smoke hanging over the Bay as if from a funeral pyre.

He shuddered as another Skyhawk swept in for attack. It was met with a hail of small-arms fire and missiles. Tracer bullets curled towards it but it passed through the curtain of lead and then peeled away, pursued by missiles.

Tensely waiting for the next attack, the noise of battle drumming in his ears, was the last thing Russell remembered about the Falklands. Overcome by pain he drifted into a state of unconsciousness. War was forgotten. Instead it was Lucy's voice he could hear. It was as if she was there, right beside him.

Russell remembered nothing at all about the journey back to England. Deeply unconscious, and kept that way by pain-killing drugs, he would occasionally drift to the edge of understanding.

His only thoughts when he did manage to open his eyes were of Lucy. He wanted her so much and he couldn't understand why she didn't come.

Weakly, hoarsely, he would call her name over and over, until his mind became blank again and he would drift back into limbo.

Now, he was in a bed. He lay for a long time trying to fathom out just where he was. The walls of the room were pale blue, the paintwork was white and it was a narrow, unfamiliar bed with white and blue curtains around it. Gradually he realised he was in a hospital.

His first thoughts were of Lucy. He closed his eyes, dreaming that she was there beside him, her golden hair fanned out around her shoulders, tickling against his face as she bent over him, her lips hovering invitingly just above his. The smell of her perfume, a rich exotic scent, filled his nostrils. He tried to stretch out and touch her but as he did so she moved . . . tantalisingly out of reach.

He opened his eyes again and as he raised his hand he found it was swathed in bandages. As if from a past life he began to dredge up memories of what had happened. He found he didn't want to remember but the thoughts came pounding in like waves, refusing to be ignored, shattering against his brain, making his head ache.

It wasn't until later, after the operation, that he discovered he was unable to move his lower limbs. The enormity of his injuries overpowered him. He lay exhausted, tears of anger and frustration rolling unchecked down his cheeks. The future seemed so bleak that he wished he had died out in the Falklands. Anything would have been better than the humiliation now engulfing him. How could he ever face Lucy like this. What sort of husband was he when he was not even sure he could still function as a man!

Chapter 29

The strong smell of antiseptic made Lucy heave as she walked down the hospital corridor. By the time she reached Gary's bedside, her stomach was churning and her legs trembling.

'You look worse than I feel,' Gary joked as she bent over to kiss him on the cheek.

'It's this place. I felt sick the moment I walked through the door.'

'What are you doing here, anyway?' His gaze raked over her, taking in the cream silk trouser suit that shimmered seductively, outlining her figure. Her blonde hair was caught back by an enormous jewelled silver slide that matched the dangling earrings that tinkled and sparkled with the slightest movement. 'I would have thought this place was "Out of Bounds" for an officer's lady,' he chuckled.

His vivid blue eyes narrowed as he looked at her speculatively. 'Have you something to tell me that I didn't ought to know?' he asked with a puzzled frown.

'I don't know what you mean,' Lucy prevaricated, avoiding his eyes.

It was not going at all as she had planned. She had intended to hint that she was pregnant, just to sound out his reaction, but she hadn't expected him to guess before she had said a word.

'I think you do!' He grinned widely as he looked her up and down. 'Or are you over-eating to compensate for being all on your own? You are certainly putting on weight . . .'

Lucy cringed inwardly. Perhaps Gary was right and it had been a mistake to come and visit him. Russell would probably be furious if he ever found out. She hadn't dared tell her in-laws. After she had received Ruth's letter telling her that

Gary had been injured and was back in England, her only thought had been to see him and find out how Russell was. She had told the Campbells she needed to go to London for a few days to sort things out at the flat.

'Why don't I come with you,' Kate suggested. 'We could have that shopping spree we are always promising ourselves.'

Lucy couldn't think of a single reason why Kate couldn't come with her, although she was well aware that if she did it would be impossible for her to visit Gary. And seeing Gary was suddenly of the utmost importance.

There had always been a special empathy between them ever since they had first met at Ruth's place when she was stationed in Ireland. She sensed her mother didn't like him but she could never understand why. She knew that when he had started to visit them, and had become friendly with Mark, her mother had forbidden him to come to the farm ever again.

It had been Gary who had introduced her to Russell. At the time she had been too starry-eyed to think very much about it, but since she had been married, and made very aware of army protocol, she realised it must have been at Russell's request.

It was funny, she thought, how she turned to Gary rather than to her brother, Mark. In some ways she treated him as a substitute father. She wished she had known her own father. From the photographs she had seen of him in uniform he looked very similar to Gary. They were both over six foot tall, ramrod straight and with the same shape face. There was even a similarity about their eyes. Someone in the village had even thought that he and Mark were brothers, she recalled.

When she turned her attention back again to Kate and the Colonel she realised Kate was saying she wouldn't, after all, be able to come up to London at the moment because it would be impossible to find someone to deputise for her on the Bench at such short notice.

'Magisterial duties must come first,' the Colonel affirmed.

Lucy hoped her restrained smile of understanding masked

the elation she felt at Kate's decision. It meant she would be able to see Gary alone and, if she could bring herself to tell him about the dilemma she was in, then he might offer some advice.

'For heaven's sake, Gary, stop teasing me. I came to visit *you*, not to talk about me,' she told him as she turned her attention back to him.

'Well, I am absolutely fine, as you can see,' he grinned, waving his plastered arm in the air and nodding his bandaged head towards his right leg, which was strung up to the bed frame by pulleys.

'But you will be A1 again . . . in time, I mean?'

'Yes, I'll mend as good as new. It will take a few months though. Still,' he smiled complacently, 'I reckon I am much better off being here than in the Falklands.'

'Don't say that,' Lucy protested, 'Russell is still out there, remember.'

'No need to worry about him, he has a charmed life,' Gary assured her. 'We were together when this happened and Russell didn't have a scratch on him.'

'When do you think it will all be over, Gary?'

'Quite soon. Don't worry, Lucy. He will be home in time to be the first to know your secret.'

'What secret . . . I haven't got a secret,' she snapped angrily, her face flushing.

'Go on, you can't fool me! I know you too well.'

For a long moment their gaze locked. Lucy was the first to look away and as she did so, Gary saw her eyes were bright with unshed tears.

'Come on, I didn't mean to upset you,' Gary said in alarm.

'You can tell though,' she choked. 'Now everyone will know. Oh, Gary,' she flung herself across his chest as her sobs heightened, 'I just don't know what to do.'

'Tell me all about it, right from the beginning,' he said, clumsily stroking her hair with his bandaged hand.

'You have guessed already what is wrong,' she said in a muffled voice. 'I am pregnant!'

'Well, that is wonderful news. Russell will be thrilled.'

'You don't understand, Gary. I don't want this baby.'

'Of course you do. An heir for Walford Grange Estate! His folks will be over the moon. Why the tears?'

'I am too young to start a family,' Lucy protested. 'I don't want to end up like Ruth, every minute of my day centred around my kids,' she added petulantly.

'Ruth is happy enough.'

'Is she? That is all you know. Ruth never has any time to do the things she wants to do. She spends her entire life cooking, cleaning and looking after the children. She never has any money to spend on herself. Sally and Anna are always needing new shoes, new clothes or something.'

'She probably gets her kicks by keeping them happy,' Gary protested.

'Does she? I doubt it. I've seen the envious way she looks at your Sheila when she has a new coat or dress. You two have had more sense than to get tied down with kids.'

Lucy was so immersed in her own problem, and so busy wiping her eyes, that she failed to see the shadow that flickered across Gary's face.

'Come on, nothing is ever as bad as it seems,' he told her. His heart ached as he looked at Lucy's petulant face. She was still so childish in spite of her sophisticated makeup and clothes. 'Go and talk things over with Ruth, or your mum, and I'm sure they will tell you the same.'

'No! I am going to get rid of it, Gary, so don't you dare say a word to either of them.'

'You mustn't do that!' Gary exclaimed aghast. 'For heaven's sake, Lucy, grow up! You wanted to marry Russell Campbell and having his children is all part of that contract. You can't have an abortion just because right this minute you are not in the mood to have a baby. It's a human life you are talking about destroying, remember!' He lay back on his pillows, exhausted. 'Go and see Ruth. She will understand, and advise you what to do.'

Ruth's reaction when Lucy told her she was pregnant was very much the same as Gary's. She absolutely refused to believe that Lucy could be serious about an abortion.

'Don't talk rubbish, Lucy. You'll feel quite differently

about it when Russell comes home.' She put an arm around Lucy and gave her a reassuring hug. 'Come on, I'll make a cup of tea and we can plan out some of the details. Have you bought anything for the baby yet? If not we will have to go on a shopping spree. I wish I had kept the cot I used to have. It was in perfect condition, but I gave it away because Hugh insists we keep our possessions down to the bare essentials. It makes moving quarters easier if we do that. Mum will want to be in on our plans, of course.' She paused. 'You have told Mum you are preggers?'

'No, I have not and I am not going to do so.'

'But you must! Phone and tell her right away. She will be thrilled . . .'

'You have not listened to a word I have been saying, have you Ruth, or you would not be saying such stupid things,' Lucy snapped. 'I may be pregnant but I am definitely not having this baby . . . I am going to have an abortion . . . now is that clear.'

'Lucy, no!' Ruth's eyes blazed. 'You must talk to Russell. It would be quite wrong to do something like that behind his back. You do understand!' She shook Lucy's shoulder fiercely.

'How can I tell Russell when he is stuck out in the Falklands?' Lucy snivelled. Her eyes misted over and her face seemed to crumple.

'He is not going to be there for the rest of his life, is he,' Ruth flared. 'Just wait until he comes back home before you make any decision.'

'That may be weeks, months . . . years, even,' Lucy said plaintively.

'Rubbish! I had a letter from Hugh just a couple of days ago and he said the end was in sight. He thought it would probably all be over in a matter of weeks and they would be coming home.'

'That is still too long for me to wait. If I'm going to have an abortion I must have it as soon as possible,' Lucy wailed, as tears began trickling down her face.

She looked so young and vulnerable that Ruth found it hard to believe that Lucy was the wife of one of her husband's superiors. Ever since she could remember, Lucy had turned to her when she was in trouble, just as she was doing now, Ruth thought as she gathered her young sister into her arms to try and console her.

'Don't take on so,' she whispered. 'Things will turn out OK. You don't have to worry, having a baby is not all that bad. Once you hold it in your arms you soon forget all the pain and discomfort.'

'That's not what is bothering me,' Lucy gulped. She pulled free from Ruth, dabbing at her eyes and sniffing back her tears.

'What is worrying you then?' Ruth asked.

'I . . . I don't want to be tied down . . . like you are with Anna and Sally.'

'But I wouldn't want it any other way,' Ruth insisted. 'I enjoy what I do for my two. I even feel lonely during term time when they are not around all day. I can't wait for it to be time to go and meet them from school. Anyway, it will probably be different for you. Russell has money, he will be able to afford a nanny if you want one. You'll see it all quite differently once you hold the baby in your arms. You will be a real family, Lucy, don't throw all that away before you have had time to talk it over with Russell.'

Although Ruth pressed her to stay on for a few days, Lucy decided to go back to Walford Grange. She suspected that Ruth only wanted her to stay so that she could try and reason with her. If Ruth was right, and the Falklands War was coming to an end soon, then she would have to move quickly if she was to carry out her plan before Russell got home.

When she arrived back at Walford Grange, and saw the stricken look on Kate's face, Lucy thought for a moment that they must have already discovered her guilty secret.

Lucy's fear turned to bewilderment, and her heart missed a beat, as Kate folded her in her arms and then began to cry, while the Colonel patted both of them awkwardly on the shoulder. Between them, they finally managed to tell her that Russell had been badly injured.

'The message came through shortly after you left for London,' Kate explained, her face white and drawn. 'We have been trying to phone you at the flat ever since.'

'I have been in touch with the War Office,' the Colonel

assured her. 'Russell is being flown home. He is due in this country any time now,' he added as he checked with his watch. 'He will have the very best medical attention so try not to worry. Everything will be all right, I am sure of that. I have told the army authorities that you can be reached here and they have promised that someone will phone to let you know just as soon as his plane lands at Brize Norton.'

Lucy felt too dazed to cry. For the rest of the day she walked round in a trance, waiting to hear he was back in England.

When the call finally came, Lucy's nerves were as taut as a violin string. She was shaking so much that she found it impossible to concentrate and had to pass the phone over to the Colonel.

The news was that Russell had been taken straight to a spinal injuries unit. When the Colonel phoned the number they had been given he was told that Russell was to be operated on immediately and he was asked to call back next day.

Sleep for all of them was out of the question. They stayed downstairs, drinking coffee and dozing fitfully until the early hours of the next morning. As dawn broke, Lucy could stand the waiting no longer and insisted that they should phone the hospital. When they did so, the news was grave, even worse than they had expected. Russell's injuries were so severe that they were warned he might never walk again.

Chapter 30

Robert and Kate Campbell went with Lucy to Woolwich Military Hospital to see Russell. She would have preferred to go on her own but the Colonel was adamant that they accompanied her.

'We wouldn't dream of letting you undertake such a journey alone, would we, my dear,' he boomed, tugging the ends of his moustache and turning to his wife for support.

'We are anxious to see him too, Lucy,' Kate pointed out.

She seemed to have aged overnight. Although as immaculately groomed and carefully made-up as ever, she looked distraught. The fine lines under her deep-set brown eyes were more pronounced and her jawline sagged. Even her shoulders drooped as if someone had removed the padding and her voice was no longer crisp and decisive but resigned and weary. Even her tailored grey slacks and the stylish black and white blouse looked wrong, almost as if she had put on the first things that came to hand instead of selecting carefully as she usually did.

When she saw Russell, Lucy was glad they were with her. The lower half of his body was covered by a cage and a wide surgical collar supported his neck and head. His face was the same colour as the pillows, and the dark shadows under his eyes added to his pallor. Only his arms seemed to be unscathed but he was unable to move even those fully because of the intravenous tubes attached to them. When she took one of his hands between her own it lay there lifeless, completely without feeling. Even when she gently squeezed it, there was no answering pressure.

It was only two days after his operation so they were not allowed to stay for more than a few minutes. When the Sister came to tell them their time was up, Kate and the

Colonel left at once, leaving Lucy a few minutes alone with Russell.

Even then he seemed unaware of what was happening. He lay with his eyes closed, as if he had already drifted back into a state of semi-consciousness, and she was not even sure if he knew she was still there. Tears blinding her she stumbled from the ward to where Russell's parents were waiting.

Everyone was so concerned about Russell, and the slow progress he was making, that the fact that Lucy was off her food and looked washed-out most of the time, went almost unnoticed. Once Kate remarked on it, but she attributed it to the fact that Lucy was upset about Russell. And Lucy said nothing to correct her.

Alone in her bedroom at night, however, Lucy went through an agony of doubt and self-reproach. She still believed she ought to have an abortion yet, since talking to Gary, she felt guilty about going ahead with it. There was the added complication that it was now impossible for her to disappear for a few days. Russell's parents expected her to be at the hospital, at Russell's bedside. Perhaps if she had told Gary everything, confided in him that the baby might be Carlile Randell's, he would have understood and not condemned her as he had done. If only she could explain everything to Russell but he was in no fit state to be troubled by such problems.

For several days Russell's life hung in the balance. Then suddenly the crisis reached its peak and he was on the road to recovery. The colour was back in his cheeks and although he still looked haggard he was showing an optimism that astonished them all.

He took the news that he might never be able to walk again with remarkable fortitude. His only concern seemed to be that he and Lucy would have to give up their fourth floor flat in London because it would be impracticable with a wheel-chair.

'It looks as though I may have to move in with you!' Russell told his parents. 'Perhaps we could turn part of the ground floor at Walford Grange into a flat. Or you could even stable me in one of the barns,' he grinned.

'Nonsense! We will install a lift,' Kate told him. His

recovery had acted like a tonic. Her own spirits restored, she was once more the efficient organiser.

'Absolutely ruin the character of the place,' the Colonel snorted, frowning angrily.

There was an uneasy silence. Kate bristled sensing that Robert was none too pleased at the thought of Russell living at home. Knowing how much he had resented the terms of her father's Will, up until now, she had let Robert act out his 'lord of the manor' fantasy to his heart's content. Now, however, if he opposed Russell's coming back home to live she would have no hesitation in reminding him of the fact that Walford Grange did not belong to him.

Once Russell's improvement was established, Robert and Kate went home but Lucy stayed on in London, welcoming the opportunity to talk to Russell, without constant inter-ruption from his parents. Her nerves were almost at breaking point. Another couple of weeks and probably it would be too late to have an abortion.

Russell, too, seemed anxious to see her alone. On her first visit without his parents, she found him propped up in bed, his mouth a grim tight line, his green eyes hard and expressionless.

'Are you in pain?' she asked after kissing him and receiving no response whatsoever.

'No. I want to talk to you . . . about the future . . . our future!'

Fear gripped her as she sat down in the chair at his bedside. She reached out to take his hand but he adroitly moved it away.

'Lucy, I think we should get a divorce.'

The bluntness of his statement staggered her. She stared back at Russell wide-eyed, wondering if she had heard aright.

From the grim set of his face she knew he meant it. She wondered what reasoning lay behind his request. Had he found out about Carlile Randell? She could not believe that either of his parents would tell him, even if they suspected, and as far as she knew, no one else had visited him. She wondered if Melany Buscombe, or someone, could have written and told him but she pushed that thought from her mind. Knowing how ill he was, surely no one could be so unfeeling.

Steeling herself, she reached out and took Russell's hand in hers. Although he didn't avoid her he let it lie there, limp and completely unresponsive, as she stroked the back of it.

'No,' she told him in a voice barely above a whisper. 'No! I want us to be together, Russ . . . always. I love you!'

He looked at her for a long moment, his eyes, diamond bright, searching her face, seeking assurance. Then, with a shuddering groan, he drew her towards him, clasping at her shoulder until her head came down to his. Their lips met in a lingering kiss, so sweet and tender that it brought tears to her eyes.

'Just get well, my darling,' she breathed. 'I want you back home where I can nurse you.'

Lucy's need of him seemed to galvanise Russell. He improved daily. A new light shone in his green eyes and there was hope in his voice. The specialist and nursing staff, were delighted by his progress.

At first, Lucy was bubbling with joy because of Russell's rapid recuperation. When she realised it meant she could no longer delay telling him about the baby, she became quieter and more withdrawn. Russell thought her change of mood was because she had suddenly realised the enormity of what would be entailed in nursing him, once he was back at home.

'The doctors say that I may be ready to leave here next week,' he told her after a day spent undergoing extensive medical checks.

Instead of looking pleased, Lucy dissolved into tears. Although she turned her face away quickly, Russell had seen her distress and his face hardened.

'My offer of a divorce still stands,' he told her abruptly. 'Don't feel you have to stay married to me for any damned stupid moral reason.'

He reached out and grabbed her shoulder, pulling her round so that she was forced to face him. 'I would hate you to stay because you felt it was your duty to do so!'

'I want to be with you!' she gulped as his gaze raked her face. 'More than you know.'

'Then why the tears?'

She shook her head, too choked to speak. When he persisted her self-control snapped and deep racking sobs shook her body.

A nerve in Russell's face twitched as he watched her agony. Then he drew her towards him, pressing her face onto his chest. Patting her shoulder, he murmured unintelligible words of comfort. When she was calmer he raised her face, holding it between both his hands he stared deep into her eyes. 'Something is troubling you, Lucy? What is it? I have to know.'

Pushing her long blonde hair back behind her ears she stared back at him, biting her lower lip nervously.

'I . . . I am pregnant.'

He stared at her in disbelief and she felt a chill of fear course down her spine. It was too late to turn back now. Slowly, his taut features relaxed and a smile of pure joy lit up his face. His eyes shone with pride.

'I don't know if it is yours or not, Russell,' she gulped before he could speak.

His spontaneous enthusiasm wilted like a frosted flower and his green eyes hardened. 'Not mine! What do you mean? I don't understand.'

In a choked voice she told him about Carlile Randell's attack on her at his stables.

Russell listened in grim silence. When she had finished he turned his head away as if unable to stand the sight of her. He had never felt so upset in his life. His temples were pounding and his throat felt tight with an implacable fury. He felt outraged and when he finally spoke, his face was contorted with anger as he silently vowed revenge against Carlile Randell.

'Have you told anyone?' he rasped.

Lucy looked at him blankly.

'Who knows you are pregnant . . . apart from me?'

'Gary and Ruth.'

'You told Gary Collins!' His face flamed. It went against the grain to think that his Platoon Sergeant had been told the news even before he had. What could Lucy have been thinking of to do such a thing.

'I had to tell someone, Russ. I was out of my mind with

worry. You were away . . . Gary has always been a friend. He's closer to me than anyone in my family,' she whimpered.

'But he has been out in the Falklands as long as I have,' Russell exclaimed, perplexed.

'He was injured . . . they sent him home. Didn't you know?'

Russell nodded without speaking. His own accident had temporarily wiped the incident from his mind. Now, it all came rushing back. He was back at Goose Green, in the centre of the square, directing Sergeant Collins on the disposal of the mountainous pile of ammunition lying there.

He winced, remembering Gary pushing him to the ground, then the tremendous explosion, flying debris and then the sight of Gary Collins lying there covered in blood and groaning. Gary Collins had risked his life protecting him, how could he ever forget!

He supposed he should be thankful that Lucy had turned to Gary. At least he knew how to be discreet, he thought, resignedly, remembering how tactful and cooperative Gary had been over introducing him to Lucy.

'No one else? Not even my parents . . . don't they know?'

'No. I intended having an abortion before you came home only . . . only Gary stopped me.'

'He was right! An abortion is out of the question.' His hand shot out and caught her arm, holding it so tightly that she winced with pain. 'When my parents visit tomorrow, we are going to tell them about the baby. Understand!'

'No!' Her face went chalk white and she tried to pull away. 'No! I don't want them to know, Russ!'

'You can hardly keep it secret much longer, now can you,' he said quietly. 'And we are only going to tell them that you are pregnant, not what happened between you and Carlile Randell. They will probably be delighted.'

'Delighted?' She stared at him uncomprehendingly. She couldn't understand what Russell meant or why he was tormenting her like this. 'You mean they will believe it is yours?' she asked shakily, her face flaming.

'Exactly! They *must* think it is mine,' he exclaimed emphatically.

'No, Russ, it would not be right to do that.' She pulled

away and there was a sadness in her blue eyes that tugged at his heartstrings but he pressed on relentlessly, determined to have his own way.

'Why not? You said yourself you are not sure whether I am the father or not,' he told her brutally.

She shivered at the savagery of his attack, then hung her head, letting her long gold hair hide her face from him.

'Listen,' he grabbed at her arm again, holding it as if in a vice. 'You must do this for me . . . for us . . . and for my parents. Don't you see, Lucy,' he added harshly, 'it is our only chance to provide an heir for the Walford Estates. I can never hope to father a child now . . . not after my injuries.'

'I can't do it, Russ. It would be . . . be like cheating.'

He pulled her towards him, until her trembling body was pressed against his chest. He could feel her panic as he tried to convince her that his solution was the right one for all of them.

'It is no good, Russ, I would never be able to tell them,' she whispered chokingly.

'I have already said that I am going to be the one to tell them, when they visit me this weekend,' Russell said in a hard toneless voice. 'I shall also confirm that we intend to sell the flat and so we will be moving into Walford Grange so that our baby can be born there.'

Lucy tried to collect her thoughts. She knew she should be blissfully happy that all her weeks of heart-searching and misery were over but her senses were spinning. Providing his parents accepted what Russ told them, and Carlile Randell never gossiped, everything was going to be all right after all and there would be no scandal. Her baby, whether it was Russell's child or not, would be brought up at Walford Grange, and enjoy all the privileges the Campbells could provide.

Chapter 31

Russell's plan to move back to Walford Grange as soon as he was discharged from hospital presented far more complications than he had anticipated. The news of Lucy's pregnancy had not been met with the enthusiasm he had expected. His mother and Mabel Sharp had both seemed to be very taken aback, hinting that having a baby around the place would increase the work load and add to their problems.

'I do hope you are going to be able to cope when the baby arrives,' Kate remarked from time to time as Lucy became increasingly cumbersome. 'Russell still needs such a lot of attention. He certainly won't be able to help you at all with the baby.'

'I am sure he will do what ever he can,' Lucy defended. 'There is nothing wrong with his hands and arms so at least he will be able to nurse it to sleep.'

'That isn't a man's job,' Mabel Sharp sniffed disapprovingly when she overheard Lucy's remark. 'Anyway, I don't approve of too much handling. It only confuses the baby and makes it fretful,' she added querulously.

Lucy refused to argue with her. Mabel Sharp was now in her eighties and in the last couple of years had become rather frail. She was crippled with rheumatism which made her very irritable. Lucy guessed that she was more than a little frustrated to think there would be a new baby at Walford Grange but she would be too old to look after it.

It made Lucy uncomfortable the way the old woman's bird-bright eyes were constantly watching her. She was not sure whether Mabel Sharp was concerned for her health or whether she harboured suspicions about the coming baby.

'You are the only one who has any reason to think it

might not be mine,' Russell snapped irritably when Lucy mentioned it to him.

'I am not so sure. She is so intuitive. I am convinced she suspects something.'

'She is bound to wonder what is wrong if you start looking over your shoulder all the time and jumping out of your skin every time she speaks to you,' he scolded.

'I can't help it, Russ!' Her blue eyes filled with tears and her under-lip trembled. 'I feel so edgy.'

As her pregnancy advanced, Lucy found that helping to nurse Russell, with all the fetching and carrying involved, was taking its toll on her strength. When she hinted as much to the Colonel he was immediately solicitous. He wanted to engage a full-time nurse but Russell refused to consider the idea. Instead, he struggled to do more for himself and became increasingly frustrated and bitter when he couldn't manage. He was often short-tempered and usually it was Lucy who was the target for his acid comments.

In November, when the weather turned wet and cold, Lucy found herself virtually a prisoner. Time dragged and she longed to visit Ruth or her mother, anything to escape the claustrophobia she felt at Walford Grange, but Russell wouldn't hear of it. Dr Elwell had warned that the baby could arrive almost any time so Russell was determined that she should take every precaution.

'This will be our only chance of a child,' he reminded her.

He was so obsessed by the idea of being a father that Lucy sometimes felt the baby meant more to him than she did. He seemed to be completely ignoring the fact that it might not be his child and she was filled with a premonition of disaster in case the baby was so obviously like Carlile that there would be no denying its parentage.

Whenever the thought came into her mind, it was as if a cold hand gripped her heart and goosebumps would rash out on her arms, causing her to shiver violently.

Lucy went into labour in mid-December. Outside, a film of snow covered the ground, and the atmosphere inside Walford Grange was almost as chilly.

Mabel Sharp, despite her infirmities, was determined to assist Dr Elwell. She had been present when Russell was born and intended to help at the birth of his child even though Lucy was adamant that she should not.

Russell wanted to stay with Lucy but Dr Elwell was opposed to the idea.

'Just for a little while,' Lucy begged, reaching out to grasp Russell's hand as a fresh wave of pain seized her.

'No, I am afraid he must wait outside, Lucy,' Dr Elwell insisted firmly. He had already noticed the stricken pallor of Russell's face and knew he was unnerved by what was happening.

Jamie Russell Campbell was born at six that evening, a bouncing, sturdy eight-pound baby with a lusty cry. Lucy lay back on the pillows too exhausted to worry whether the baby was Russell's or not. The tears that streamed down her face were not of guilt or remorse but thankfulness that her physical ordeal was over.

Through a mist of tears, she studied the baby's tiny features. As she saw the down of burnished bronzed hair a wave of relief and happiness swept through her. Her spirits soared. Even his hands, with their long slender fingers were replicas of Russell's.

As Kate and the Colonel pushed Russell's wheelchair into the room there was no need for words as Lucy's eyes met Russell's and he saw the joy in their blue depths. The furrow that had become a permanent scar between his green eyes, lifted and a smile transformed his haggard look into one of boyish happiness.

Cradling the baby in the crook of one arm, Lucy held out her other hand to Russell. As their fingers met, a tingle of excitement locked their grip. Then Russell leaned forward to gently stroke the baby's soft downy head and trace the outline of cheek and chin.

'Do you think he is like you?' Lucy asked shyly.

'Of course he is,' he asserted proudly, smiling down at his son. 'He has the Russell family's features and hands.'

'But has he the family birthmark?' Mabel Sharp cackled.

'Birthmark?' Lucy met the challenge in the birdlike eyes fearlessly. 'What birthmark, Nanny?' With tremendous effort Lucy refused to flinch but stared back until the old woman looked away.

'I'll show it to you . . . if he has one, that is.' Mabel Sharp bent over the baby and unwrapped the enveloping shawl. High on the inside of the baby's thigh was a small brown smudge, almost like a crescent moon.

Tears blurred Lucy's eyes as she stared at it. When she looked up she found Mabel Sharp watching her, an inscrutable gleam in her narrowed eyes.

'I think we should make this a double celebration,' the Colonel declared, producing a bottle of vintage champagne. 'Let's drink to the new baby,' he ordered, as he charged their glasses, 'and to Russell's future success.' His eyes locked with Kate's as he added, 'I think it is high time I stepped down and left the management of the Estate to Russell.'

'Hold on, a minute,' Russell begged. 'It might sound like a great idea to you but I don't know a thing about farming . . .'

'You'll soon pick it up. I did,' the Colonel assured him.

'You knew something about farming and, even more to the point, you were interested in it. My only concern has been that there was a horse in the stables for me to ride. What is more, when you first took over, Grandfather was around to advise you!'

'And you will have me on hand if you need any assistance,' the Colonel boomed magnanimously.

'Well, I hope so. I'll need all the help I can get.' He grinned widely. 'They say things always come in threes, so raise your glasses again.'

'What else is there to celebrate?' Kate asked frowning.

'Well, I've just become a father, I've just been handed a plum job for which I have no qualifications whatsoever and,' he paused and looked round at them all, 'I've just received a letter from the hospital giving me the results of the last set of tests and X-rays . . . They say it may take a long time but I will be able to walk again.'

There was a moment of stunned silence then an outburst of excited chatter. Lucy felt ecstatically happy. For her, only one thing marred an otherwise perfect occasion, the fact that none of her own family were there.

'Could one of you phone and tell my mother about the baby?' she asked, looking first at Kate and then at the Colonel.

'Good heavens!' Robert Campbell looked at his watch. 'Is that the time! We phoned your mother as soon as you went into labour. She was staying in London, with your sister. I've invited them all down for a few days and I must go and collect them from the station.'

'But . . .' tears blurred Lucy's eyes. 'We can't have them here . . . Russell's position . . .'

'I'm a civilian now . . . remember,' Russell told her, manoeuvring his chair closer to the bed. 'Your mother, and your sister can visit us any time you want to see them. From now on, there is no protocol to worry about,' he added with a twinkle in his green eyes, 'we can even invite Gary Collins for a weekend!'

Lucy gave a sigh of sheer happiness. It was as if an unbearable burden had been removed. She raised her face to Russell's and their lips met in a long and lingering kiss.

'Thank you for my son,' he murmured, huskily, as he gently stroked her damp hair back from her brow.

'He is wonderful, isn't he!' She sighed contentedly. 'We will have to watch out or he will be spoiled . . . like his father,' she teased.

'Not him. The eldest always has to take care of all the others,' he told her, a meaningful twinkle in his green eyes.

'I thought . . . ?'

'The doctor has said there is no reason why we couldn't have a dozen more . . . should we want that many,' he added hastily.

As she lay back, she slid her hand underneath the pillow and her fingers curled round a newspaper cutting she had hidden there. It was a wedding photograph of Melany Buscombe and Carlile Randell. The caption stated that after their honeymoon in Paris they would be living in New Zealand.

She had intended showing it to Russell. Now, as she looked down at the baby sleeping peacefully at her side, she knew there was no need to do so. Every phantom had been quelled. Carlile was out of her life forever, Russell was going to walk again and she was free to mix with her own family whenever she wished.

'Jamie Russell Campbell, you are one of the luckiest babies

in the world. You have a charmed life ahead of you,' she whispered happily as she gazed down at the baby sleeping contentedly in the cot alongside her bed.